ON A RIDGE ABOUT THREE HUNDRED YARDS AWAY, A SOLITARY RIDER SAT FACING ME, ASTRIDE A ROAN HORSE WITH NO SADDLE.

The figure's hair hung down in plaits on either side of its naked chest. It was holding a rifle upright with the butt resting upon one thigh, a cloth of some sort drooping from its barrel and stirring ever so slightly in the minimal breeze. I was only dimly aware that this was Pere Jac's beloved calico shirt. The Indian looked as if he had been there for hours, which was impossible, since I'd just looked in that direction a few minutes before and seen nothing. The slimy thing crawled back down my backbone.

"Page Murdock." Warped and distorted by distance, the unfamiliar voice was felt rather than heard, stroking my eardrums in such a way that it set my teeth on edge. "You have the choice of dying in the mission with your friends or dying out here alone. I await your answer."

Books by Loren D. Estleman

The Hider
The High Rocks
Stamping Ground

Published by POCKET BOOKS

STAMPING GROUND

Loren D. Estleman

PUBLISHED BY POCKET BOOKS NEW YORK

All of the characters in this book are fictitious,
and any resemblance to actual persons, living or dead,
except for historical personages, is purely coincidental.

POCKET BOOKS, a Simon & Schuster division of
GULF & WESTERN CORPORATION
1230 Avenue of the Americas, New York, N.Y. 10020

ISBN: 0-671-41861-0

First Pocket Books printing February, 1981

10 9 8 7 6 5 4 3 2 1

POCKET and colophon are trademarks of Simon & Schuster.

Printed in the U.S.A.

For Louise Baraksadic Stamenoff,
my grandmother—the last pioneer

From an Old Commander

As near as I can estimate, there were in 1865 about nine and a half million of buffaloes on the plains between the Missouri River and the Rocky Mountains; all are now gone—killed for their meat, their skins and bones.

This seems like desecration, cruelty, and murder, yet they have been replaced by twice as many *neat* cattle. At that date there were about 165,000 Pawnees, Sioux, Cheyennes, Kiowas, and Arapahoes, who depended on these buffaloes for their yearly food. They, too, are gone, and have been replaced by twice or thrice as many white men and women, who have made the earth to blossom as the rose, and who can be counted, taxed and governed by the laws of nature and civilization. This change has been salutary and will go on to the end.

—General William Tecumseh Sherman to William F. Cody, June 29, 1887, as quoted in the latter's autobiography, *Life and Adventures of Buffalo Bill*.

STAMPING GROUND

1 . . .

"Simmer down, Page. Northern Dakota isn't the end of the world."

As he spoke, Judge Blackthorne ran the fingers of his gavel hand through his raven chin-whiskers. I suppose he thought that made him appear wise and fatherly, but the effect was more satanic than usual. His gaunt, Lincolnesque features were set off by steady gray eyes with soaring brows and a high, shiny forehead peaked with a great mane of black hair of which he was more than a little vain, there being not a breath of silver in it. His dress when he was not on the bench was dudish: Prince Albert coats and Vanderbilt ascots tucked inside the collars of ruffled shirts and secured with a tiny golden horseshoe studded with diamond chips. His resemblance to Lucifer was heightened by a constant, tight-lipped smile. Something had gone wrong with his teeth when he was down in Mexico helping the U. S. Army show the natives their error in refusing to cede several hundred million acres of land now known as California, Nevada, Utah, New Mexico, Arizona, Colorado, and Wyoming to their neighbors to the north. He had a nice new set of white porcelains, but found them uncomfortable and never wore them except when eating or in the courtroom; they made a most authoritative clack when he set his jaw. The result when he smiled without them was straight out of *Paradise Lost*. The last time he had presented me with this particular expression was during the Panic of '73, just before he cut my salary. And now he was telling me that northern Dakota was not the end of the world.

"That's easy for you to say," I retorted. "You aren't going there."

I'd almost said, "You've never been there," but changed my mind. I was fairly certain he hadn't, but he was forever surprising me, bringing forth reminiscences I hadn't known he possessed to support his argument, and I wasn't about to blunder into *that* trap. If he had visited our neighboring territory, however, he knew why I objected to going there. I'd passed through Dakota on a cattle drive to Montana six years before and had seen enough of sudden blizzards, spring floods, and Mormon crickets to last a lifetime. When I'd learned at the end of the drive in Helena that the trail boss was planning to return to the ranch along the same route, I'd turned in my rope and taken the first job that was offered me, namely that of deputy U. S. marshal for the court of Judge Harlan Blackthorne in the territory of Montana, the place of my birth. Neither his nor the usurped power of President Rutherford Birchard Hayes was going to make me go back without a damned good reason.

He busied himself with the case records on his broad oaken desk. The one on top dealt with a French Canadian fur trapper who had been apprehended in Deer Lodge trying to sell a load of beaver skins bearing the mark of a small band of Blackfeet found murdered the month before near the Canadian border. But Blackthrone had sentenced the Canuck to hang earlier that week, so I knew he was stalling.

I sighed and sat down in the straight-backed wooden chair that faced his desk, hanging my hat on my knee.

Daylight shone through a ragged rent in the crown where a renegade Crow had come within an inch of separating my scalp from my skull with a tomahawk before I altered his plans with three grouped shots from my English revolver in the center of his face. "All right, spill it. What's the real reason you're sending me?"

He pretended to interest himself in the case of the executed trapper a moment longer, then abandoned the pose. He had a keen sense of the absurd, which was one of the reasons I tolerated him as an employer. Our gazes locked.

"I owe a friend a favor," he said at length. "Abel Flood, the federal judge in Dakota, is an old classmate. If not for his intervention on my behalf, I would have lost the appointment in Helena back in sixty-four to a young pup from North Carolina." He drawled the name of the state exaggeratedly. His contempt for the South was equaled only by his distrust of youth in general. "He's short on marshals at the moment—they've all been gobbled up by the army for scouts, the Indian situation being what it is—and he's called in my marker. I promised him my best man. You're going to Bismarck."

"Is that supposed to be an argument on your side? I'm supposed to drop everything and go to that privy-pit because you owe somebody a good turn? I thought you knew me better than that."

"You wanted the truth. Besides, it can't be as bad there as you paint it. I understand the territory's going through the biggest land boom in its history."

"The railroads can sell manure to hog farmers."

That isn't exactly the way I said it, but a thing like that sounds better in person than it looks on the printed page. He rose. When he did that he lost a good deal of his authority. In a pair of high-heeled Texas boots he would still have had to stretch to see over a five-and-a-half-foot fence. It was his turn to sigh.

"I wish you'd be a little more co-operative about this, Page. You know how much I hate to pull rank."

"About as much as a whore hates to charge."

"You leave me no choice." He donned his courtroom scowl. "Page Murdock, I'm placing you under arrest for the murder last year of Lucas Church, the bounty hunter."

That one took me by surprise. "It won't wash," I said, after the shock had worn off. "You know as well as I do that that was a case of self-defense. He was trying to take Bear Anderson away from me for the bounty when I was bringing him in on the scalp-hunting charge. I turned in a detailed report at the time."

"It will be introduced as evidence."

"A case like that will take a week to unravel!"

"More like six. The wheels of justice grind slowly and exceedingly small."

"What will I live on in the meantime?"

"Bread and water, most likely. That's up to the jailer. Of course, I could take another look at your report and reconsider the case."

"While I'm in Dakota?" No answer. I glared at him. "Did you ever find out who your father was?"

"Be sure and pack your waterproof," he said, plainly fighting off the return of the diabolic smile. "I'm told it's wet on the Missouri Plateau this time of year."

Here I had the choice of complying or handing in my badge and being done with it. He had no case and he knew it. But I'd found my niche and, in what the papers back East referred to as the "emerging West," jobs were scarce for thirty-five-year-old ex-rawhiders who knew nothing but how to handle a rope and where to place a bullet so it will do the most good. I could always cheat on my expenses. Anyway, six years was a long time.

Maybe Dakota had changed. And maybe elves lived in General Grant's beard.

It was all steamboat travel from Helena down the Missouri to the railhead of Bismarck. It would have been rail all the way had not the Panic ground construction and just about everything else to a halt five years before, but wishing didn't straighten out the bends in the river. My fellow passengers, aside from a group of close-mouthed prospectors on their way to the gold strikes in the Black Hills, included an aged Scandinavian with a two-word English vocabulary and a battered brass trumpet screwed constantly into his left ear, and a woman who was on her way to visit her husband, the adjutant at Fort Abraham Lincoln. Neither had much to say in any language, both were ugly, and the only thing we appeared to have in common was an all-consuming dread of our destination.

I didn't recognize the place when I got there. The tent town I had passed through riding drag for Ford Harper, then known as Carleton City, had given way since the coming of the trains and the gold rush of 1874 to a city of neat wooden and log buildings, every other one a saloon, complete with courthouse and the requisite number of churches. In my time the settlement had been a mile or so farther downriver, but when the railroad came through in 1873 it was decided to move the tracks north of the ford to beat the land-grabbers out of their profit. When it came to stealing, the Northern Pacific brooked no competition. The new location was dubbed Point Pleasant, but troopers from nearby Fort McKeen called it Whiskey Point for obvious reasons. Gold mines opening around Deadwood two hundred miles south brought in the rough element, and the city's bloodstained history dates from that time. Now, construction was going on everywhere and the streets were jammed with traffic, evidence enough that the much-vaunted Dakota land boom was more than a figment of some railroad magnate's imagination.

I picked out a likely looking hotel from the dozen or so that confronted me upon leaving my torture cell of the past several days and struck off in that direction carrying my valise. It was a hot day for June—in northern Dakota it was unprecedented. Stepping into the narrow coolness of the shallow lobby was like plunging fully clothed into a lake. The room was deserted except for a sallow youth who sat behind the desk flipping through the latest dime novel from Fargo. He didn't look up as I approached.

The thud of my valise hitting the floor from two feet up brought him lazily to his feet. He marked his place in the novel with a forefinger. "Yes?" He was younger than I'd thought. He had long, slicked-back dishwater-brown hair and a thin face mottled with clusters of pimples. His eyelids drooped insolently behind steel-rimmed spectacles. The gray suit he was almost wearing had to have looked better in the catalogue or the fellow who had worn it before him would never have ordered it.

I asked for a room. His upper lip curled.

"We're full up. Happens every spring, when the prospectors come in from Deadwood to pick up equipment. Try us in September." He opened his book and started to sit back down.

"Tell me something." I leaned my elbows on the desk. This put my grimy, unshaven face inches from his relatively clean one. He paused, knees bent. "What would you do if an important visitor from another country showed up without warning and asked for a room?"

The lip curled farther. I decided that was his smile. "Well, in a case like that, I suppose we could always scrape up something."

I eased my gun from its holster and laid it atop the desk. "This was made in London. We room together."

His eyes dropped to the gun, then roamed the lobby, looking for law. That made him fresh from the East. After a few months on the frontier you get out of the habit. I grunted, reached inside my breast pocket, and plunked the tin star down beside the gun. One glance was enough. He swung the big register around, dipped a pen into his inkwell, and handed it to me.

I scribbled my name and flung down the pen, squirting watered-down ink over the page. "Where's the nearest tub?"

"The Chinese Baths are just around the corner." He frowned at the spots on the yellowed cream paper. Then the lip curled again. "Of course, there's Amity Morgan's place on Third Street. If you're not too tired—"

"I'm too tired." I put away the gun and badge, lifted my valise, and headed toward the stairs, leaving him there with his mouth open. Apparently there were some things you didn't admit to in Bismarck, and being too tired for a roll between perfumed sheets was one of them. I was too tired to care.

The End of Track Saloon, located at the north end of Mandan Street, was as new as its name. Construction was still going on inside and the smells of fresh lumber and turpentine held their own against the more insidious odors of beer and sweat and brimming spittoons. It was dark inside, oil being sold at gold-rush prices out here where it was hard to get. I welcomed its cool interior even more than the hotel's, since the Chinese Baths had opened my pores and I was sweating freely beneath my clean clothes. Even at that early hour the place was packed. Gritty miners up from Deadwood literally rubbed elbows with fat land speculators just off the train and dusty troopers on leave from the adjacent Fort

Lincoln. I shouldered my way up to the bar and shouted for whiskey over the clatter of the carpenters' hammers. A bartender with furry forearms and heavy Prussian features splashed amber liquid into an unchipped glass, shoved it at me, and scooped up the coin I dropped without a wasted movement. I wondered if he was one of the immigrants a destitute Northern Pacific had lured there by naming the 'settlement after Germany's Iron Chancellor. If he was, it didn't look as if he thought he'd gotten the best of the deal.

Liquor in a new glass was too rare a thing to waste at a crowded bar. I had beaten two unsuccessful-looking prospectors to a freshly vacated table in the far corner and was toasting my good fortune when a pair of hand-tooled Mexican boots with a man standing in them stopped beside my chair. I ignored him and went on drinking. There was a good deal of Missouri River in with the Minnesota whiskey.

"Deputy Murdock."

It was a declaration rather than a question. Something about the tone in which it was delivered lifted the hairs on the back of my neck. I raised my eyes from the glass as slowly as possible. That trick had saved my hide more than once, for the tension it created could usually be counted upon to force the hand of a would-be gunslinger before he was ready. If it didn't, then I was up against someone with experience, which was good to know. This time it didn't. I raised them past pin-striped brown pants and a well-fed belly over which was buttoned a vest and a hip-length coat, to a huge black handlebar moustache and a vulture's beak of a nose the color of raw iron. A pair of bright blue eyes glittered beneath the shade of a black hat so new it gleamed in the pale light filtering through the open front door. There being no holster visible, I looked to the next most likely place and noticed a familiar bulge beneath the man's left armpit. I noticed something else as well: two points of a star poking out from under the lapel of his coat.

"I'm Murdock. Who are you?"

"A. C. Hudspeth, federal marshal, Dakota Territory. I got a complaint you threatened a hotel clerk a little while ago with a gun."

"It got heavy in my holster. I put it on top of the desk to rest. Like this." I lifted the five-shot .45 from my lap and deposited it, still cocked, atop the table. His buzzard's beak turned crimson.

"Where's your badge?"

I flashed metal.

"Why don't you wear it?"

"For the same reason I don't paint a big red bull's-eye on the back of my coat."

"You need a lesson in good manners," he said. "Judge Flood's expecting you over to the courthouse. He's been waiting ever since we got word an hour ago you were in town. He don't like to be left hanging."

"Neither do most of the defendants in his court. But that doesn't keep them off the scaffold."

That was a shot to the groin. Abel Flood's record of hangings was no worse than that of any other judge in the territories, where prisons were a long way apart and lumber for building gallows came cheaper than armed escorts. But when they leave openings like that, I leap through.

All of Hudspeth's emotions showed in his nose, which was beginning to resemble a railroader's lantern. It was a knotted lump of flesh trussed like a rodeo calf with hundreds of tiny burst blood vessels. You saw a lot of noses like it in canteens throughout the West, not uncommonly on men who wore badges, but seldom on federal marshals, who, like cavalry officers, were usually selected for their heroic good looks and little else. I decided he was probably a pretty good lawman, because he certainly had nothing else going for him. I might even have admired him if he weren't such a pain. I let him stew while I tossed down the rest of my drink the way they do in the dime novels, in one confident jerk. You could do that when most of it was water.

His voice was choked, as if he'd emptied the glass himself. "If you're through, the judge wants to see you. Now."

I took just enough time leathering the five-shot and getting up to let him know what I thought of his implied ultimatum without seeming self-conscious about it. I found when I stood that he had a couple of inches on me and that I'd been all wrong in thinking him soft. Although he was thick in the middle, his weight was pretty evenly distributed upon a heavy frame, and solid. His eyes were as clear and bright as bullets fresh from the mold.

"Strictly speaking," Judge Blackthorne had explained before I'd left Helena, "Bismarck shouldn't even have a federal judge, Yankton being the territorial capital. But there's talk in Congress of dividing Dakota in two once it becomes a state, and it's a sure bet it'll *be* the capital of the northern half soon now that the railroad's in. That's why Flood keeps his chambers in the county courthouse."

This structure was a squat log affair within smelling distance of the river, identified by a sign that swung from a rusted iron rod with crude letters burned into the wood. Hudspeth entered without knocking and tracked mud across a big room with a judge's bench, three rows of seats, and empty echoes in the rafters. An American flag, spanking new (nothing in Bismarck was old), hung on the wall behind the bench at a discreet distance from a much-missed spittoon near the witness-box. Beyond that was a door before which the marshal stopped and rapped upon with a ponderous fist. A voice like two blasts on a steam whistle bade us enter.

Fat law books crowded the shelves of the corner cubicle in which Flood shared chambers with the county magistrate. He got them in sets straight from New York City and never read them, or so I divined from the lack of wear on the expensive leather bindings. Unlike Blackthorne, who had scrimped and worked nights to buy a book at a time while putting himself through college, and had studied each until he knew it by heart, Flood had come from a family of rich eastern politicians who had been only too happy to grease the skids. "Don't let him fool you, though," the judge—my judge —had warned. "The old bastard knows more about human nature than you'll find in any legal record, and that's all it takes to dispense the brand of justice our founding fathers talked about."

A quarter ton of flesh wrapped in twenty yards of black broadcloth was seated in a stuffed leather armchair near the window as we entered, that day's edition of the Bismarck *Tribune* spread open across his fat knees. His bald head shone like a wet egg in a nest of cobwebby fringe, and black-rimmed pince-nez wobbled astride his round pink nose. He was clean-shaven except for fluffy side-whiskers. The knot of a narrow black necktie was obscured beneath the folds of his chin. He looked as if he had never been out of that chair. The room had been built around him while he sat there reading his newspaper. Looking at him, I wondered how I had ever thought of A. C. Hudspeth as fat. A gold watch was attached by a chain to his swollen vest, and this he was consulting in the palm of a pudgy flipper.

"One hour and six minutes," he bellowed, snapping shut the face of the watch. "I'll have the accountant deduct that from your salary at the end of the month."

I was to learn presently that this was his normal

speaking voice, and that he was almost deaf. The trials over which he presided, I was told later, with both sides shouting to be heard by the man who wielded the gavel, could be followed from halfway across town. The *Tribune*'s court reporter had only to sit next to an open window in the newspaper office and take notes.

I didn't say anything, but scooped out a handful of crumpled scraps of paper from my left hip pocket and dumped them over the newspaper in his lap.

"What's all this?"

"Receipts," I said, and repeated it in a louder voice when he cocked his ear. "Food. Boat fare. A bath. Whiskey. Judge Blackthorne said you'd reimburse me."

"For the necessities! The taxpayers of the United States will not subsidize your self-indulgence!"

"All right, forget the bath."

The top of his head grew pink. His scalp and Hudspeth's nose made good barometers. I took pity on him and stopped being smart.

"I'm kidding. The whiskey's on me."

To my surprise, the fat judge broke into a guffaw that set the window behind him to rattling in its frame. He handed the receipts to the marshal.

"See that Deputy Murdock is compensated for his expenses. All of them, including whiskey." He returned his attention to me. "I'm a man of temperance myself, but I can appreciate the importance of that first drink after the journey downriver. Henceforth, however, the spirits will indeed be on you. Well, what do you think of our little community?"

"The prices are too high and it's full of bastards. Aside from that it's a nice little trap."

That didn't amuse him at all. I was having difficulty getting his range.

"Well, no matter," he said finally. "You won't be here long. Tomorrow I'm sending you to Fargo."

"Why Fargo?"

"You're picking someone up."

"A prisoner?"

"No." He smiled secretly—the kind of expression you get by practicing for hours in front of a mirror—and removed his pince-nez to polish them with an acre of white silk handkerchief taken from his breast pocket. His eyes, in contrast to the marshal's, were vague and lifeless. "Not yet, anyway. It'll be your job to make him one. The gentleman's name is Ghost Shirt, but as far as the Dakota Cheyenne are concerned he's the Second Coming of Jesus Christ. The families of one hundred and forty-nine men, women and children massacred by his band in the Black Hills last year might not agree. I hope you find the rest of the territory more to your taste than Bismarck, Deputy. You're likely to see a lot of it before you finish this assignment."

2 . . .

The Indian they called Ghost Shirt might have died a minor sub-chief of the Cheyenne nation had not George Custer's 7th Cavalry discovered gold in the Black Hills of southern Dakota in 1874.

The following year, frustrated by its consistent failure to reach a treaty with the resident Casts No Shadow and his Cheyenne followers, the federal government opened the hills to gold-seekers in an attempt to force the Indians out. Casts No Shadow, a provincial brave who had never ventured east of the Red River of the North, struck back by attacking and slaughtering the first wagon trainload of prospectors that rolled into his stamping ground. Then the army came, and after the chief's two sons were killed in a skirmish with the cavalry, he lost heart, surrendered himself, and was hanged six weeks later for his part in the massacre. His brother, Kills Bear, who had departed with half the tribe for Montana at the time of the surrender, threw in his lot with Sitting Bull at the Little Big Horn and, in the charged aftermath of Custer's slaughter, fled to Canada in '77 to escape the vengeance of the new administration in Washington City.

With him was Ghost Shirt, a young nephew filled with an all-consuming hatred for the white man nurtured throughout the three years he had spent in the East learning the ways of the enemy. During the trek north he grew restless and peeled forty braves off the main shaft for his own foray into the Black Hills. The immediate result was the Dry Hole Massacre.

Dry Hole was a tent city erected near the gold strikes fifteen miles from Deadwood, where some seventy miners had settled with their families while they eked out a bare living chipping away at an anemic vein above a tributary of the Belle Fourche River. Ghost Shirt and his warriors came upon the settlement one morning soon after the men had left to work their claims. Without warning the Indians swept down on the women and children who remained behind. The few miners who heard the commotion in time to go back and do something about it ran straight into an ambush. By the time the others returned in force, they found their tents and wagons in flames and the camp a litter of corpses. The Indians had salvaged everything of value and fled.

That was the first. Others were to follow. Names like
Teamstrike and Crooked Creek and Blind Man's Hollow conjured up images of smoldering bodies and
babies dashed against trees and women in the final
stages of pregnancy writhing at the ends of lances skew-
ering them to the ground. The newspapers back East
were crammed with wild-eyed descriptions of how the
renegades ate the hearts and livers of their victims and
wore leggings made of human flesh. These last were
fabrications, but the troopers sent out to investigate the
disturbances knew that the reality was far worse.

The near eradication of a large cavalry patrol from
Fort Abraham Lincoln by the diminutive band of
braves at Elk Creek in December of '77 opened the
floodgates. With Sitting Bull and Kills Bear in Canada,
Ghost Shirt became the Red Man's Great Hope. From
all over the Northwest they flocked to his standard—
Cheyenne, Sioux, Arapaho, and even a disgruntled few
of the despised Crow, all united for the first time in
living memory. Rumor had it that the battle-wise Cheyenne who had accompanied the old chief into exile were
trickling south to join the "loinclothed Messiah," as
General of the Army Sherman referred to him bitterly
during an unguarded moment at a press conference.
The War Department made hurried preparations for a
stepped-up Indian war. New forts were planned, while
existing ones as far away from the seat of trouble as
Fort Buford near the border of northern Montana were
reinforced to capacity, and a massive recruitment campaign was launched throughout the eastern states in an
effort to bring the peacetime army up to its Civil War
strength. Within two months of Ghost Shirt's return, all
of Dakota had become an armed camp.

On New Year's Day, 1878, four hundred troopers
under the command of General Baldur Scott descended
on a Cheyenne camp south of Castle Rock and slaugh-

tered everything that moved. When the carnage was over, it developed that Ghost Shirt was not present and that most of those killed were old men, women, and children. Never one to let slip an opportunity, Scott ordered everything burned so that the warriors would have nothing to come back to and then took off in pursuit.

Ghost Shirt now was on the run for the second time in his young life. At the head of his band of homeless braves, he struck out across the Badlands toward Canada, but was forced to turn east when two cavalry regiments from Fort Yates opened fire on them at Thunder Creek, and crossed the Missouri River below Mobridge. A forced march followed, with pursuers and pursued covering a hundred miles in two days. The Indians were nearly overtaken at Napoleon and again at Jamestown, only to escape with bullets singing about their ears. Outnumbered two to one, they made a stand, aptly enough, at the Sheyenne River and were all but annihilated at the cost of one hundred and twenty-six troopers. Ghost Shirt was wounded in the leg and taken prisoner along with three warriors. The rest fell in battle. The survivors were incarcerated at Fort Ransom and tried within the week for the Black Hills massacres. The verdict was guilty. At the age of twenty-two, the nephew of the last chief of the Cheyenne nation was sentenced to hang.

He and his trio of condemned followers were kept in the guardhouse under close watch while work progressed on a special gallows designed to accommodate four men at once. Shortly after the changing of the guard on a starless night in March, an argument broke out among the prisoners, blows were exchanged, and Ghost Shirt collapsed. The guards thrust bayoneted rifles between the bars and held the others at bay while the door was unlocked and a delegation entered to examine the stricken man. Suddenly a strangled cry rang out. A sergeant who had been stooping over Ghost Shirt reeled back, clawing at a bloody shard of wood protruding from the socket where his right eye had been. In the confusion that followed, one of the Indians snatched the rifle out of the hands of a guard and placed the bayonet point against a paralyzed troopers' throat. Then Ghost Shirt, who had sprung to his feet after attacking the sergeant, relieved the private of his side arm and got the drop on the remaining trooper in the guardhouse. It was all over within seconds.

With one of their comrades in his death agonies and two more in the hands of the prisoners, the troopers outside the cell were forced to stand and watch while Ghost Shirt and his companions prodded their hostages before them through the opening and backed across the compound into the shadows along the east wall with them in tow. Not until they were out of sight did the soldiers act. They ran for the wall, raising the alarm as they went, and snapped off shots at gray figures spotted scaling the ladder to the battlements. One brave, Standing Calf, fell at the foot of the ladder when a bullet crashed through his brain. Another, identified later as Ghost Shirt's cousin Bad Antelope, was struck twice in the back as he teetered atop the wall, and toppled into the Sheyenne River on the other side. A third, a Crow called Silent Dog because his tongue had been cut out when as a youth he had been captured by the Iroquois, was taken prisoner before he could reach the ladder but was killed later under mysterious circumstances which the army was still investigating. Ghost Shirt was nowhere in sight.

The bodies of the two troopers who had been taken hostage were found lying in pools of blood at the bottom of the ladder, their throats slashed by the captured bayonet.

The next day, a search party discovered Bad Antelope's corpse bobbing against a rock at a bend in the river a mile south of the fort. When a week of searching failed to turn up either Ghost Shirt or his tracks, it was decided that he had perished while trying to swim the rapid waters of the Sheyenne at spring thaw, and that his body was already halfway to Minnesota, if it hadn't snagged on a fallen limb in some uninhabited part of the territory. The search was called off after ten days, and Washington began processing new orders for the now unnecessary reinforcement troops in Dakota.

Then, two weeks after the escape, a Swedish farmer was found murdered in his cabin two miles east of Fort Ransom. A neighbor who called on him from time to time became alarmed when the immigrant, and aged widower, failed to answer his knock, and entered through the unlocked front door. The house was a shambles. Someone had gone through the cupboards, scattered their contents over the floor, overturned flour barrels, dumped out the woodbox, torn out drawers, and pawed through the linens and clothing inside. Amid this confusion lay the elderly Swede, naked except for a nightshirt, the latter stained where he had been disemboweled with some sharp instrument the moment he stepped out of his bedroom.

Further investigation revealed that there was not a scrap of food left in the house. Missing also was the dead man's only weapon, a pre-Civil War Colt pistol which he was known to have kept next to his bed. That he had been carrying it when he went out to investigate the strange noises in the other room seemed a reasonable assumption. His buggy horse was gone as well. The hasp on the barn door had been forced with great difficulty and the animal removed by a man wearing moccasins—as shown by the tracks left in the soft earth inside. The considerable effort that had gone into breaking the hasp was borne out by the shattered half of a bayonet blade found in the grass beside the door.

The discovery sparked panic among settlers throughout the territory. The commanding officer at Fort Ransom issued a hasty statement to the press declaring the evidence inconclusive, but as no other explanation was forthcoming his words went unheeded. Washington was bombarded with telegrams demanding protection from the Antichrist in the settlers' midst. Congress, still involved with its investigation into the more interesting legacies of the Grant Administration, sent a terse directive to the General of the Army: Either deal with Ghost Shirt once and for all or learn to get along without allocations from next year's budget. Sherman's immediate reaction to this ultimatum went unrecorded, as this time no reporters were present. Nevertheless the laborious process of reassigning men who were already enroute to their new posts was begun.

The turnaround was too slow. In mid-April, while the troop strength at Fort Ransom was still at low ebb, Ghost Shirt, accompanied by twenty renegades believed to have been recruited from among the disgruntled Sioux south of the Red River Valley, raided the post armory and made off with a wagonload of rifles and ammunition, enough to equip a force five times as large. They struck while the troopers were busy fighting a fire the braves had set at the north wall, and, in a bloodless battle—the first such since the trouble had begun—shot their way out through the gate, wagon, horses, and all. The weapons stolen were part of a new shipment of unissued .56-caliber Spencer repeating rifles, which made the outlaw braves among the best-armed Indians in the West. The average cavalryman was still carrying the single-shot Springfield that had helped lose the Civil War for the Confederates. A pursuit patrol dispatched within minutes of the raid came upon the wagon half a mile west of the fort, its bed a jumble of empty crates. After that the fates appeared to be on Ghost Shirt's side, as at that moment one of those sudden downpours for which the region surrounding the Red River of the North was notorious opened up and washed out all traces of the Indians' escape route.

Nothing more was heard of the renegades or their activities after that. Repeated forays by the U. S. Cavalry between the Black Hills and the Minnesota border failed to turn up the slightest hint as to their whereabouts. This time, however, no one was optimistic enough to advance any theories regarding the death of Ghost Shirt. It was believed that he was busy raising a brand new army with which he would launch a series of massacres that would make those in the hills pale by comparison. If the current land boom was any indication, Easterners were confident of the Indians' imminent capture or destruction, but as far as those already in residence were concerned, the entire territory was a powder charge primed and ready to blow as soon as Ghost Shirt lit the fuse.

I was aware of all this, but as it gave me time to study the angles, I let Judge Flood prattle on until his thunderous voice grew raspy at the edges. Then I broke in.

"What's Fargo got to do with it?"

The fat judge cleared his throat, a sound that reminded me of coal sliding down a chute. "A people who call themselves the métis keep a small camp a couple of miles south of there," he said. "They're part Algonquin, part French, and they know more about the territory than any other friendly Indians you're likely to find. You'll want to engage one or two of them as guides. Also, Fort Ransom is only three days' ride to the southwest. The commanding officer, Colonel Broderick, is an acquaintance of mine. I'll give you a letter of introduction and he'll fill you in on the latest details. Any other questions?"

"Several hundred. To begin with, what am I supposed to do that the army can't?"

"The reason that bunch has been so hard to find up until now is that the cavalry can't move without being heard for miles. Too many men, too much equipment. But one man or a small band, provided they know what they're doing, can penetrate that region unobserved. Since half the problem is locating them, you'll have a head start."

"What do I do once I've located them? Surround them?"

"You won't be alone. I'm sending Marshal Hudspeth with you."

"Dandy. That makes the odds only ten to one."

"That's why time is of the essence. Army intelligence has reported a general exodus from Sioux and Cheyenne reservations throughout Montana and Dakota over the last few weeks. It's no mystery why they're leaving. Your job will be to capture Ghost Shirt and bring him here for hanging before they can join up with him. Otherwise there'll be hell to pay."

"I thought he was scheduled to hang at Fort Ransom."

"He was." All this time Flood had been polishing his spectacles. Now he stopped and held them up to the light. Apparently satisfied with their sparkle, he placed them in a hinged leather case, snapped it shut, and slid it into his breast pocket along with the handkerchief, neatly folded. "I've rescheduled it for Bismarck because I feel it's imperative that the citizens of Dakota witness the execution. The present situation hasn't affected the land rush so far, but if Ghost Shirt is captured and hanged in some remote place like Fort Ransom there's going to be talk that he wasn't apprehended at all, that the army's covering up, and accusations like that have a habit of sticking. Right now our sole advantage is that Bismarck is the end of the line. By this time next year that will no longer be true. The Northern Pacific plans to resume operations next spring. Let one suspicious rumor get started and the settlers will keep going as far as the rails will take them. The only way to prevent such a situation is to make this a civil matter and invite the public to the hanging."

"And you expect this Colonel Broderick to co-operate?"

"He has no choice. If Ghost Shirt is not brought to justice soon he faces court-martial for criminal negligence. You will find him most eager to help."

"What's your interest in this?"

A fresh guffaw exploded from him. "Harlan was right, by thunder! You're nobody's fool. Very well, I'll be honest." He folded his hands upon the swell of his stomach, which for him was quite a reach. "I have interests in seevral hundred acres of land situated along the railroad right-of-way. If the land boom fizzles, so do my interests. But that's only a small part of it. I'm genuinely concerned with the welfare of the territory, and I'll make use of all the power I possess to insure its future. It will never be anything more than a rest stop between stations if everyone who passes through thinks he has to hold onto his scalp with both hands for fear of losing it. It's in your power to change that. Will you accept the assignment?"

"I didn't realize I had a choice."

"Of course you do. I can't order a man to go on a mission from which the odds are he won't return. Hudspeth has volunteered. If you wish, you can be on the next boat back to Helena and no one will think less of you because of it."

"What makes you think I can do the job at all?"

He smiled, I think. At least, something stirred his mammoth jowls. "I've done my homework. Anyone who takes on the entire Flathead nation as you did last year and lives to tell about it is capable."

"You're doing your damnedest to make it impossible for me to refuse."

He shrugged.

"What the hell?" I said. "I couldn't face another boat ride so soon anyway." That kind of breezy nonchalance fit me like a tent, but something was going on here that he wasn't telling, and since I had gone to all the trouble of coming to my least favorite spot on earth I decided I might as well find out the reason. I figured he'd buy my vanity act, that being the West's most available commodity. "When do we leave?"

"Tomorrow morning, on the six-fifteen to Fargo. As I said, time is of the essence."

I put on my hat. "In that case I'll be seeing you. I've got just enough time to grab a meal and a bath and get some sleep."

"I thought you had a bath." This from the marshal, in a suspicious tone. He was still holding my receipts.

"Don't worry. I won't charge this one to the taxpayers."

Hudspeth leered. "Amity Morgan," he said knowingly. "Just be sure and keep an eye on your poke. Her girls would steal the pennies off a dead man's eyes."

"I'm not dead yet."

I looked to the judge to see if that was worth another belly laugh, but he didn't appear to be paying attention, frowning as he was at his enormous paunch and pushing his lips in and out. He was preoccupied with something, and I had a pretty good idea what it was. I'd been overconfident in assuming he hadn't seen through my act. I should have known better. A liar is quick to recognize a peer.

3 ∎ ∎ ∎

Hudspeth didn't like trains. That much was obvious once we had taken seats in the coach and, precisely on the stroke of six-fifteen, jolted into motion. He gripped the arms of his seat as if clutching the brasswork of a storm-tossed clipper and held on, eyes staring straight ahead and the veins in his nose standing out, until we had left the station and topped off at a steady twenty-five miles per hour. Then he relaxed by degrees until his teeth stopped grinding and the color returned to his knuckles.

The seat opposite us, like most of the others in the car, was empty. But the crowded runs west more than made up for the deadheads away from the land of opportunity. I settled back into the plush upholstery and stretched out my legs in the half acre that separated the seats. Space was George Pullman's long suit.

"You don't look like the kind that volunteers," I ventured after five or six miles. I watched the telegraph poles flitting past the window. They were more interesting than the flat scenery beyond, scrawny and misshapen as they were. Trees were scarce in northern Dakota, and the linemen made use of what they could get.

"Neither do you." His voice sounded almost normal. "So how come we're here?"

"I asked you first."

He grumbled some and shifted around on the cushions. But he could see that didn't satisfy me, so he sighed and stared at the floor. That bought him some more time. "I won't lie," he said at length. "I've petered down to considerable less of a lawman than I was when I started out. My eyes ain't half what they was, and you can cook and eat a fair-size meal in the time it takes me to get a gun out of a holster. That's why I hide it under my arm."

"I noticed. It's obvious as hell."

He scowled, as at the unwanted logic of an impertinent child, and went on. "I got two years before my thirty's in, then I can retire and collect my pension. That's if I can stick it out without getting fired. The judge has been handing out some heavy hints lately, mostly about my drinking. He's a damn dyed-in-the-wool teetotaler, and in his thinking every man who takes a sip now and then is a drunk. Anyhow, he doubts my ability to carry out my duties, he says, and with the territory filling with settlers like it is he's wondering if some young jackanapes from out East might be more suitable. Then he brings up this Ghost Shirt business. It's blackmail, pure and simple, but what've I got to put up against it? I'm too old to drive teams any more, and that's all I know how to do besides enforcing the law."

"I guess all judges are alike," I said, and related how I came to be in Dakota. He snorted.

"Them law schools ought to be made illegal. They turn out more crooks than the prisons."

I agreed. "Flood, for instance. Assuming we can pull off the impossible and beat the army to Ghost Shirt, what's he to gain? I don't for one minute buy his story about land interests, and that's easier to swallow than the one about saving this glorious territory." I waved a hand toward the window just as we happened to be passing a group of ragged bone-pickers reaping the rotting harvest of last winter's buffalo slaughter along the railroad right-of-way.

"The White House. That's what he's got to gain." The marshal slid a metal flask from the inside breast pocket of his coat and uncorked it. As he did so, the coat buckled and I caught a glimpse of the gun reposing in a special pocket of his vest beneath his left armpit. Small wonder it bulged. It was an army-size Smith & Wesson .44 caliber, christened the American, big and heavy enough to drive nails with the butt. The Deane-Adams English .45 I carried in my hip holster looked insignificant by comparison. This one was about as suited to be carried beneath a man's arm as a grand piano was to be played in a third-floor cathouse. He took a long pull at the flask's acrid contents—the odor of bad traveling whiskey assaulted my nostrils—replaced the cork, although without conviction, and returned the container to his pocket. His bright little eyes clouded for an instant, then cleared brighter than ever.

"The White House?" I prompted.

He nodded. "Flood ain't been satisfied just being judge since he first clumb onto the bench. He made two tries for governor of the territory and damn near got the appointment the second time. He would of, too, if some nosy reporter on the *Tribune* hadn't wrote that he took money from the Northern Pacific back in seventy-one to clear a track foreman of a charge of murdering a Chinaman on government property."

"Did he?"

"Kill the Chinaman? I reckon so."

"Not that. Did Flood take the money?"

"Oh, that. Who knows. I'd be mighty damn surprised if he didn't. Everybody takes money from the railroads.

The only reason the choice went against him is he got caught. That didn't cool him off any, though. He just aimed higher." Hudspeth went for the flask again, then changed directions and, instead, loosened his gun in its leather-lined sheath as if that had been his intention all along. I recognized the standard drunk's way of cutting down: Take plenty of liquor along just in case, but only hit it half as hard. Flood's threats worried him more than he would admit. "Ever since Custer got it," he went on, "being an injun fighter brings in more votes than promising to cut taxes. The judges figures if he can get to Ghost Shirt ahead of the army and hang him in Bismarck, he'll collect enough publicity between now and eighteen eighty to step into Hayes's shoes."

"In that case, why send just us? Why not a posse?"

"That's easy. If the posse gets wiped out, he has to explain to Washington City what they was doing butting in on the army's business, and probably get himself impeached, or whatever it is they call firing a judge. This way, if we don't make it back—which strikes me as more than likely—he can say we was acting on our own or at most just offering our services to the authorities already involved. Two more scalps on Ghost Shirt's belt don't make a hell of a lot of difference in them drawing rooms back East. Besides, the judge can spare me, and since you ain't his man anyway he can afford to toss you down the same hole. It's like betting someone else's money on a fair hand. He's got nothing to lose and the whole pot to gain."

"He's told you this?"

"A skunk don't have to announce himself for you to know he's there. My nose is as good as any lard-bucket newspaper reporter's."

"Greedy, isn't he?"

"Your judge ain't?"

I returned my attention to the landscape beyond the

window. We were shuddering now through the buttes—huge, flat-topped stumps of weathered granite whose red sandstone caps glistened with the remnants of a recent rain. Beyond them to the northeast, gunmetal-colored clouds were gathering for a fresh offensive upon the newly planted, still vulnerable crops in the Red River Valley. If it wasn't torrential rains, it was drought. If it wasn't drought, it was grasshoppers, "Mormon crickets," that swarmed in by the hundreds of millions to blight everything in their path. Fate and the elements stood in line for a lick at the unsuspecting settlers who dared take a plow to God's country. For the rest of us He saved the Indians and the politicians.

"I hate Dakota," I said.

The canvas-to-clapboard story in Bismarck found its echo in Fargo but intensified a hundredfold. Here, where the busy, backward-flowing Red River of the North transected the railroad jumping-off point for merchants and developers laden with hard-to-get goods and peddled dreams from Minnesota and points east, Chinamen, Scots, Germans, French and Scandinavians teemed the muddy streets and temporary shacks in greater variety than anywhere else west of the Old World. Hudspeth and I hoisted the bedrolls, slickers, saddles and rifles (his a single-shot Springfield, mine a Winchester so new it squeaked) that were our only luggage down from the rack and stepped into the sea of humanity on the platform in search of a livery.

"It used to be over there," said the marshal, pointing out a building two blocks down the street, which now, if the sign was to be believed, sheltered the Golden West Emporium and Tonsorial Parlor.

"It's come up in the world," I observed.

On our third try we found someone who spoke English well enough to direct us to a livery on a street with the optimistic name of Broadway. There, we haggled with the stony-faced old Scot who ran the place over some serviceable-looking horseflesh, including a pack animal, and at length agreed upon a mutually unreasonable price, for the payment of which we asked for and were given receipts made out in flowing European script that neither Flood nor even a skinflint like Blackthorne could doubt. One hour, a meal, and four exorbitantly priced drinks later we were astride our new mounts and on our way to a métis camp which the bartender at the Old Fargo Saloon assured us was two miles south of the city limits. We were still riding five miles beyond that point.

"I thought you said you knew where the camp was," I growled at Hudspeth. Light was fading fast and the weeks between me and my last hard ride were beginning to tell in various places.

"I did once. I can't help it if they moved."

"They must move a lot. The bartender said they were camped an hour's ride back just last night."

"You can't believe everything a bartender says."

"You should know."

Half a mile farther on we spotted scattered fires in the distance, and another twenty minutes found us on the outskirts of a village of primitive lodges and skin tents. The usual menagerie of yapping mongrels heralded our arrival. Despite the racket, the dogs were all that crowded around us, snapping at the horses' heels as we made our way through the camp. I was unprepared for this reception, or lack of it. Where I came from, a visit by whites to an Indian camp was an event worthy of note, if it was anything less than suicide. A brave who let a stranger, any stranger, within a mile of his lodge without raising the alarm wasn't worth his feathers. We had gone a hundred yards before we came across the first sign that the place was inhabited at all. This was a boy with long black hair cropped straight across the back of his neck at the nape, wearing a bright calico shirt and new Levi's cut down and stuffed into the tops of calf-high moccasins (the only part of his attire that could have come from inside the village), who was busy sewing up a rip in the side of a lodge covered with scraped buffalo hides. He paid us no attention as we rode up to where he sat cross-legged on the ground bent over his labors. Although he couldn't have been older than ten or eleven, he manipulated the bone needle and gut thong with the assurance of an old squaw stitching a new ornament onto her warrior's tunic.

"We're looking for Pere Jac," Hudspeth announced.

The boy looked up uncomprehendingly. The light of the torch that blazed before the lodge fell across a set of features finer than I'd expected, set off by flashing black eyes and lashes that swept his dark cheeks. The marshal repeated the query, or one like it, in bastard French. After a moment the boy nodded and pointed with the needle toward the rusty glow of a large fire east of camp. Hudspeth thanked him and we moved off in that direction. The boy resumed working.

"Do they all get that excited over white men?" I asked the marshal.

"What did you expect? They're more than half white themselves."

The métis, I was to learn, were no less mongrel than their pets. Also called *bois brûlés,* or "burnt wood," because of their swarthy complexions, most were descended from Huron or Algonquin women and foreign trappers who had come west in the middle of the last century and married into the tribes. Since then interbreeding had become a way of life, until now there was precious little to separate them from the equally dark French Canadians who were prevalent in the area. Nevertheless they retained their essentially Indian ways. They were nomadic and depended for their existence almost entirely upon the buffalo of which they were undisciplined butchers. They also knew every rock and bush in Dakota territory by its first name, which was the reason we were here.

Whatever was going on inside the circle of firelight, it was receiving the full-throated approval of the colorfully clad mob that surrounded it. Their shouted encouragement was a stew of English, French, and one or two other languages I couldn't identify. It was so loud it almost drowned out the sound of blows.

The free-for-all was well in progress by the time we got there. In the center of the circle, cheered on by the howling spectators, half-naked men shining with the sweat of their exertions wrestled and fought in a tangled throng, grunting, snarling and muttering oaths in a variety of tongues as colorful as their audience's garb. Kicking seemed to be in, as was biting and eye-gouging. It was an elimination contest. Every now and then a man battered and torn beyond his limits staggered or was carried from the action over the outstretched forms of his predecessors, while in the middle the melee raged on without flagging. Those left sported shiners and smeared lips like I hadn't seen since the bank runs in the early days of the Panic. All about their feet bloody teeth twinkled in the firelight.

One brawler in particular, a squat breed whose powerful build belied the iron-gray hair falling about his shoulders, looked to be giving more than he got, as he answered his opponents' blows with Helena Haymakers that sent them reeling back into the crowd of spectators. Little by little, as Hudspeth and I watched from the backs of our horses, the heaving mass dwindled until only a handful remained to slug it out among themselves, with the old man in the heart of it. The air was heavy with the rank smell of turned earth and sweat.

All in all, I reflected, this spectacle was playing hell

with what I'd been told about the gentle ways of the métis. But then there are exceptions to every rule.

Down to the bare boards, the rules of combat underwent a subtle change. The younger men, apparently recognizing the threat to their reputations should they fall to someone thirty years their senior, stopped fighting each other and teamed up, at odds of six to one, to take out the old man. They whooped and hollered and charged headlong into a beehive.

He was a magnificent specimen, this old breed who could have been anywhere from fifty to seventy-five but fought like a Blackfoot brave in his twenties. Muscles writhed beneath his naked torso like snakes beneath a sheet, and scars thick as cables crisscrossed his great chest and shoulders. He reminded me of a king buffalo I had once seen defending its throne. Old and grizzled though he was, he was still more than a match for the youngsters who challenged his authority. Besieged from all sides, he met them in silence, snaggled teeth bared in a determined grin as he felled this one with a blow and hooked that one viciously in the groin with the toe of a moccasin. Those lucky enough to connect found their best shots glancing off him like a blacksmith's hammer bounding from an anvil. Then a clout from an axe-like fist would bring their participation to an end. In this manner he disposed of four assailants in as many minutes.

He had both arms wrapped around a fifth and was bear-hugging him into unconsciousness when the sixth, a lean young breed with features more Indian than white, snatched up a chunk of wood from the fire and charged him from behind, swinging the glowing end above his head. I have no special love for rules, but this seemed to be going astray from the spirit of healthy competition. I drew my revolver and was debating whether I should drop him and risk the hostility of the

tribe or gamble on a dime-novel try at shooting the
club out of his hand, when a shot like the Fourth of
July in Chinatown crashed within a foot of my left ear.
The young breed shrieked, dropped his weapon, and
clapped a hand to the side of his head. It came back
bloody.

Every eye in the vicinity, including mine, swung to
the big man astride the horse next to my own. A plume
of metallic gray smoke wandered from the snout of the
Smith & Wesson in Hudspeth's right hand while with
the other he struggled to keep his startled mount under
control. He had drawn the clumsy thing from its un-
likely position beneath his left arm and fired while I was
still figuring the angles. And he said he was slowing
down.

The old man wasn't one to let the grass grow.
While his would-be attacker was still hopping around
and lamenting the loss of his right ear, he whirled and
slung the limp breed he was holding six feet into the
other's arms. One hundred and sixty pounds of métis
struck him full in the chest, tore the wind from his
lungs in a loud *woof,* and bore him, a tangle of arms
and legs, to the ground on the other side of the fire.

For a long moment there was silence. Then the air
erupted and the crowd surged forward, closing in on
the old breed, the women babbling excitedly, the men
pumping his hands and slapping him on the back. Our
presence was forgotten. A half-full whiskey bottle was
produced from some hoarder's lodge and, after it had
been admired for a while, was presented to the victor
with a flourish. He seized it in a bloodied right hand
and tipped it up, letting the contents gurgle down his
throat without seeming to swallow. Two more tilts and
he slung the empty vessel away over his shoulder. It
bounced once in the grass and rolled after the retreating form of the vanquished breed as if pursuing him.

Everyone seemed to find that amusing. Everyone, that is, except the old man, who caught the eye of a dark-skinned young woman standing on the edge of the crowd and jerked his head toward the injured man. She nodded and moved off to follow him. The old man's will, it appeared, was law—rare among Indians, where a leader usually led by example only and would not presume to issue anything so harsh as an order.

"Hey, Pere Jac!" called Hudspeth, dismounting.

"A.C.!" The aged métis squinted through the gathering gloom. "A.C., is that you?"

"Who the hell else would waste a bullet on your worthless hide?" He started leading his buckskin in that direction. I stepped down to follow.

Pere Jac barked something in French to the man nearest him, who took the reins from Hudspeth and those of my bay and led them toward camp.

"They will be fed and rubbed down well," the old man explained. He had a French accent you couldn't suck through a straw. "How are you, A.C.? That was respectable shooting." He seized the marshal's out-stretched hand and shook it every bit as energetically as his own had been shaken moments before.

"Not as good as it looked," said the other, wincing as he disengaged his hand from the other's grasp. "I was trying to put one between his eyes."

"I am glad that you did not. He is my sister's only son." He looked at me curiously. He was almost a foot shorter than I, but built like a warhorse. He had well-shaped features despite the numerous bruises and swellings, and eyes of washed-out blue in contrast to the mahogany hue of his skin. His jaw was fine, almost delicate, his face shot through with tiny creases and wrinkles, as if it had been crumpled into a tight ball and then smoothed out again. His gray hair, dark with sweat, hung in lank strands to his shoulders. Perspiration glistened on his skin in the firelight and trickled down the cleft that divided his chest into twin slabs of lean meat. Yet he was not the least bit winded.

Hudspeth introduced us and we shook hands. His grip wasn't much, if you were used to sticking your hand inside a corn-sheller and turning the handle.

"Page Murdock," he said, with unfeigned interest. "You are the man who brought Bear Anderson out of the Bitterroot Mountains last winter, one step ahead of the Flatheads."

I said that I was. I could see that those were the words someone was going to carve on my tombstone.

"And yet you do not look like a foolish man," he observed.

I grinned. "Pere Jac," I said, "you and I are going to get along."

"My name is Jacques St. Jean. Marshal Hudspeth and these others insist upon calling me Pere Jac because for a brief period in my foolish youth I sought the clergy. The clergy, alas, did not share my enthusiasm. Now I content myself with reciting the Scriptures and instructing my people in the ways of the Lord."

"That was some Bible-reading we caught just now," said Hudspeth dryly.

"Man is an imperfect animal, full of hostility and sin. He must be given the opportunity to cleanse himself of both from time to time if he is ever to pass through Purgatory."

"You do this often?"

"Every other Wednesday, without fail."

"How about sin?"

"Sin is for Tuesday. But you have not come all this way to speak of religion, A.C."

"We need an experienced tracker, Jac, and unless there's someone around here who reads sign as good as you I guess you're it."

"That is what I thought. Come with me to the river." He signaled for a torch to be brought. When one was handed him, he motioned the others to remain where they were and strode away, carrying the flaming instrument. As we hastened to catch up: "How much are you offering this time, A.C.?"

"I was thinking four cases."

"A man's thoughts are his own, *mon ami*. But that one is beneath notice."

"That's the price we agreed on last time!"

"The last time was four years ago. It costs much more to subsist in these days of revolution and expansion."

"We're talking about whiskey, not money. And you got no more bellies to fill now than you had four years back. All right, six cases. But that's as high as I go. We're talking about taxpayers' money."

"I do not think that ten cases would upset the economy."

"Ten cases!" Hudspeth stopped walking. At the base of the grassy slope, the Red River hissed and gurgled at high water. But the métis kept walking, so he had to sprint to catch up.

"Seven cases," he said.

Pere Jac made no reply.

"Eight, damn it! But you'd better guarantee results."

We were at the river now. The old man handed me the torch and stepped off the bank, Levi's, moccasins and all. He dipped his swollen and bleeding hands into the water and splashed it over his face and chest.

"Eight it shall be," he said at last. "But I guarantee nothing." He dug a finger into his mouth, withdrew a loosened tooth, saw it was gold, and thrust it into a hip pocket. "Who are we going after, A.C.?"

"A Cheyenne by the name of Ghost Shirt."

The dusky-skinned woman Jac had sent earlier to look after the wounded breed appeared bearing a bundle of clothing. She held out a calico shirt while he stepped out of the water, and helped him on with it. I figured her for his granddaughter; she turned out later to be his squaw. He shook his head at her offer of a dry pair of leather leggings, accepted a military-style red sash instead, and knotted it about his waist. "I think, A.C.," he said finally, "that you had better give us the whiskey in advance."

4 . . .

We were Pere Jac's guests for the night, which meant that despite our protests, he, his woman and his three children slept outside and the lodge was ours. This was the same structure we had seen being repaired earlier by the boy who turned out to be Jac's son Lucien. Sleeping on buffalo robes didn't come easy after an extended period of city life, but I'd got along on worse and so had Hudspeth. We drifted off in short order— me from exhaustion after the unsettling activity of the past few days, the marshal after reacquainting himself with the flask in his pocket.

It rained sometime during the night without our knowing it. There were puddles on the ground the next morning and the air had that damp metallic smell, but the sultry and unseasonal heat that had dogged me since leaving Montana had not been washed away. If anything, the atmosphere was more oppressive than ever. It hung from last night's burned-out torches, beaded on the outside of the lodges in droplets of moisture, clung like moldy rags to our throats and the insides of our nostrils when we tried to breathe. The very act of taking in oxygen was exhausting. Two steps outside the shelter I felt as if I hadn't slept at all.

Our host and his family were wet but cheerful—the métis' natural state—and greeted us warmly in order of rank. We muttered something in response and sat down on the ground to a breakfast of dried buffalo meat and herbs fresh from the soil. That finished, Hudspeth mounted his buckskin and took off to fetch supplies and the pack horse we had left in Fargo, and to make arrangements for the delivery of Pere Jac's eight cases of whiskey, while I stayed behind to get to know our guide. This was more important than it sounds. Armed men forced to travel in each other's company for an indefinite period are well advised to get acquainted before they set out, or the first argument on the trail could well be the last.

I had nothing to worry about in Jac. He packed no side arm but carried a Sharps carbine and rode an unprepossessing paint pony, and the confident but careful way he handled both as he made ready for the trip reflected a familiarity with the rugged life that earned my approval. One of his few concessions to the white man's way was a weatherbeaten McClellan saddle complete with a pair of army issue bags. Into these he packed a leatherbound copy of the Scriptures and enough pemmican to last three weeks on the trail— roughly an ounce and a half of dried buffalo, berries and sugar pounded into a hard cake the size of a cowboy's brass buckle. These were his only provisions.

His woman's name was Arabella. Save for the dusky brown of her features and a thoroughly Algonquin mode of dress, from the polished snail shells strung around her neck to her elkskin moccasins, there was very little about her that said she was part Indian. Her hair was chestnut and hung in braids to her breasts. Her eyes, more oriental than native, rode at a slight tilt atop high cheekbones. Her mouth was wide but handsomely sculpted, the line of her jaw strong but not stubborn. She seldom spoke in Jac's presence. In that respect at least she was all squaw.

The children took after their father in looks, with Lucien, the oldest at ten, already beginning to show in the girth of his chest the beginnings of Jac's warrior build, and Jerome, six, and little, black-haired Paulette, three, watching every step of the preparations for departure with identical pairs of the old man's pale blue eyes staring out of their chocolate faces.

This, I had been told over breakfast, was Pere Jac's second family. His first wife had been killed fifteen years before when a herd of buffalo spooked prematurely during a hunt near Pembina and trampled the camp. His first son, now grown, left shortly before Jac's second mating along with his own squaw to start a new métis settlement below the Nebraska line. The old chief had taken Arabella as his bride after her first husband, his brother, succumbed to smallpox in the epidemic of '67. Jac remarked with pride that two of his five grandchildren were older than Lucien, and that Arabella was expecting another child in November.

Once the paint and my bay were saddled and ready to go, we sat down in the shade of the only tree for miles, a cottonwood beginning to die out at the top, and swapped a lie or two about past manhunts while he charged a stubby clay pipe from a pouch he carried on his belt and lit it with a sulphur match. Then we sat and listened to a faint breeze too high to reach us stir the branches twenty feet above our heads.

"Ghost Shirt," I said then. "What do you know about him?"

"Only what I have heard." He was having trouble keeping the tobacco burning. He struck a fresh match, puffed at the anemic glow in the bowl, got it going, shook out the match. Bluish smoke curled before his bruised and weathered features. "There is nothing haughtier than a full-blooded Cheyenne in his prime. Tell him that he is Christ reborn, as they have done with Ghost Shirt since he was old enough to understand, and he becomes impossible. Ten days before his birth, it is said, Ghost Shirt's father, Paints His Lodge, dreamed that he saw the sun rising from his squaw's loins. When the story was repeated to him, the tribal shaman prophesied that a son would be born who would lead his people to greater glories than had ever been known, a son who was destined to be a god, yet who would remain on earth to guide the Cheyenne to their rightful place as conquerors of the land.

"It did not help matters that the boy proved himself a superior athlete long before the time came for his test of manhood, nor that when that time came he fulfilled all of the requirements with ease. Sent east to study the white man's world, he returned after three years seething with hatred for the entire race. He commanded the right flank of his uncle Kills Bear's warrior band in the Custer fight and proved himself an adept tactician as well as a born leader of men. Had the Little Big Horn never happened, Ghost Shirt might have enjoyed limited authority for a number of years and attained the rank of chief sometime in middle life. As it is, he has risen too fast too soon. He is a rash young man with more power than he knows what to do with. Unfortunately, of late he has been finding uses for it."

"Is he as crafty as they say he is, or just lucky?"

"Craft and luck are difficult things to separate. A

man must have a little of both if he is ever to be successful. Ghost Shirt is fortunate. Moreover, he is brilliant. It is a dangerous combination if you are not on his side."

"You're describing a young Sitting Bull."

"Or a young Napoleon," said Jac.

He thought about it, then shook his head. "No. Not like Sitting Bull. He at least has learned to temper his distaste for the white man with wisdom. There is no wisdom in Ghost Shirt's brilliance. Only hate. He cares not for the future of his people, only for revenge. He will be the ruin of the Cheyenne nation. You have a saying for it: He burns down the barn in order to destroy the rats."

Pere Jac was silent for a time. A dead seed came rattling down between us from the cottonwood's upper branches. A crow had come to light upon a high twig and began to scold us raucously. A newcomer, screaming for those already there to leave. Thus harangued, I understood for a moment the feelings of Ghost Shirt and his followers. But only for a moment.

"You are to kill him?" asked Pere Jac.

I hesitated, thinking at first that he was talking about the crow. "No," I said, catching his drift. "We've strict orders to bring him back alive for execution in Bismarck."

"That is a foolish thing. Dead, he is a threat ended. Alive, he remains an open sore. There is always the hope among his people that he will return to lead them. If we are able to capture him, our troubles will just be beginning."

"Look at the bright side. We won't live long enough to take him prisoner."

He laughed and brushed at the sparks that had showered from his pipe down onto his leather leggings. "You are right, Page Murdock," he said. "We are going to get along."

We basked in the warmth of that for a while. Then the sound of galloping hoofs shattered the late morning stillness and Hudspeth, the loaded pack horse tethered behind his own mount, reined to a dusty halt in front of us and heaved himself out of the saddle, nearly going down on one knee as he landed on his feet with a jarring thud. His nose was flame-red and his eyes held an urgent glitter. He barely gave us time to scramble out from under the tree before he thrust a crumple of paper into my face.

"This was waiting at the telegraph office," he announced. "It's from Judge Flood. A force of twenty injuns ambushed a patrol out of Fort Ransom last night and killed Colonel Broderick and twelve others. Ghost Shirt was leading them."

5 . . .

"Why?" I looked up from the scrap, torn and wilted from being jammed into a pocket and carried across eight miles of Dakota territory.

"How in hell should I know why?" Hudspeth demanded. "He's crazy mad. He'll do anything."

"I don't think so. If he were that crazy he'd have

been dead long ago. Ghost Shirt must have had a reason to attack that patrol."

"It don't much matter if he did or didn't. What matters is he went ahead and attacked it. I wired Flood to tell him we got the message, and Fort Ransom to let them know we're coming."

"Any answer from the fort?"

He shook his head. "Likely they're on alert. Operator's too busy hunting up reinforcements to acknowledge." He grunted and flicked a drop of sweat from his beacon of a nose with the tip of a blunt forefinger. "The only good thing about this whole business is now we know he ain't met up yet with the Sioux and Cheyenne from around the territories."

"Maybe. Or maybe it's a trap."

"We'll know soon enough." He swung back into the saddle. "Mount up. We're heading out."

I straddled the bay. "What'll we do once we get there?"

"We'll think of something on the way." He wheeled west.

Pere Jac didn't move. "Where is my whiskey, A.C.?"

The marshal reached into a saddle bag, hoisted out a quart bottle full of tobacco-colored liquid, and tossed it to the breed, who caught it in one hand. "There's ninety-five more coming day after tomorrow," Hudspeth told him. "You want to see the receipt?"

Jac drew the cork and helped himself to a swig. "I trust you, A.C.," he said, wiping his mouth with the back of his hand.

The métis slid the bottle in with his other belongings, said his good-byes all around, and stepped into the paint's leather with the ease of a man forty years his junior. Five minutes later we were clear of camp and heading southwest, fifty miles of which separated us from our destination.

We reached the Sheyenne at dusk. There, a shallow ford stretched between us and the fort, which was a purple blemish on the muted red glare of the setting sun. No sooner had Hudspeth set a hoof in the water than a shot rang out. Riding behind him, I heard a *thup* and saw his broad-brimmed black hat tilt over his left ear. He hauled back on the reins to keep his horse from spooking, but it was too late. The buckskin kicked up its heels and arched its back, whinnying and trying to turn so it could bolt. The marshal spun it around three times before dizziness took over and the animal stopped to regain its bearings.

"Halt! Who goes there?"

A lanky trooper stood up to his knees in water in the middle of the river, a rifle braced against his shoulder, smoke draining from its barrel. The challenge lost a great deal of its force, however, when the young voice issuing it cracked in the middle.

Hudspeth let out a roar and sprang to the ground. He hit the water running, tore the rifle from the trooper's hands before he could react, and sent it spinning far out into the river. Then he swept the trooper off his feet and prepared to send him after it.

"Do it, and you'll be dead before he hits the water." A harsh croak, dry and empty as a spent cartridge. It crackled in the charged air.

The marshal froze, legs spread apart, the trooper squirming in his arms. He turned his head slowly in the direction of the voice.

Three soldiers were mounted on horseback on the opposite bank, each with a rifle snuggled against his cheek. The broad brims of their dusty campaign hats left their faces in shadow. Two of them, anyway. The man on the left, although obviously cavalry, wore the cocked forage cap of an infantryman, a style of headgear made famous by both sides during the late unpleasantness out East. A rain cape hung to his waist, performing double duty as a duster. His features were invisible against the sun. Softer now, the wallowing light glinted off gold epaulets on the square shoulders of the man in the middle. A hammer was thumbed back with a brittle crunch. Late, but persuasive as hell. Hudspeth returned the trooper, a callow youth with blond hair and freckles, to his feet. He put several yards between himself and the marshal as quickly as possible.

"Hands up, all of you."

We did as directed, raising our open palms above our shoulders. Hudspeth was last to comply.

"Now suppose you tell me who you are and what you're doing here."

"We're federal officers," growled Hudspeth, after a pause. "I'm Hudspeth. The mean-looking one is Murdock. Here from Bismarck on the injun problem. I got a letter from Abel Flood, federal judge for the territory of Dakota, for Colonel Broderick." He started to reach inside his coat but stopped when all three rifles rattled.

"Keep your hands up!" The command was metallic. "Colonel Broderick is dead."

"I know. I wired you this morning to tell you we was coming."

The officer turned his head a fraction of an inch toward the soldier Hudspeth had just released. "Go to the telegraph shack. See if there's a wire from someone named Hudspeth." When the youth had gone: "The Indian. I suppose he's a federal officer too."

"He's our guide, and I bet he's got more white in him than you."

The pause that followed put an extra twist in the tension.

"You make a bad first impression, friend." The words were bitten off.

After about a year of silence, the trooper returned

bearing a telegraph blank with a spike-hole in the center of it. The officer glanced at it, then handed it back. He lowered his rifle. At a signal from him the others followed suit a moment later. Then he spurred his big black forward into the water. He stopped in front of Hudspeth and ran his eyes over the three of us. They were brown eyes, with flecks of silver in them. His heavy brows were startlingly black in comparison, downward-drawn and prevented from running into each other only by a thin pucker line that went up until it disappeared beneath the forward tilt of his campaign hat. His beard too was black and cropped close to the skin so that it resembled General Grant's. That came as no surprise. In spite of his dismal presidency, in spite of the endless congressional investigations that had hounded him during his last days in office and after, Grant was still the hero of Appomattox, the hard man on the white horse whose preference for whiskers had inspired men from New York to California to lay aside their razors. Among army officers there were two distinct types, the Grants and the Custers, and you didn't venture into many posts without finding yourself virtually surrounded by either long-hairs in buckskin jackets or silent men who fingered their beards meaningfully when they could think of nothing significant to say.

This officer—a major, now that I could make out his insignia away from the sun's glare—had a long, one might say Roman, nose and the beginnings of jowls beneath his whiskers, which had undoubtedly contributed to his decision to grow them. The sun had burned his flesh to match the red Dakota dust on his saddle. His eyes were not the steely type one expected in men accustomed to command, but large and luminous and cowlike, strangely unintelligent—like Grant's. His physique beneath the coarse blue tunic (buttoned to the neck, even in that heat) was powerful but beginning to loosen around the thighs and belly. I placed his age at about forty.

His side arm was an Army Colt with a smooth wooden grip, the rifle he held across his lap, a Spencer. Like his uniform, both were covered with a skin of fine dust. Beneath him his horse was lathered and blowing.

He took in my face, clothes, horse, the Deane-Adams in my holster, the Winchester in its scabbard, then went on for a similar inventory of Pere Jac. Then he returned to Hudspeth.

"You owe the U. S. Government the price of a new Springfield rifle, Marshal."

"Tell them to take it out of my taxes."

I stifled a grin. Either the lawman had qualities I hadn't suspected or a little of me was beginning to rub off on him. I was starting to enjoy my subordinate role in this thing.

He wasn't finished. "I told you who we are. It's polite to introduce yourself back, ain't it, Lieutenant?"

"It's Major," snapped the other. "Major Quincy Harms, acting commanding officer at Fort Ransom until Washington City appoints a permanent replacement for Colonel Broderick. I'm sorry, Marshal, for all the inconvenience, but you must understand that the situation here is tense. We can trust no one." There was no apology in his tone.

"So you shoot everyone on sight?"

"Trooper Gordon will be reprimanded for his lapse in judgment. I believe you mentioned a letter from Judge Flood." He held out a hand.

The marshal drew out the paper Flood had given him the morning of our departure and handed it over. Harms unfolded it and read. The muscles in his jaw twitched. Then he thrust the letter inside his tunic.

"Sergeant Burdett, relieve Trooper Gordon of his

duties and place him under house arrest until further orders."

An infantryman, the private had no side arm to be taken from him. The man in the forage cap merely leaned down, screwed the muzzle of his rifle into the other's collar, and began walking his horse forward. Rather than be trampled, the trooper let himself be prodded along like a stray calf. Somehow I got the impression that he was going to be punished not so much for firing a premature shot as for allowing himself to be overpowered by a civilian.

"Come with me, please, all of you. Bring your horses." The major reined his black around and splashed through the water toward the fort entrance. The third rider, a middle-aged corporal with a plug of tobacco bulging beneath his lower lip, followed him.

"Damn tin soldiers," muttered Hudspeth as he mounted the subdued buckskin.

One half of the huge double slat gate swung inward to allow us entrance, then was pushed shut by two troopers and secured with a timber bar that must have been shipped, like the logs of which the fort's framework was constructed, downriver from Montana or by rail from Minnesota. From there we rode past crowds of hard-eyed men in uniform who watched us with hands clasped tightly around their Springfields and Spencers. They had the desperate look of animals left too long at the ends of their tethers. Before the post livery a company of troopers was dismounting wearily, their horses, faces and uniforms covered with a mud of sweat and dust. Among them was a pair of empty mounts bearing the army's brand.

From the porch overhang of a long adobe building swung a sign that identified it as the garrison commander's office. The major and corporal left their saddles in exhausted unison, their square-topped boots double-crunching on the carted-in gravel. Jac and Hudspeth and I dismounted more earthily and hitched up at the watering trough, where the horses wet their noses eagerly. Harms handed his reins to the corporal.

"The right front needs reshoeing. And see to it that our guests' mounts are rubbed down and fed. They're dead on their feet."

The corporal saluted and led off his and the major's mounts.

The office smelled of coffee and stale tobacco. The walls were bare adobe reinforced by wooden timbers, and the floor was made of pine planks eight inches wide and scrubbed white as bears' teeth by some miserable trooper on punishment detail with a scouring pad and a toothbrush for the cracks. The desk was battered, scarred in numerous places where matches had been struck against its scaly surface, and covered by a large-scale map of eastern Dakota. Holes in the corners and a pale spot on the wall behind the desk indicated that the map had been taken down recently for close study. A curled corner was held in place beneath a white china mug with damp brown grains clustered in the bottom. Behind the desk stood a high-backed swivel chair, its dark wood covered to within an inch of the age-polished edges by hard, dry leather secured with large brass tacks. From fort to fort, the decor never varied.

Major Harms peeled off his hat and pegged it beside the door. His hair, like his beard, was jet black, short at the temples and neck and full on top. A bald spot the size of a ten-dollar goldpiece showed defiantly at the back of his head. He made no attempt to conceal it. He stepped around behind the desk and dropped into the swivel chair in a cloud of powdery dust. His forehead just beneath the hairline was ringed unevenly with several different shades of tan where he'd settled and resettled his hat under the scorching sun.

Hudspeth sat down on the edge of the sturdy captain's chair that faced the desk as if easing himself into a scalding tub of water. Evidently it had been some time since he'd sat a saddle as long as he had during the past few days. I chose a bench that ran along the right wall and wished it were the back of my horse, it was that hard. Pere Jac remained standing. In his dusty half-Indian, half-white man's attire, his pewter-colored hair loose about his shoulders, eyes impassive as the heads of newly driven nails, he might have been posing for the stamp on a penny. The mingled scents of leather and dust and sour sweat and, faintly, old bear grease wafted from him. Aside from the grease, I was at a loss to determine how much of it was his and how much mine.

"Frankly, gentlemen, I don't see how I can help you, nor why I should try." Harms folded aside the map on his desk, revealing mottled traces of green blotter paper beneath a pattern of dead black ink.

"The letter calls for your co-operation," Hudspeth rapped.

"Not mine, Broderick's. And it calls for something which was not his to give. He had no authority to bring in an outside party. Hostile Indians fall within the jurisdiction of the U. S. Army and no other. Their crimes are not a matter for the civil courts."

"Judge Flood thinks different."

"Judge Flood can go to bloody hell." The words came lashing out. He fell silent, rolled the map back farther, found a hand-worked wooden humidor standing on the corner of the desk, and removed the cover. He drew out a cigar the length of his wrist, struck a match—placing a fresh groove on a previously unmarred section of desk—and ignited it. Blue smoke came billowing out in true Grant style. I don't smoke, but it would have been nice if he'd offered us one. He used the same match to light a lamp with a milky white glass shade on the opposite corner and sat back as the soft glow gulped up the shadows.

"Forgive me, gentlemen," he said. This time he sounded sincere. "I've been in the saddle eighteen hours straight. We're short-handed, but it's important we show the enemy a stern face. I'm tired and my patience is on a short halter."

"Any luck?"

He looked at me quickly. "Luck? Doing what?"

I didn't answer. Finally he shook his head.

"We hit every arroyo and dry wash between here and Jamestown. No trace of Ghost Shirt or his warriors. Two of my Indian scouts deserted. They're afraid the Great Spirit is on the other side. Superstitious heathens!" He puffed furiously. His features swam behind an azure haze.

"You're lying, Major."

He stared. Something akin to rage glimmered in his dull brown eyes. I went on before he could blow.

"Your horse was heaving and covered with froth. They don't get that way unless they're ridden fast and hard. Two riderless horses came in with the patrol, and I know enough about Indians to know they don't desert on foot in this country. My guess is you buried what was left of those scouts after Ghost Shirt got through with them, then took off in pursuit. Where's he holed up?"

Harms made a thing out of picking all the lint off his cigar.

"We sent them on ahead to scout out the territory." He spoke slowly. "When they stopped leaving sign we tracked them to the James River. We found them hanging upside down from a cottonwood over a smoldering fire. Their skulls had exploded from the heat."

"Ghost Shirt. Where is he?"

For a moment it looked as if he might answer. Then his dazed expression cleared and the stubborn glint returned to his eyes. "That's army business. So far all the casualties in this quadrant have been sustained by the military. I won't take the responsibility for any civilian deaths here."

"Colonel Broderick—" Hudspeth began.

"Colonel Broderick was a good soldier, but he was weak. He worried more about holding onto his command than keeping the peace in his sector. As a result he lost his own life and those of a dozen of his men while on routine patrol. There will be no such blunders beneath my command. As long as you three are here you are welcome, within limits, to the facilities of the post, but you will not be allowed to leave until the situation is in hand." He started to rise.

"What was a full colonel doing leading a routine patrol?" I pressed. "That's a job for a captain or a lieutenant."

He looked at me again. A faint smile played over his lips but fell short of his eyes. "You served?"

"I was with Schoepf at Mill Springs and with Rosecrans at Murfreesboro. A ball smashed my leg there and I sat out the rest of my enlistment in splints."

"I thought I'd noticed a slight limp. You must have been very young."

"I was nineteen when I signed up."

"Why did you leave?"

"I don't like officers."

That ended the friendly conversation. He stalked toward the door and clapped on his hat. "Sergeant Burdett will be in to show you to your quarters."

"You didn't answer my question, Major," I said.

He ignored me and tugged open the door. I went on. "Colonel Broderick was tracking Ghost Shirt, wasn't he? He got too close and the Indians attacked. Which means you have a fair idea where their stronghold is."

He turned back. Beyond his shoulder, purple twilight had settled over the compound, silhouetting the sentries on the wall in liquid black. "What makes you think it's a stronghold?"

"You took thirty men and came back with twenty-eight. If you'd met Ghost Shirt in the open you'd have killed at least a few of his braves and lost more than two scouts. The only explanation is they're holed up someplace where you can't dig them out. All I'm asking is where."

"Suppose I told you. What can you do that we can't, one underarmed deputy and two old has-beens?"

The marshal sprang from his chair and lunged toward the major, who clawed at his holster. I stuck out a leg, tripping Hudspeth. He threw out his arms and struck the floor hard on his face. The china mug fell from the desk, clunked against the planks, and rolled around in a lazy circle, coming to rest against the lawman's left boot.

Pere Jac remained rooted in the middle of the floor. He hadn't moved. I had already pegged him as a born survivor.

"You're forgetting that one of these old has-beens almost turned one of your men into fishbait a little while ago," I reminded the major.

He put away the Colt and secured the strap that held it in place. "It's a moot point, Deputy," he said. "You're confined to the post for the duration."

"We can make it as hot in here as it is out there." I slid out the Deane-Adams and pointed it in the general direction of his groin. He kept his calm.

"I don't think you will. You're sworn to uphold the law."

I grinned and pulled back the hammer. As I did so I heard another weapon being cocked behind me. It could have been an echo. I knew it wasn't.

Harms smiled, this time all the way. "It might be a good idea to give me the gun." He came forward with his hand outstretched. "Sergeant Burdett has a Spencer rifle pointed at the back of your head."

"He speaks the truth, Page." Jac's tone was noncommittal.

I shifted my head just far enough to take in the outline of the man leaning through the open window behind my right shoulder, a rifle in his hands. I held onto the revolver. Something in my expression halted the officer in mid-step. His smile drained from his features.

"You know," I said, "everyone thinks the gun at a man's back is deadlier than the one in his hand, but that's not true. They both kill just the same."

Drops of moisture sparkled on Harms's tanned forehead. This wasn't his game, I could tell. He was used to shooting it out with rifles and howitzers across several hundred yards of open ground until one side or the other gave up or ran out of ammunition. Here there was no room for his brand of bravery. Face to face with .45-caliber death in that narrow room, he felt fear for what was probably the first time in his career.

In that instant I threw myself from the bench, hit the floor, and rolled. There was an explosion and a cloud of splinters near my head and something hot seared my right cheek, but I kept moving. I came up flat against the wall with my gun still in my grip.

As the sergeant maneuvered to get something worthwhile in his sights, I grabbed the Spencer's barrel with my free hand and jerked it downward. It throbbed in my hand, belched flame. One of the broad white planks in the floor splintered and split down the middle from one end of the room to the other. The simultaneous roar set my ears to jangling and brought dust and loose dirt showering down from the rafters. I twisted the gun from Burdett's desperate grasp and pulled it through the window.

Harms went for his Colt. He was pretty fast. He had the strap almost undone by the time Hudspeth, back on his feet, hauled out his Smith & Wesson and clapped the muzzle to the major's temple.

"Go for it," he said. "Please go for it."

Harms left the Colt where it was.

I had Burdett covered with the Deane-Adams. Short and thickset, he had sunken eyes overhung with black, bushy brows and a cleft chin bunched up like a fist. Tiny blue specks peppered the left side of his face just beneath the leathery skin. Some time or other he had come within a hair's breadth of having his head blown off by a shotgun blast. His left eye glittered unnaturally in the lamplight, and I knew it was glass. His nose was an incongruous pug, but he had filled the gap between it and his wide mouth with a thick black moustache. I counted to ten, then extended the Spencer to him. He stared at it as if he'd never seen it before, then, gingerly, as if he thought it might blow up, took hold of it and hauled it back through the opening. Hudspeth watched, thunderstruck.

"What the hell—"

"Three men don't stand a lot of chance against a garrison full of soldiers." I handed Harms my revolver. He took it hesitantly. "Give him yours before somebody gets hurt," I told the marshal. I was having trouble talking. I relaxed my face muscles and realized I'd been grinning all this time.

It took a few seconds, but finally Hudspeth sighed and turned his weapon over to the major.

"One underarmed deputy and two old has-beens, Major." My resistance to temptation never was much to speak of.

Harms rattled the revolvers together, stared from one face to the other. Then:

"They're all yours, Sergeant. Put them up in Colonel Broderick's quarters and post a guard at the door. And try to resist the urge to give Murdock your rifle again." He turned and strode out stiffly. The troopers who had crowded around the door at the sound of gunfire stood aside to let him through.

"Some fight, A.C.," said Pere Jac on our way out.

"Sure you was close enough to see it?" snarled Hudspeth.

"It is the meek who shall inherit the earth. I fight only for what is mine."

"At least you didn't try to break my neck." Bright eyes slid murderously in my direction.

"Better a broken neck than a bullet in the belly," I said.

Burdett told us to be quiet.

Broderick's late home, one of a row of officers' quarters housed in a single building near the north wall of the fort, was equipped with a sitting room and a bedchamber with two narrow beds. We were told he had shared it with his wife before the Indian troubles had forced her to return to their permanent home in Ohio. The furnishings were spartan and, except for the handsewn lace curtains beginning to yellow on the windows of the bedroom, masculine. The rooms smelled strongly of bootblack.

Hudspeth and I wrestled for a while with a supper of stringy longhorn beef and vegetables taken from what was left of the colonel's wife's garden, which was brought in to us by a seasoned-looking horse soldier, then we gave up and pushed our plates aside. Only Jac, his teeth and gums toughened by years of gnawing at leather-tough pemmican, went on eating. His chewing and the ticking of the clock on the mantel were the loudest sounds for some time. Outside, the boards on the porch creaked beneath the shifting weight of our restless guard.

"This is your stamping ground, Jac," Hudspeth said finally. The sound of a human voice after all that silence made me jump. "Where's the best place around here for a bunch of injuns to hole up?"

"The possibilities are endless." The old métis dipped a spoon in the gravy on his plate and began drawing lines on the bare surface of the table. "There are many buttes and sheltered washes, any one of which would serve Ghost Shirt's purpose. The best is here, just west of the James River." He made a wet X on the other side of the line that represented the body of water. "An abandoned mission, once used by Mormons and built to withstand fierce attack. Twenty well-armed braves could stand off an army from its battlements for months."

"You think that's it?"

He shrugged. "Who is to say? If he is the brilliant chief the stories claim he is, that is where he will be. But I have never met him, and so I have nothing else on which to base my judgment."

"I've heard them same stories, so there must be something to 'em. I'll gamble on it. Murdock?"

"I'm in the pot." I had gotten up from the table to listen for the guard. I laid my hand upon one of the rock-solid timbers that held up the wall of our prison. "Now all we have to do is figure out a way to get past the guard, fight our way through a hundred or so armed troopers, and scale a sixteen-foot wall. I hope one of you has something in mind, because I'm fresh out of suggestions."

" 'The foolish despise wisdom and instruction,' " quoted Pere Jac approvingly. Something in the way he said it made Hudspeth and me look at him. Smiling, he was tracing pagan symbols absent-mindedly on the table with the edge of his spoon.

6 . . .

They made quite a pile, the lighter items such as Mrs. Broderick's lace curtains and the sheets and ticking from the beds on the bottom with the colonel's heavy uniforms and whatever else we could find that would burn heaped on top. Hudspeth and I had done most of the work, gathering the stuff and throwing it into the middle of the sitting room floor while Jac supervised. All of this was done with a minimum of noise and with one ear cocked toward the door, where the squeaking and groaning of the porch boards beneath our guard's feet told us whether he was listening at the keyhole or just pacing back and forth. When the pile was four feet high Jac signaled us to stop, picked up the coal-oil lamp from the table where we had eaten, extinguished it, and saturated the linens and woolens on the floor with its contents. Then he struck a match on the edge of the table.

"You sure this will work?" whispered the marshal. "I always wanted a funeral with an open coffin."

"I offer no guarantees." The métis watched the sulphur flare and waited for it to burn down to the wood. "This is not the sort of thing one can practice. Since there is no other way out of this fort, however, we must convince Major Harms that it is in his own best interests to release us."

"Ghost Shirt made it out without all this."

"Ghost Shirt lost three men doing it and killed that many soldiers. I assume that you wish to spill as little of your own countrymen's blood as possible."

"Meanwhile," I pointed out impatiently, "the smell of that coal oil is drifting toward our friend outside."

"Quite right." Pere Jac squatted and touched the match to the hem of a lace curtain.

The flame caught, burned slowly at first, then spread to engulf the pile with a hollow, sucking sound. A pillar of oily black smoke rose to the ceiling and sent greasy curls unwinding into all the corners of the room. The choking stench of burning rags followed. We got down on the floor where the air was sweeter and waited for results.

We didn't wait long. There was shouting outside the door and pounding, and then a key rattled in the lock and the trooper on guard, a grizzled old campaigner with leathern features and a great swelling belly solid as a sack of lead shot, burst into the room, coughing and digging his fists into his eyes as a wall of smoke hit him square in the face. He stumbled about, clawing at the air and calling for assistance between fits of hacking. In another moment the room was full of troopers in varying states of undress, but all of them armed. Finally buckets of water were produced and emptied in the general direction of the flames, which hissed and spat and sent up thicker and more fragrant columns of smoke than before. The firefighters' curses were colorful and, as a rule, had to do with someone's ancestry. A muck of water and soot darkened the muted colors in the Brodericks' carpet, which was the kind you bought out East and had shipped back here.

Quincy Harms came striding in just as the troopers were slapping out the last of the flames with coats and army blankets. He was in his shirtsleeves, and the scrubbed cleanliness of his face and hands in contrast to the grimy cross-hatching on his neck and wrists indicated that he had been shaving, or more likely trimming his beard, when the alarm had sounded. His suspenders were twisted from having been hastily drawn up over his shoulders. He circled the room, taking in the smoking, charred debris on the floor, the soot on the walls and ceiling, the objects overturned and smashed in the commotion that had followed the troopers' arrival. Our guard, his face streaked black and glistening with sweat, saluted and began to tell his side of the story, but the major cut him off with a slashing motion.

By this time the air had cleared and the three of us were sitting around the table with innocent expressions pasted on our faces. Harms kicked aside a smoldering scrap of tunic and stalked up to us, fists clenched at his sides. He was livid.

"Something wrong, Major?" I was seated nearest him.

His left fist caught me on the corner of the jaw. I went over backwards, chair and all, and hit the floor hard. I bounced up quicker than he expected and cocked my own left.

"Page."

Jac spoke warningly. I shifted my gaze, followed his, and got a spectacular view of the inside of the old trooper's Army Colt pointed at my breast. I lowered my arm.

At a nod from Harms the gun was returned to leather. Cutting loose had calmed him somewhat. His color was closer to normal, but the silver flecks in his eyes swam and glittered in the light of the one lamp left burning.

"What did you gain by that?" He addressed himself to Hudspeth.

"We're expensive pets to keep," I replied, making him face me. "We just wanted to show you how expensive we can be."

"Is that a threat? Because if it is I can throw you in the guardhouse and be done with it."

"You did that with Ghost Shirt."

"We've learned a bit since then."

"Like what?" Hudspeth put in. "Doubling the guard? You can't spare that many men with things like they are. You said yourself you're short-handed."

"The fact of it is, Major," I went on, "we're more trouble than we're worth. You can take away our guns and our matches, tie us up and throw us in a deep hole, and we'll still make it hot for you and your men. You can weather it, but why should you have to? You've enough to worry about with all hell breaking loose outside."

While I had been speaking, patches of color had appeared on his cheeks, glowing as if from fever, and I braced myself to meet another blow. But he held himself in check. When he spoke, the strain showed in his voice, raising it from its normal moderate level to a quivering tenor.

"Just whose side are you on, Murdock?"

"That's easy. Mine."

This time I was sure he was going to make a move, but he fooled me again. For an hour, or maybe it was just ten seconds, he stood there staring at me without seeing me. Then, without turning, he spoke to the old trooper.

"See that their mounts are saddled and their pack horse loaded and ready to go. They're leaving tonight."

"Tomorrow morning's soon enough," I said magnanimously. "We promise not to burn down any buildings before then."

"I wasn't offering you a choice. It's tonight or never." The glint in his cow eyes was as steely as it got. "I'll read Scripture over your grave, Murdock."

Half the stars in the sky were blotted out behind a black overcast as we saddled up (never trust that job to anyone else, least of all a trooper who hates your guts), and by the time we were ready to move out they were all gone and thunder was belching faintly in the distance.

Our guns were returned to us in the livery by the old trooper who had been our guard. I slid my Winchester into its scabbard, inspected the Deane-Adams to make sure it was still loaded, and caught the horse soldier's eye over the cylinder. He avoided my gaze.

He was old enough to be a general, but his faded blue sleeves bore a single stripe. Most likely he'd risen in rank and been busted back down more than once, probably for brawling. The scar tissue over his eyes and fistlike, many-times-broken nose gave me that much. Those eyes were deep in their sockets and shadowed beneath shaggy white brows. They wouldn't blacken noticeably no matter how many times they were hit, nor how hard. He wore his handlebar a third longer than Hudspeth's. Also white, it was stained yellow at the fringe—chewing tobacco—and at the moment its ends were being gnawed by a set of mail-order teeth that buzzed when he spoke, which he hadn't done for some time. Unlike Blackthorne, he appeared not to mind wearing them. His complexion was breadcrustbrown and cracked all over like a riverbed gone dry. The sagging flesh beneath his chin was gathered together at the buttoned collar of his field-stained tunic. Crisp white stubble showed where his razor had missed that morning, a circle of sticking-plaster where it hadn't. We played tag with the eye contact for a while and then I lost my patience.

"All right, disgorge." I holstered the five-shot. "You look like you swallowed a powder keg."

"I can't do it," he said. His voice fell somewhere between a whisper and the sound you get when you try to rack a shell into the chamber of a repeater with sand in the action. "I don't care if they bust me again, I can't watch you three go out there without telling you what's waiting."

Hudspeth gave his cinch a yank and then all was silence. The ticking of the blacksmith's forge as it cooled grew loud. Somewhere a horse snored.

"Well?" The word exploded from the marshal.

The trooper lurched ahead without further preamble. His eyes were black hollows beneath the heavy brows. "I'm Hoxie, Jed Hoxie. Twenty years in the service, not counting the two I spent with Stonewall Jackson. I was with that patrol that got hit last night. Cap'n Francis—he was one of them got kilt—he headed it up till one of the injun scouts found the trail of a couple dozen unshod ponies this side of the James. It could of been friendlies, maybe even métis, but nobody believed that for a minute. None of them has budged a inch from their camps and reservations since this whole thing started, except to hunt, and there ain't no hunting along the Jim this time of year. No, we knowed who it was all right. When you been out here as long as some of us you get so you can smell 'em. Francis ordered halt and sent a messenger back to the fort for orders from Colonel Broderick. But instead of sending 'em, the old man rode back hisself and took charge of the patrol. He said it was time the job got done right, and he wasn't going to trust it to no one else. There was forty of us—more than enough, I guess he figured, to deal with Ghost Shirt.

"Their trail crossed the river a couple of miles south of Jamestown. It was so fresh there was puddles of water in the tracks on the other side. We caught sight of dust clouds a hour or so later. There wasn't much, what with all the grass, but you can always count on twenty horses kicking up a little when they're rid hard. This was the hilly country in the Drift Prairie, and the dust was all we seen of 'em. Broderick called column of twos and we give chase at a canter. We was still following the dust cloud when they hit us.

"They come at us from two sides, one half hitting us in the flank from the left, the other taking us at a angle near the front from the right, just like a pair of scissors. Neatest split cavalry charge I ever did see. They come out of nowhere, whooping it up to beat the band and pounding away with them Spencer repeaters they took from our armory. Broderick went first. Bullet tore clean through his left eye and knocked off the back of his head on its way out. Captain Francis took two in the chest and one in the thigh and bled to death before we could get him back to the fort. We lost our bugler whilst he was blowing recall. He went down with one in his back, wailing on that horn like a sick calf. Bullets was flying all over the place. Once I felt someone tugging at my sleeve, but when I turned to see who it was, there was nobody there. What was there was a hole in the elbow where a hunk of lead kissed it. The injuns made one pass, then turned around and done it again, only backwards, and all the time they was pouring lead into us like grease through a tin horn.

We'd of lost a hell of a lot more than twelve men if injuns was any kind of shots."

"Did you hit any of them?" I asked.

He shook his head, working his store-bought teeth like a mouthful of chew. "Can't say for sure. There was a lot of metal buzzing back and forth, and the way them injuns shriek you don't know if they're hit or just mad. But if we didn't at least nick one or two of 'em it'd be a miracle."

"Was Ghost Shirt with them?"

"Oh, he was with 'em all right. I seen too much of him when he was here in the stockade not to recognize him when I seen him again, and he wasn't wearing no war paint like the others. He rode point on the bunch that hit us from the front."

"Why wasn't he wearing paint?"

"How the hell should I know? Them injuns don't think the same as people. All I know is that paint's supposed to turn away bullets. Maybe he figures he don't need it."

"Whose dust were you following when they attacked?" Hudspeth asked. He peered into the buckskin sack of cartridges he carried in his saddle bag to see if they were all there.

"Likely that belonged to the womenfolk, dragging buffalo robes and bushes behind their horses to make it look like the whole party. It's the oldest trick in the book, but it works most every time. Hell, what can you do to fight it?"

"You can go back to the fort." This from Pere Jac, without intonation. The comment drew a hostile glance from the horse soldier.

"I'd expect that from a breed," he snarled. "We're the army. We're trained to fight."

"And die," said the other. "In the end, what have you gained?"

Hoxie's complexion turned a high copper. I stepped between him and the métis.

"Steady, soldier. We're all on the same side."

"I don't take to nobody with injun blood in his veins calling me a fool," he said. But his violent mood had subsided.

"Nobody called anybody anything. Where was this fight?"

He grew furtive. "I said enough. If the major finds out I told you what I done already he'll bust me out of the service. I just didn't want nobody running off and getting kilt without knowing the score. What you do now is your business." He tugged his hat down and took a step toward the stable door. I laid a hand on his shoulder. It felt like a chunk of the scrawny meat we'd had for supper. He stopped and glared up at me from his inferior height, eyes glittering beneath the shelf of his brows.

"If you tell us where Ghost Shirt is hiding, the major will never know you told us anything."

He started as if slapped in the face. For a moment disbelief and consternation chased each other across his features in the greasy glow of the coal-oil lantern that hung on a rusty nail beside the door. His eyes searched mine for some sign that I was bluffing. He didn't find anything. I sit a good game of poker.

"That stinks," he said.

"To high heaven," I agreed.

"They give him a lot of slack out here. He could call it high treason in time of war and have me shot."

"That's up to you."

"Even if I get away, he'll send Sergeant Burdett after me. Broderick used to sic him on deserters like a trained hunting dog. He never brought any of them back alive."

I said nothing. The forge had grown silent, and now there was only the liquid hiss of the lantern behind me to underscore the stillness. At last the trooper fixed me with an expression that made me feel the way I'd felt when I looked down the barrel of his gun in Broderick's quarters. I rested a thumb on the butt of the Deane-Adams, just in case.

"There's a old stone building six, eight miles west of the river, a fort of some kind. Sergeant Burdett told me that Harms's patrol got within a couple of hundred yards of it this morning when a bunch of bucks on the wall opened fire and the major called retreat. It'd take a force three times what we got a month to blast its way in there. A twelve-pounder wouldn't knock the mortar out from between the rocks in the wall."

"The Mormon mission," said Jac.

I nodded. "Thanks, Private. You're clear with us."

He muttered something indelicate and stamped out.

The first drop banged my hat while I was mounting up outside the door. It was the last individual drop I heard. The rest came down in a roar so sudden Hudspeth and I were thoroughly soaked by the time was got our black slickers out and on. Pere Jac merely removed his nice calico shirt and stored it safely in a saddle bag, facing the elements half naked.

"Couldn't wait till tomorrow to get kicked out, could you?" grumbled the marshal.

Jac smiled and quoted something from Mark, or maybe it was Matthew.

The water was streaming from the brims of our hats —those of us who had hats—as we rode out through the open gate. It glistened on the old breed's broad back, magnifying the scars of battles old and new. There was a light in the window of Major Harms's office, and I knew he was bidding us good riddance. I considered tipping my hat, thought better of it, and kicked the bay into a canter just in time to splatter mud over the uniforms of the troopers waiting to close the gates behind us. Whatever they called me was drowned out by the downpour.

7 . . .

The wind rose and lightning stabbed at the ground, throwing the landscape into dazzling negative, as we stopped to camp on the high ground west of Fort Ransom. But the hard rain was over, and that which hissed down around us now was the kind that could go on for days, flooding the lowlands and washing away farmers' crops as it fed rivers still swollen from the spring thaw. Hudspeth and I used our rifles to make tents of our oilcloth slickers and crawled under them while Pere Jac wrapped himself up from head to foot in his saddle blanket and began snoring almost immediately. If I slept at all I never realized it, shivering in my wet clothes and listening to the drops drumming the surface of my temporary shelter as I thought about how nice it would be to hear them tapping the roof of the officers' quarters back at the fort from the depths of a warm featherbed.

It was still raining when I arose at sunup to find the

marshal already at work over a small fire, frying bacon in the cast-iron skillet he carried in one of his saddle bags. The smell of sweet grease clawed at my stomach, reminding me that I hadn't eaten anything to speak of since breakfast the day before. The longhorn beef at Fort Ransom didn't count. I swigged water from my canteen, sloshed it around and spat it out to clear away some of the fuzz, and stepped closer just to smell.

"Where in hell did you find dry wood?" I asked him.

"Not wood, buffalo chips." His voice was hoarse and thick with phlegm, the way it was every morning. After several days with him I knew that it didn't begin to clear until he'd been up half an hour. "Best damn fuel there is, and it never gets so soaked you can't start it burning with a little work."

"I'm surprised the métis have left buffalo in Dakota to make enough to get a fire started." I glowered at Pere Jac, who sat on his wet blanket gnawing at his pemmican. I resented the ease with which he had fallen asleep the night before. He went on chewing as if he hadn't heard.

The bacon was a little too crisp for my taste, but after nearly starving to death I wasn't complaining. Jac preferred the saddle leather he was eating, but he did accept a tin cup of coffee when it was offered. I did too, but only to wash the grease from the roof of my mouth. The stuff tasted like burnt grain. We crouched around the fire sipping in moody silence.

"What are we doing out here?" growled Hudspeth. "Bouncing around all over the territory, getting saddle sores and wet asses, and for what? A hunk of lead between the eyes and six feet of Dakota on our faces."

"Flood's your boss, not mine. You tell me." I swallowed the dregs in the cup carefully, having already scalded my tongue and throat with the first gulp. I hooked the pot out of the fire with my kerchief wrapped around my hand and poured a second cupful. Glutton for punishment, that's me.

"Me I can answer for." He produced his flask and poured a ration of whiskey into his coffee. "I'm out of a job if I don't. Jac's got whiskey coming, if the rest of his tribe don't drink it all up before he gets back. You're the one I can't figure. What's in this for you?"

"The thrill of the hunt, the glory of the kill."

"No, really."

I warmed my hands around the tin cup. "I've never walked away from anything once it's started. I suppose this was as good a place to start as any, and I probably would have if I hadn't risked my scalp fighting the Flatheads in the Bitterroots last year. If I didn't turn my back on that, why should I do it now? Besides, I'd kind of like to see if we can get away with it. So do you, but you won't admit it."

"Maybe so, but it's a damn poor reason to get killed."

"I've yet to hear a good one."

He threw the dregs of his coffee into the fire and got up. That was another of his quirks. He never drank the last of anything, not even whiskey. "Well, if we got to die, it might as well be sooner as later. Saddle up." He kicked mud and clumps of wet grass into the fire. It went out grudgingly.

Pere Jac drained his cup and rose with none of the complaints you expect from an old man climbing to his feet after a long interval. He shook out his blanket, wrung it out thoroughly, used it to rub down his shivering paint, wrung it out again, tossed it over the pony's back, and saddled it. I did the same, using the bay's blanket for rubdown, then wringing out my bedroll and strapping it behind the cantle of my saddle. We fed the horses two handfuls of grain apiece and were on our way by the time sunlight turned the sky from black to charcoal gray.

It was twenty-five miles from where we'd camped to the James River, with mud the color of rust squirting up around the horses' hoofs at every step. There's nothing exciting about a trek across the flat country east of the Drift Prairie, especially with rain bleeding down and turning everything a mildewy gray. Suffice it to say that one Dakota river basin looks pretty much like all the others.

By the same token, there was nothing spectacular about the James, even at high water. Sodden, grassy banks dotted sparsely with scrawny cottonwoods and box elders sunk to their lower branches in muddy, liver-colored water do not inspire great poetry. The current was swift but hardly torrential, so the damned thing didn't even have danger going for it. It was just another river in a territory chock full of just anothers. Nevertheless we had made pretty good time in reaching it, as there was still an hour of daylight sitting somewhere beyond the overcast when we got off to water the horses and fill our canteens.

"We'll camp here tonight," I said. "Cross in the morning."

"What for? It's early yet." Hudspeth wiped his running nose on the sleeve of his coat and removed a clot of floating grass from the mouth of his canteen between thumb and forefinger.

"I don't know about you, but I'll sleep better with a river between me and Ghost Shirt."

"Afraid?"

"Yes."

There were no fires that night, nor the next morning. Even if there had been buffalo chips available, the chance of an Indian spotting the smoke was too great. We ate some of the salt pork Hudspeth and I had bought in Fargo—Jac stuck to his pemmican—and washed it down with water from our canteens. That night we took turns standing watch, me first. I kept awake slapping at the mosquitoes that descended over me in swarms.

The rain had stopped by the time we were ready to pull out, not that it made much difference with the sun still hidden by clouds and the wet grass cloying around our knees and a strip of water thirty feet wide waiting to be crossed. I dreaded that. Horses hate to cross the stuff at the best of times, but when it's over chest-high they forget who their masters are and make for the nearest dry land regardless of what happens to the weight on their backs. I felt the bay gasp when the bottom fell out from under it. Before it could spook, I grabbed a double armload of its neck and raked its flanks with my spurs. It screamed and swam for dear life. I closed my eyes and held on until there was solid ground beneath me once again. Hudspeth was there waiting for me, the pack horse in tow. Pere Jac crossed over a moment later.

"How far?" I asked the latter.

"Seven miles." He pointed toward the southwest. "It is the only building around still standing."

"What's the best way to approach it?" asked Hudspeth.

"With the cavalry."

We decided to risk a frontal approach rather than lose another day by circling around, and headed southwest. Half an hour later the sun broke through the overcast. Droplets of moisture sparkled on the blades of tall grass like broken glass after a barroom fight. Gradually the flat plain gave way to rolling prairie. The landscape was deceptive. From a distance it looked as if you could see everything for miles, but you could miss half the Cheyenne nation hiding in the hollows between the hills. We slowed our pace accordingly.

After four miles we came to a broad swath running

from north to south where what grass that had not been trampled beneath many hoofs was grazed almost to the ground. The horses nickered when we stopped, and shifted their weight nervously from hoof to hoof. The métis dismounted, crouched, and spent some moments studying the turned earth. Then he rose with a grim expression on his weathered countenance.

"Unshod ponies," he said. "Heading south. One, perhaps two hours ago."

"Ghost Shirt?" I suggested.

He shook his head. "Not unless he has picked up many new braves."

"How many?"

"More than I can count."

He climbed back into the saddle and we continued for another hour. Jac reined in at the crown of a hill and thrust a long, wrinkled finger at arm's length before him. "There!"

I followed his gesture. At first I couldn't see anything. Then I spotted it, an irregularity on the horizon, hardly more than a blur, but obvious enough against a skyline nearly devoid of trees.

"The mission?"

Jac nodded.

"I can't see a damn thing." The marshal drew a battered army-issue telescope from his saddle bag, extended it to its full length, and screwed it into his left eye socket. He spent some time twisting it. "Yeah, I see it," he said then. "It's—" He stiffened.

"What is it?" I demanded, after a couple of seconds had slithered past in silence.

"I think we're too late." He handed me the glass.

I trained it toward the object atop the distant rise. It was a stone fortress, thirty years old if it was a day, with broken battlements along the top of the front wall and a ravaged bell tower rising from the middle, the bell intact and naked to the elements. I panned away from the structure, saw something belatedly, went back. I twisted the scope for sharper focus.

A mounted phalanx of perhaps three hundred Indians loaded down with full war regalia was on its way toward the mission's yawning entrance from the north. Even as they approached, a small group of similarly attired warriors galloped out to meet them. When they were a hundred yards apart they stopped, and the leader of each band peeled off for a private parley in the center of the clearing. The glass wasn't powerful enough for me to make out their features, but it didn't really matter. Never having seen Ghost Shirt, I wouldn't have recognized him anyway.

8 . . .

"You're the injun expert," Hudspeth informed me sourly. "What do we do now?"

I played for time, studying the doll-size figures on horseback in the center of the magnified circle. Short of a Great Southwestern desert after a brief rain, when everything is in blossom and the sagebrush looks like it's on fire, there's nothing more colorful than a large group of Plains Indians girded for war. Many of them half naked, the rest wearing fringed and beaded vests or jackets or the remnants of blue cavalry tunics with the sleeves cut off, the warriors had painted their skin red and black and yellow and white and decorated themselves with shells and beads and the claws and teeth of various predators. The braves from the mission were all armed with rifles, the others with only an occasional firearm among the lances, clubs, and bows and arrows, all of which were lowered as a gesture of peace and good faith.

They wore buckskin leggings and wolf pelts and summer moccasins with fringes that dangled below the bellies of their mounts. Coup sticks trailing eagle feathers and the traditional Cheyenne and Sioux symbols of strength and virility, fashioned of leather and polished wood and rattling at the ends of buckhide thongs knotted to the buffalo bone crosspieces, stuck up at crazy angles above the heads of the warriors holding them. Here and there the white bulb of a bleached human skull decorated the top of a pike.

One Indian—he who had ridden out alone to greet the leader of the newcomers—wore neither paint nor decoration. Naked to the waist, he was attired only in leggings, moccasins, and a breechclout of what looked like faded red burlap, dyed by a squaw's patient hand. It was the only splash of color on his person. He rode bareback astride a muscular roan with a white blaze and stockings, whose full sides suggested grain and not grass feeding—hardly an Indian pony. A couple of hundred yards closer and I might have been able to make out the army brand on its sleek rump. The rider was built thick about the chest and upper arms, and his nut-brown flesh glistened with grease or sweat or both. He wore his black hair long. That was as much as I could tell about him from my vantage point. He didn't look much like a god, but then I'm no authority.

The other chief was decked out in fine buckskins and

a feathered headdress whose tail descended below his waist and rested on the back of one of those hide-stripping wooden saddles with which some savages insisted upon torturing their mounts. Strips of ermine dangled in front of his ears, and when he turned once to gesture with a long, fringed arm over the Indians at his back the sunlight shone on a row of polished stones in the headband. It was a sight that kings and Russian grand dukes came halfway around the world to see, only to return home in disappointment when they didn't. Somehow, though, in the presence of the other's unadorned simplicity, the visitor's splendor came off as pompous and a shade ludicrous. I passed the telescope to Pere Jac.

"The one in the headdress. Recognize him?"

The métis was unfamiliar with the instrument. Carefully he placed it against his right eye, waved it back and forth a little, settled down finally, and sat motionless for about a minute. Then he returned the glass to me.

"His name is Many Ponies," he said. "He used to trade with the métis before the wars. Some of the Miniconjou Sioux elected to follow him at the time of the breakup following Custer's death. The last I heard of him he was in Canada."

"He's back."

Jac went on. "Tall Dog, also a Miniconjou, is there as well. I was told he had retired to the Standing Rock reservation. Also Broken Jaw, a Cheyenne warrior, and Blood on His Lance, who was a sub-chief under the great Oglala Crazy Horse. The others I do not know."

"That's all right. That's enough."

"So what do we do?" repeated the marshal.

"Why ask me?" I swung the glass back to him. The movement startled him. He jumped, then grabbed the instrument with both hands. "You're the ramrod in this outfit."

"You've fought injuns. I never been closer to one than a cigar store."

"I shot at a few. That's not the same as fighting them."

"It's close enough for me."

"While we are arguing," Pere Jac put in, "I suggest that we get down behind this hill before they see us against the horizon."

"Congratulations," I told him. "You just became our new Indian expert."

We wheeled our horses and withdrew below the crest of the rise. There we dismounted and squatted to confer, holding onto the animals' reins in the absence of a place to tether them. We kept our voices low, which was ridiculous, considering the distance that separated us from the Indians at the mission. Fear does strange things to people.

"It is obvious that one of us must go back for the soldiers while the rest remain here to keep an eye on the Indians." Jack took out his stubby pipe and sucked air through it noisily. "The question is, which of us shall it be?"

We exchanged glances for a while, but no one seemed inclined to volunteer. There was no telling what kind of reception awaited the one who returned to the fort alone. Ghost Shirt, however, was something on which we could count. At length the métis shrugged and plucked a handful of stiff new grass from the ground at his feet. He spent some time sorting through the blades, decided on three, discarded the others, then made a show of clearing his throat, like the foreman of a jury milking his moment in the sun before delivering the verdict.

"We will draw straws. The holder of the short straw will go."

I shook my head. "I don't like it."

"Why not?" Hudspeth demanded. "It seems fair enough."

"That's why I don't like it."

Jac shuffled the bits of stubble in such a way that we couldn't see what he was doing, and held out a fist from the top of which the ends barely protruded.

Hudspeth selected the first one and held it up. It was about two inches long. His breath came out in a sigh.

I stared at the two remaining until the breed began to show signs of impatience—which, taking into account his natural stoic disposition, should give some idea of how long I stalled. I took a deep breath and plucked out the one on the right. It fell just short of an inch.

We looked at Jac. He was enjoying his role. He kept us in suspense for as long as was prudent, and when Hudspeth's nose began to flush he opened his fist. A straw an inch and a half long lay in the hollow of his palm.

"I told you I didn't like it." I threw down the evidence and got up to remount. "I'll be back when I can." The bay grunted in protest when I swung a leg over its back, as if it knew where we were going.

"Just a minute." Hudspeth took hold of the bit chain. "If you bring the army and they help us catch Ghost Shirt, how are we going to get him away from them to hang in Bismarck?"

I leaned forward and, taking his wrist between thumb and forefinger, removed his hand from the bit. "You worry too much," I said. "We'll never live to see Bismarck again anyway."

"Good luck, Page." Pere Jac's expression was blank.

I could see he really meant it, so I choked back the response I had all set, nodded curtly, and laid down tracks east.

The rain in Dakota, I learned, doesn't stop during the

wet season. It just moves on, leaving the places where it's been to dry and cake and the crops to wither while it washes away what's left of the green that's already given up waiting for it elsewhere. The storm that had hit us after leaving Fort Ransom was in the north now, a black crescent on the skyline looking like the charred fringe of a towel left too close to the fire, dumping water over the higher country up around Fargo. The prehistoric lake bed that stretched from the Drift Prairie to the Red River took the runoff and channeled it into the James River. At that point the lazy stream we had crossed a couple of hours earlier became a snarling torrent forty feet wide at its narrowest point and swift enough to sweep downriver a horse and rider faster than a man can curse. I no longer recognized it.

I wasted half a day riding up and down in search of a place to cross. A mile north of the spot where we'd come over, the river broadened into a lake, which was no good at all, and the farther south I rode the swifter grew the current. It was late afternoon when I gave up and turned back toward the mission, and damned near sundown before I galloped up the rise where I'd left my companions.

At least I thought it was where I'd left them. Those swells all looked alike when there was no one there. I called their names a couple of times, being careful to keep my voice from carrying as far as the mission. When after two or three minutes there was no answer, I rode to the top of the hill and looked around. There was the mission on the skyline, looking to be about the same distance away as it had been that morning. There was no sign of life on any of the other hills in the area. I turned and cantered back below the crest for a second look.

It was the spot, all right. Dismounting, I saw that the ground was chewed up where our horses had stood

fidgeting and pawing the earth while we squatted talking, and in a bare spot I saw the pointed toe of a foot-
print that could only have been made by one of Hudspeth's fancy Mexican boots. As I bent over to study it,
something cold and slimy slithered up my spine. I
mounted again and spurred the bay back to the crest.
What I saw there made me reach back automatically to
grip the butt of my revolver.

On the ridge about three hundred yards away, a
solitary rider sat facing me astride a roan horse with no
saddle. The figure's hair hung down in plaits on either
side of its naked chest. It was holding a rifle upright
with the butt resting upon one thigh, a cloth of some
sort drooping from its barrel and stirring ever so slightly in the minimal breeze. I was only dimly aware that
this was Pere Jac's beloved calico shirt. The Indian
looked as if he had been there for hours, which was
impossible, since I'd just looked in that direction a few
minutes before and seen nothing. The slimy thing
crawled back down my backbone.

"Page Murdock." Warped and distorted by distance,
the unfamiliar voice was felt rather than heard, stroking
my eardrums in such a way that it set my teeth on edge.
"You have the choice of dying in the mission with your
friends or dying out here alone. I await your answer."

9 ...

I waited until the words died away before, slowly, as if a sudden movement might spook my game, I squeaked my Winchester from its scabbard and raised it to my shoulder. Ghost Shirt didn't stir. I wondered if he thought his flag of truce might save him, or if he really believed he was indestructible. If so, his brilliance was overrated. Allowing for distance and the updraft from the hills that rolled between us, I drew a bead on a point just above his left shoulder and took a deep breath, half of which I planned to let out before I squeezed the trigger. Still he didn't move.

But something did.

Thirty feet in front of my nose, the ground heaved and spewed up a dozen black-faced braves on horseback. They exploded over the crest of the next ridge, teeth bared white—or as close to white as Indians' teeth got—against the ebony goo they had smeared over themselves from hairline to breechclout, Spencer repeaters braced one-armed against their biceps in that impossible-to-hit-anything way they had. At that range, however, they couldn't *all* miss. They were all over me in two blinks, stabbing the bay's bit before it could rear, snatching the carbine out of my hands, jerking my

Deane-Adams from its holster. I was overpowered by the stench of hot sweat and bad grease, of lathered horseflesh and paint. No hands reached for me. They didn't have to. I was ringed in.

They were Cheyenne. One, a brave with a nose like a razor and a lightning-streak of yellow slashing diagonally across his blackened features, wore one of those human-finger necklaces for which the tribe was notorious, its macabre pendants brown and wrinkled and shrunken so that the nails stood out like claws. They didn't look as if they had ever strung a bow or braided beads into a horse's mane or, to put an even grimmer face on it, drawn a needle through an embroidery hoop or followed a passage in a family Bible. Interspersed among these were tiny medicine bags that looked to have been fashioned from human flesh. The ornament carried strong medicine, too strong for an ordinary warrior. But there was only one chief in Ghost Shirt's crowd, so he must have been no more than a sub-chief or a brave who had proved himself in many battles. Possibly a medicine man. In any case, he seemed to be the leader of this band, as my Winchester was turned over to him without hesitation by the Indian who had seized it. He eyed it lovingly, passed a hand over the engraving on the action, then, decisively, thrust his own dusty Spencer into the hands of the brave nearest him and tucked the carbine under his arm. He grunted a terse order. The point of a broad-bladed knife was thrust inside my left nostril and hands rooted around inside my saddle bags. At length my cartridge boxes were produced and tossed to the ranking warrior. The sharp scent of steel tickled the hairs inside my nose. I controlled myself with an effort. A sneeze now could have cost me a substantial amount of blood, to say nothing of what a startled Indian might do. Not that I was going to live long enough to see the last of the sun, wallowing now in a blood-red pool behind the fortress on the distant ridge.

Another order was given in guttural Cheyenne and my horse began moving with no encouragement from me. In a mass we struck out toward the mission. I glanced in that direction, but Ghost Shirt was no longer there. Having served his purpose as bait, he had left the situation in the hands of his subordinates and returned to his stronghold. Such confidence in the obedience of his warriors bordered on arrogance.

Up close, the wall of the mission turned out to be constructed of weathered stone, tightly mortared and forming a barrier nearly twenty feet high around the buildings inside. Three decades or more ago it had served as a place of refuge for the settlers who had dwelled nearby in farmhouses long since reduced to their foundations by fire and the elements. A few pulls on the great bell that swung in the central tower and the Mormons would come streaming in for protection from Indians, blizzards, or religious persecution, three of the many dangers they had learned to live with in order to uphold their creed. I wondered which of the three had brought an end to it all in this lonely quarter, or if they had simply thrown everything over to join Brigham Young's exodus to Utah. Whatever the reason, only this fire-blackened, bullet-chipped fortress remained as a monument to the brotherly existence they preached.

The gate was made of logs bound and pegged together vertically, all but petrified with age. It swung open in one piece to admit us, then was secured by a handful of Indians who lowered another log into steel cleats on either side of the opening, much as at Fort Ransom. The ground inside the enclosure had been pounded over the years into a dust fine as face powder and loosened by the activity of the present occupants to form a layer two inches deep. It puffed up around the horses' fetlocks in reddish clouds that drifted across the compound like gunsmoke across a busy battlefield. Fresh rope ladders hung from the catwalks on all four walls, atop which Sioux and Cheyenne sentries stood watching me, their eyes hostile slits in faces dried and cracked beyond their years by constant exposure to sun, wind, and grit.

There were women and children in the compound, which surprised me, although there was no reason it should have. Sex and age were of little consequence among a people for whom hardship and danger were a way of life. It didn't matter to the children running naked, their ribs showing beneath their brown hides, that there was a war on, nor to the stout squaws who hardly glanced at me as they sat cross-legged in the hot sun chewing on large squares of buckskin to make soft leggings for their braves or lugged clay pots of water and baskets of dried buffalo chips to their cooking fires. They were doing the work their mothers and grand-mothers had done before them, all the way back to when the Earth-Shaker fashioned the first woman out of clay to mate with and free the first brave for hunting and making weapons.

Except for the stone bell tower, now in the early stages of decay, the structures inside the compound were made of less sturdy stuff than the wall. Soddies mostly, with here and there a long, low adobe building scattered among them, its thatched roof sagging in the middle like a Conestoga wagon, they were ramshackle affairs slapped together more for shelter during the hours of sleep than for actual living purposes, and had begun falling apart twenty years before. Cones of buf-falo hide strewn about the grounds offered mute testi-mony to some Indians' contempt for the white man's idea of quarters.

The foundation of the tower—which, if the weather-beaten wooden cross pegged into the mortar on the front of it was any indication, had once been the mission chapel—was square, sunk below the ground, and entered by means of a shallow flight of earthen steps leading down to a low plank door. Rough hands yanked me from my horse and half-carried, half-dragged me to the top of the steps. Teetering on the edge, I was patted all over for hidden weapons, relieved of the knife I carried in my right boot, and shoved head first down the stairwell. I sailed through the air just long enough to experience that eerie weightless sensation you get when falling in a dream, then, suddenly, slammed into a great blank wall of nothing.

Someday, when they build a home for retired lawmen, they'll have to provide a row of chairs in which those fortunate few who survive the profession may sit while they stare at the wall. I had scarcely gotten rid of the headache I'd acquired last winter when a wife-murderer I'd been escorting back to Helena had parted my hair with a rock during an unguarded moment, and now, as I swam to consciousness through a pool of thick, multicolored glue, I wondered why Grant and Lee were fighting the Battle of the Wilderness, complete with thundering twelve-pounders and rattling musketry, all over again inside my skull.

I was flat on my back on what had to be the hardest stone floor this side of Yuma prison. My first act, after the necessary vomiting, was to raise a gentle hand to the top of my head to see if anything was leaking out. A white-hot bolt of pure pain shot straight down to my toes when the tip of my index finger stroked a lump the size of a cobblestone in a nest of matted, sticky hair. After that I quit. At least this time my skull was in one piece. That was a relief, even if whatever was locked up inside it was pounding to get out. Nobody ever told me if we're allowed more than one cracked head to a lifetime.

I decided that I was inside the chapel. If so, I now saw where the work that had not gone into the other buildings on the mission grounds went. I ran a palm over the surface of the floor. It was made of flat rocks, polished to as high a finish as sandstone ever achieved, and bunted up against one another so snugly that in places I couldn't squeeze my fingertips between them. Above me, the crudely vaulted ceiling opened into a shaft that shot straight up to the sky, where the rusted bell stood out in sharp relief against the jagged, moon-washed square beyond. The thing must have weighed half a ton. One good tug on the frayed old rope that dangled down between the rotted rafters, I thought detachedly, and the great hunk of iron would come singing down and squash me like a roach. With my head in its present condition I didn't much care.

Now and then a solitary bat flapped its pendulous course to and fro inside the rim, the framework of its membrane-covered wings etched starkly against the pale sky. The sight of it jarred me into reality. How long had I been out?

"Two hours."

My head jerked around in the direction of the unexpected voice, the pain following close behind. When the popping lights and purple spots faded, I saw moonlight playing over the angular bones of Pere Jac's face in the darkened corner where he was sitting. The orange glow of his pipe brightened as he sucked on the other end, then faded as he took it from between invisible lips. He was shirtless, which came as no surprise since I'd seen the garment hanging from Ghost Shirt's rifle earlier.

"It is the third question a man asks when he comes to after a blow," he went on without salutation. "First he asks himself where he is, then what happened. When he has answered those he is left with the passage of time, to which only another can reply."

"Sounds like the voice of experience." My tongue moved sluggishly. My face began to burn and I realized that my forehead and the bridge of my nose were skinned where I had come into contact with whatever I had come into contact with.

"A man who has reached my age without being knocked senseless at least once has not lived. They carried you in here after it became apparent that they could not open the door simply by throwing you against it. Not that they did not come close. Two of the boards you sprang will never be the same."

"Neither will my head." I rolled over onto my side so that I could see him without straining my eyeballs, which creaked in their sockets. It was then that I discovered that every muscle in my body was in the same condition as my skull. "Where's Hudspeth?"

"Beside me, sleeping. Can you not hear his snores?"

I'd thought it was the foundation settling. Now I became aware of the rhythm in the rumbling noise coming from the blackness at the base of the wall. I had to hand it to the marshal. He could sleep on the gallows.

"Care to tell me the story?"

"It is very exciting." The red glow arced upward, flared, faded again. Black against the milky-water color of the moonlight, threads of smoke unraveled up the shaft. "An hour after you left we decided to bed down the horses so that they would be fresh for whatever would be expected of them when you returned. I heard a noise on the other side of the hill as I was unsaddling. I was reaching for my Sharps when a Cheyenne lance pierced my right shoulder. A.C. shot the brave in the throat with his revolver while he was turning to draw his knife at the top of the hill. The bullet nearly took his head off. Before he hit the ground fourteen or fifteen Indians came whooping and shrieking over the crest, waving rifles and those hatchets my French ancestors traded their great-grandfathers for furs and blankets. A.C. killed two and wounded a third, but there were too many of them and they were too fast, even on foot. They fell on him and would have torn him to pieces then and there had not Ghost Shirt stepped in to prevent it."

"That doesn't fit in with what I've heard about him."

"I think that he has something special in mind for A.C."

And yet he slept. I shook my head in wonder. Judge Flood didn't know the quality of the iron he was getting set to toss on the scrap heap.

"How'd they know you were there?" I asked Jac.

"Perhaps they spotted us when we were watching them earlier. It is more likely that someone noticed the sunlight glancing off the lens of the spyglass."

"Seems to me I should have heard the gunshots. I wasn't that far away."

"You wouldn't. These hills soak up noise."

"That's not all they've soaked up. How's the shoulder?"

He shrugged, then right away regretted it. I heard a sharp intake of breath in the darkness. He let it out carefully, through his nostrils. "They have applied a bandage, of sorts. The medicine man—Lame Horse, I think he is called, my Cheyenne is rusty—said some words over it. I shall live in spite of them."

"Decent of them to have left you your pipe, matches and tobacco."

"We are the only things here that will burn. Am I to assume that the army is not coming?"

I told him about the river. He sighed.

" 'For it is better,' " he quoted, " 'if the will of God be so, that ye suffer for well doing, than for evil doing.' "

There isn't much you can say to a thing like that, so I let it stand. Hudspeth's snoring dominated everything for a time. Then, from outside, a high, thin wail was borne in on the night air. An unearthly sound, brazen and eerie. It raised the hairs on the back of my neck.

"What in hell was *that?*"

"A bugle." He knocked out his pipe against the wall at his back. A shower of sparks fell to the floor, glowed there for a while, then blinked out, one by one. "Captured, I suppose, when they attacked Colonel Broderick's patrol. They have been taking turns blowing it for the past hour. Probably they hope to use it to confuse the soldiers next time they fight."

"It won't work unless they know the calls. The way they're blowing it sounds chilling as hell."

"That is the next best thing."

We listened to it for a while.

"How come we're still alive?" I asked then.

He hesitated. "I have been wondering the same thing. It worries me."

"Hostages?"

"I think not. What would they have to bargain for? They have their freedom. No, I fear that they have some other use for us. The reason I fear is that I have no idea what it is."

Outside, the bugle fell silent. We listened to that for a while.

I said, "Ghost Shirt knew my name."

"Of course he did. I told him."

That took a minute to sink in. I'd suspected it, of course, but I hadn't expected him to admit it so readily.

"What do you plan to do with the thirty pieces of silver?" I asked then.

He chuckled, without humor. "Page, you have an exaggerated sense of your own importance. He asked me who was with us. I might have said no one. He would have read the ground and seen that there were three sets of tracks, not counting those made by the pack horse. Hudspeth and I would have been strung up by our heels over a fire until we either talked or our skulls burst. I thought it best that we were all spared the trouble. Can you honestly say that you would have acted differently?"

"I might have made him work for it a little."

"That is where our characters differ. I fight only for what is mine. It is enough that I lost a fine shirt. Besides, once he had us dangling over that fire he would not have bothered to have us cut down whether we talked or not. This way it was more of a burden for him to do it than to undo it."

There was no arguing with logic like that, but I was in that kind of mood, so we hashed it out for another five minutes or so. We were so busy neither of us noticed when Hudspeth ceased snoring.

"Can't you bastards shut the hell up and let a man sleep?" He sat up, lifting his head and shoulders into the pale light. His face was a map of cuts, swellings and bruises. One half of his handlebar was cocked upward where his upper lip was puffed and crusted over with dark blood.

"Jesus, you're hard to look at," I said.

"That's your problem." Absent-mindedly he reached for his flask, grumbled when he came up with a handful of air. "One of them black-faced sons of bitches took the time to lift my whiskey whilst the others was kicking me around." He hawked and spat out a jet of what looked to be blood that had collected in his mouth. It splattered loudly on the stone floor.

"It is fortunate that they did not lift your scalp as well." Jac blew the sludge out of his pipe with a sound that put me in mind of a boy blasting on a broken whistle.

"Wouldn't much matter if they had, since they're going to anyway. This ain't no weekend in St. Louis we been invited on."

"They don't usually take the scalp of an enemy not killed in battle," I said. "They might, however, hollow out your skull and use it for a bowl to grind meal in. That is, if it isn't solid bone."

"You should talk. You took a look at that door you knocked on with your forehead?"

I had a snappy retort all ready, but I didn't get to use it. Pere Jac made a noise like steam escaping from a boiler and clutched our wrists in a vise grip, listening.

A short scraping sound, such as might have been made by a human foot wrapped in dead animal flesh scuffing hard earth, reached us from just outside the door. A heavy bolt was shot back and moonlight fanned out across the flagstones. Two Indians stood outside the doorway, one a little behind the other because there was not enough room for them to stand side by side in the narrow passage. Cold light painted silver stripes along the barrels of their rifles. The one in front signaled for us to stand up. When we obeyed, he covered us with his rifle while his companion slid in past him, carrying coils of what looked like buckskin thong. He stepped behind us.

I knew what was coming. I put my hands behind me so he'd have no excuse to yank, and in a few seconds he had the first cord wound tightly around my wrists. Tight as it was, though, he gave it an extra tug that almost pitched me forward onto my face, then secured it and spat on the knot. He did the same with Jac, but when he got to Hudspeth he surpassed himself, forcing the marshal to curse through his teeth when the knot was set. That finished, the other Indian came in and joined his partner. Steel dug into my back and we started forward.

"I feel like a bride on her wedding night," I whispered to Pere Jac as we approached the steps. "What do you say when you meet a god?" Then the gun punched me behind the ribs and I shut up.

10 . . .

Dakota nights being cool the year around, there was a snap in the air as we made our way across camp, our Indian escorts close behind. I shivered in my thin canvas coat and wondered how Pere Jac, naked to the waist, managed to keep from turning blue. But he was a native and accustomed to extremes of temperature. The fact that his breath, like mine and Hudspeth's, was visible in gray jets of vapor seemed to bother him not at all. He seemed equally unconcerned with the boiled strip of buffalo hide that swathed his injured right shoulder, which, now dry, must have chafed his skin at the edges like dusty barbed wire. The blood had dried into a yellow-brown stain on the hide. Around us, firelight glimmered cozily behind panes of oiled paper in the windows of the soddies and huts and behind the skin walls of the tipis. The smell of wood smoke teased my nostrils and caused my stomach to grind when I detected in it the sweet aroma of roasting meat. I hadn't eaten since I'd shared a piece of salt pork with the marshal that morning, a hundred years ago.

We were conducted to a large adobe building near the south wall, which had, I supposed, served as a place for the Mormons to meet and be preached at and marry their legions of wives. The door had long since been blown off or taken down and chopped up for firewood or used for lumber in a country where wood fetched higher prices than whiskey, and now a buffalo robe hung in its place over the opening. The barrel of a Spencer blocked my way as I was about to step inside. Its owner, one of our guards, held us at bay with the business end while his companion went in. Half a minute later he returned and pulled the robe aside for us to enter. The other brave resumed his position behind us as I stepped across a threshold worn hollow by foot traffic, followed closely by Jac and Hudspeth.

The room was long and narrow, the mud-and-timber walls unpaneled, the floor earthen. At the far end a fire of wood scraps and buffalo chips burned bluish and smokeless in the grate of a large stone fireplace, casting its buttery light over the floor and walls, where giant shadows licked and flickered against a dingy yellow background. The owner of one of them sat in a rickety wooden chair with his back to the fire, a colorful blanket draped shawl-like over his bare shoulders and my gun belt buckled around his waist, the Deane-Adams resting in its holster. That came as no surprise. The five-shot was a rare piece this side of the Atlantic. Any Indian, even a Messiah who had been educated at the hands of the white man, would find it enough of a novelty to prefer it over Hudspeth's Smith & Wesson or any of the other more common firearms seized over the past several weeks. There was no sign of my Winchester, but then it was dark in the room and I doubted that he'd let a weapon so obviously superior to the Spencers his tribe was using get very far out of his sight, even if it had already been claimed by someone else.

Seen up close, his features, which had once been described as "satanic" by a newspaper writer who had never been west of Manhattan, were rather ordinary, although even enough to be considered handsome by some moon-eyed schoolgirl with visions of being abducted by a virile savage to a tipi in some far-off prairie. His nose was strong but hooked only slightly, his lips full for an Indian and sculpted, his chin square. Somewhere along the line someone had told him his eyes were hypnotic, and he played them for all they were worth, glaring at each of us in turn from beneath drawn brows, like Napoleon in his portraits. He did his best to make the rough-hewn old chair look like a throne by sitting as erect as possible, and I have to admit that the effort wasn't altogether unsuccessful. He might even have pulled it off if he weren't suffering from a bad summer cold.

His eyelids were puffy and he wiped his nose from time to time with the edge of the blanket, but that only made his sniffles worse. The idea that he was prey to the same ills that plagued the rest of us plainly bothered him more than the cold. It showed in his expression. His face was more easily readable than the average Indian's, which irritated him no less. He would be that kind, I thought, growing more disgusted with himself each day for his inability to live up to his reputation. It was a weakness he shared with many another legend I had known. I filed the knowledge away in my memory for future reference.

All the same, he made me feel old. At the age of

twenty-two I had been a penniless veteran with a game leg and no prospects. Thirteen years had healed my leg and improved my outlook, but that was about all. At twenty-two, Ghost Shirt was the undisputed chief of all the renegade tribes in the Northwest, with more braves flocking to his standard every day. Is it a white man's trait always to be comparing his lot with others? In any case, we did have one thing in common, and that was that in our respective occupations we both stood a better than even chance of being dead tomorrow. At the moment, however, the odds of it happening to me were much the stronger.

But there must have been something to the god theory, because it wasn't until I had exhausted myself on Ghost Shirt that I noticed the room's other three occupants. One, a scruffy, grime-yellow dog of uncertain forebears, lay stretched across the hearth with its chin on its front paws, bright eyes resting on Ghost Shirt, whom I took to be its master. Its tail had been bobbed, from the look of the ragged stub, by a jack knife or some other instrument just as inadequate. It twitched whenever the chief's eyes flickered in that direction. The others in attendance were not seated— partly, I assumed, out of respect for the chief and partly because most Indians were uncomfortable sitting on chairs, and the floor was too hard and cold even for them. For some reason I knew that the Sioux standing near the farthest of the four windows was the Miniconjou whom Jac had identified earlier as Many Ponies, even though I had seen him before only at a distance and he had since doffed his paint and feathers. But he carried himself like a chief, and the strong, beak-nosed face, partially in shadow, was too old and seamed to belong to a warrior one would choose to take along on such an arduous campaign as this. He appeared to be more interested in the moonlight-drenched scenery beyond the window than anything inside the room. The third was a nervous sort with a sharp face and lean brown body set off by sun-bleached buckskins, who hadn't stopped pacing since we'd entered. He too had scraped off his paint, but I recognized him instantly as the streak-faced warrior who had commanded the party that had taken me prisoner. He had exchanged his necklace of human fingers for a more conventional one of copper and semiprecious stones. Apparently he felt no need for strong medicine in the presence of his chief. I hadn't noticed it before, but now that he was on foot I couldn't miss his withered left leg, which looked as if it had been shattered in his childhood and stunted, so that his foot dragged sibilantly across the floor as he paced up and down the length of the room.

On the long, low table that stood before Ghost Shirt, chunks of lean red meat, the remains of a meal, floated in a pool of bloody juice in a pottery bowl. My stomach began to work all over again at the sight of it. I tried to devour it with my eyes, but that was less than satisfying. But since it was the next best thing to eating I kept my eyes on it from then on. I even imagined that I could smell it, although there was no steam rising from it and it was probably cold as ice. As far as I was concerned it was tender sirloin hot off the griddle.

The warrior with the game leg was holding forth in a harsh guttural I took to be Cheyenne. His voice was a nasty bleat and he spoke with a pronounced, buzzing lisp. He was angry as hell about something and his tone reflected it as he continued to pace rapidly in spite of the dead limb, gesturing agitatedly with his long, bony arms. Although he pointedly avoided looking in our direction, it was plain enough who were the subjects of his tirade. Ghost Shirt waited until he had finished, then blew his nose on the edge of the blanket and said something over his shoulder to Many Ponies. His voice was moderate but high strung. It's unfair to pass judgment on a man's tones when he's speaking in a foreign tongue, and more so when his adenoids are swollen, but I blamed the tension on the pressure of command. You'll hear the same quality in the calmest of voices at an officers' cotillion if you've an ear for it.

He didn't say much, but whatever it was it had a question mark on the end of it. Reluctantly, as if afraid he'd miss something outside, Many Ponies turned his face from the window long enough to flick his eyes over us, then returned them to the landscape beyond the empty pane. His lids were bald where he plucked his lashes, and deep crow's feet pulled them down at the corners, giving his elderly face—he might have been forty-eight, far past prime for an Indian—a sad expression. His reply, in Sioux, was brief and without inflection.

Gimpy launched a fresh tantrum—or maybe it was the same one—as if he'd been holding it back during the others' exchange only with great effort. But he pulled up short when Ghost Shirt held up a callused palm. Annoyance glittered in the lame brave's eye. He'd had more to say.

Unlike his fellow tribesman, the Cheyenne chief kept his attention fixed on one or the other of us all the while he spoke, and he spoke at length. He was calm for the most part, but certain words brought out his emotions from time to time, twisting his face into a mask of hatred and rasping harshly off his tongue like the buzz from a snake's rattle. Once I caught the Sioux word for the Arapaho nation—uttered, no doubt, for the Miniconjou's benefit—when it came lashing out in this manner. I wondered about that, since the Cheyenne and the Arapaho were supposed to be like brothers, but perhaps this was a matter of personal preference. From there he dovetailed deliberately into more placid speech.

Broken occasionally by interruptions from the gimp, which were themselves cut off when Ghost Shirt resumed as if unchecked, the monologue went on for about five minutes, at the end of which stretched a silence complete enough to reveal that the warriors in the compound had returned for a fresh go at the bugle. I could have sworn once that I heard the opening bars of "The Campbells Are Coming," but it was probably just coincidence.

We had not been addressed, nor had we heard a word of English since we'd been ushered into the room. It wasn't ignorance, because Ghost Shirt had spent enough time in the East to have picked up at least the rudiments of the language. I saw his strategy. As long as he refused to acknowledge our intelligence by speaking to us, we were less than human. He had nothing to gain by it other than revenge, but then that must have been one of the things that ate at him when he was locked up at Fort Ransom. It meant something else as well, although I dared not put it into anything so dangerous as a hope: As long as he preferred to play this kind of game with us, we were going to live.

Evidently this was lost on Hudspeth, who had also seen Ghost Shirt's motives, as his flush had spread beyond his nose over his forehead and down into his collar. His buckskins creaked as he worked his wrists. Before he could blow I ground my heel surreptitiously into the toe of his Mexican boot. Rage gurgled in his throat and he glared murder at me out of the corner of his eye, but he held himself back. I had succeeded in splitting his anger into two channels and preventing him from saying or doing something that would cost us our hides.

The lame Cheyenne plainly didn't like what was going on. He stamped around a few seconds longer, flapping his arms and dragging his useless foot and not looking at us, slid an eye toward the door as if longing for the nerve to stalk out, gave up finally, and turned his back on the room to see what was outside the window that Many Ponies found so diverting. At that point the Sioux apparently decided that anything the other might find worth looking at wasn't, and turned his attention to the rafters atop the opposite wall. I got the impression the two were less than eager comrades.

A pair of sharp notes delivered on the bugle seemed to bring the young chief out of the funk into which he'd fallen. He said something to the guards, waving a hand toward the door. One of the Spencers nudged Jac and we turned to leave, but not before Ghost Shirt spoke his first two words in English.

"Here, Custer," he said, and leaned down to set the bowl of meat scraps on the floor for the dog.

Back in the chapel, Hudspeth waited until the door was slammed shut and barred, then sat down on the floor and tugged off his left boot. "You damn near busted my foot!" He massaged the injured area.

"Better that than some buck wearing our fingers on a cord around his neck." I rubbed my wrists to get back the circulation cut off by the thong, which had been removed.

"The hell with that! First you trip me, then you try to screw my foot to the floor. You're more dangerous than the injuns!"

I ignored him, looking at Pere Jac. "What was that all about, anyway?"

The activity had started the métis' wound bleeding again. He leaned back in the semidarkness and staunched it by pressing the heel of his hand against the bandage and holding it there.

"They argued over us. Lame Horse—the one who limps, he is the medicine man who dressed my wound—wanted us dead. It seems he has dreamt that white men in their midst will bring them ill fortune. He was quite vehement about it. Colorful, too. You should have heard what he wanted to do with your head, A.C."

The marshal muttered something unintelligible and wiggled his toes to see if they still worked.

"What about Many Ponies?" I asked.

"He had no opinion about it one way or the other. He has brought a new squaw with him and he was anxious to get back to her. When Ghost Shirt asked him how he voted, he said that he would go along with whatever the others decided."

"And Ghost Shirt?"

Jac's brow furrowed. "He is not so simple. He hates us worst of all, and I think that if he had his choice he would agree with Lame Horse. But he has other things on his mind. Many Ponies has not been able to deliver as many braves as promised. The Sioux sub-chief, Blood on His Lance, has a child down with fever and could not come to tonight's meeting as he is the medicine man of his band. The Cheyenne lost three of his best braves in the fight with A.C. this morning. The fourth is not expected to survive the night. I think he was strongly tempted to see us roasted to a turn."

"So why aren't we roasting?"

"I am getting to that. Now that the army knows where he is, he has decided to leave the mission before more soldiers come. Spotted Cat, the Arapaho chief, is camped with eight hundred warriors just this side of the Black Hills. Ghost Shirt plans to meet up with him there and, with his help, fight the blue coats on his own ground. He knows now that final victory is impossible, but he wishes to teach the whites a great lesson before he goes to join Kills Bear and Sitting Bull in the land of the white grandmother. He wishes, he said, to make the whites speak his name henceforth in whispers, like old women around a campfire."

"He's a fool. Eleven hundred Indians don't stand a chance against the U. S. Army."

"Against the entire army, no. But they can do great damage to a single garrison that is not expecting them, to say nothing of what will happen when they descend upon the unprotected gold camps in the Black Hills. Further, there are as many as two thousand Indians unaccounted for on reservations throughout the Northwest. Once the news of what Ghost Shirt is up to spreads, there is little doubt around whom they will rally, and then many lives will be lost."

Here the métis smiled sardonically. The tight-lipped expression reminded me of Judge Blackthorne and made me homesick all over again. "Spotted Cat," he said, "is no friend of Ghost Shirt's. But he needs Spotted Cat's warriors, and he is confident that a generous gift will seal the rift that separates them, at least for the time being."

"Let me guess," I said. "We're the gift."

He nodded, still smiling. The mirth fell short of his eyes. In front of the door, Hudspeth stopped playing with his foot and gaped at him.

"Torture is Spotted Cat's speciality." His bleeding under control now, the breed got out his pipe and blew lint from the bowl. Then he began poking tobacco into it. "Moreover, he shares Ghost Shirt's sympathies concerning white men and half-breeds. The Cheyenne feels that the gift of two white federal lawmen and a métis will ensure his alliance in the forthcoming struggle." His face was bathed briefly in the flare of the match as he puffed life into the pipe. Then he shook out the flame and retreated into shadow once more.

"So when are we leaving?" Hudspeth demanded.

"First light."

Later I wished the marshal hadn't asked that question. I was the rest of the night trying to get to sleep.

11 . . .

Three hundred warriors, their women, dogs, three prisoners, and assorted children don't set out on a long journey at the drop of a hat, but the dust had hardly settled on the crown when we began moving through the heavy mist of dawn of what was shaping up to be another humid day. War ponies and their riders were first out the gate, followed by the relief string herded along by the women, with travois of all sizes bringing up the rear behind plugs too old and worn out for any other duty. These last contraptions were simply lodge poles roped together to carry weapons and ammunition and folded tipis and jerked buffalo meat and infants, which had to be dragged slowly to keep down the dust and friction, standard hazards among a people who had never developed the wheel. Once outside, the warrior band split into thirds, with Ghost Shirt riding point at the head of his Cheyenne and Many Ponies and Blood on His Lance, a Miniconjou who looked to be in his late twenties and wore his hair in plaits braided with otter skin, protecting the flanks with their Sioux. None of them wore paint, but then they weren't anticipating any fights just yet or they would have been stripped down to keep the wounds clean. Jac, Hudspeth, and I ate

112

dust astride our own mounts behind the leading band of Cheyenne.

At least we weren't traveling on empty stomachs. Even Ghost Shirt had been forced to admit that dead men made poor torture victims, and so we had each been treated to a heaping bowlful of half-raw horse, or maybe it was dog. If the latter, it wasn't the one Ghost Shirt called Custer, as I saw him darting in and out among the horses' shanks later as we'd been getting ready to leave. Whatever it was, it stayed down, and that's all I'd been asking of my meals for some time. Nobody had bothered to tie us up, which was a compliment to our common sense. You don't outrun an Indian on horseback, not astride anything that eats grain or grass.

I'd thought riding with two partners was dusty but I hadn't seen clouds like this since the army. Tying my kerchief over my nose and mouth wasn't much help. The stuff was so fine it came right through the cloth into my nostrils and down my throat. By midday I'd eaten that peck of dirt we're allotted during our lifetime. Reddish mud caked my clothes, skin and horse. My armpits were chafed raw from the grit, my eyelids gummed so tight I had to pry them open with my fingers to see. I could only imagine what it was like at the rear of the column.

We traveled slowly, climbing the Missouri Plateau twenty miles west of the James River shortly before sunset and camping on the edge of a watering hole just beyond effective rifle range of the buttes that lined the eastern ridge. For supper we were issued buffalo jerky and warned, in the halting English of the glowering Cheyenne who gave it to us, to make it last because that was all we were going to get between now and trail's end. I gnawed at my portion in silence and, after the same brave had bound my hands and feet, turned in without a word to my companions. After all the time we had spent together we had very little to say to each other.

The blue-coated Indian was standing atop the central ridge of the nearest butte when I awoke the next morning. Not for long, though; one moment he was there, the next he had vanished. I kept still about it until our guard had cut us free of our bonds and walked away to attend to other matters.

"See him?" I asked of my fellow prisoners as we crouched together, grinding away at our jerky.

Jac nodded. "Crow, most likely. Or Arikara. Some of them still scout for the army. He has been with us since before dawn."

"What do you think they'll do?"

"Follow us until their messenger brings back reinforcements from Fort Abraham Lincoln, or Fort Yates, or both. Then they will attack, probably while we are preparing to move out."

I glanced around. We were not the only ones who had noticed our observer. Here and there a brave was smearing black paint over himself from a hollow horn, while others tested their bowstrings or loaded their rifles, stopping at one or two shells because ammunition was limited and some Indians believed that a fully loaded rifle led to extravagance. A Sioux crouching a few yards away used the point of his knife to scrape a cake of excess powder from the action of his Spencer. I winced. Give an Indian a brand new firearm and inside of a month he'll turn it into junk.

"What makes you so sure they won't hit us now, while we're sitting?" asked the marshal.

"For the same reason that cavalry does not storm an artillery emplacement without infantry support," Jac said, chewing. "They would be cut to pieces. Besides, there is a little matter of their being outnumbered nearly two to one."

"In that case, why don't the injuns force a fight right now?"

"They are unaware of their advantage. Only we know Harms's strength. And even if they did, the soldiers will not fight with the odds so strong against them. We would be here forever. In the meantime Spotted Cat may move beyond Ghost Shirt's reach. Here he will not gamble. So all the paint you see being applied will go to waste."

"How long before the reinforcements come?" I asked.

Pere Jac shrugged his good shoulder and thrust his jerky away inside his left moccasin. "If the messenger heads north and waylays the train from Fargo to Bismarck, three days. Otherwise, a week. Give or take a day. Two riders left this camp an hour ago, heading west. I suspect their mission is to try to catch and kill the messenger. If that fails, it will be a forced march all the way to the Black Hills."

I followed his example and put away my own strip of jerked meat. "Why don't they wire the other forts?"

"If Ghost Shirt has not had the telegraph line cut by now, he is unworthy of his reputation."

"All the same it's stupid," said Hudspeth, still gnawing. "That's what alerted Fort Ransom."

"He had no choice. It was either that or take the chance of finding himself knee-deep in soldiers before he reached the Missouri River."

"Hell of a note, us being scared of our own army."

Jac said, "Now you know how the Indians feel."

Lame Horse approached, shuffling his dead foot and carrying a buckskin sack. He was painted and wore his grisly necklace and something new, a headdress made from a wolf's head with the fangs of the upper jaw encircling his brow and a fur mantle hanging down the back of his head like a cowl to the shoulders. His deformity was concealed beneath a buffalo robe that swept from his neck to his heels. The flame-yellow streak knifing diagonally across the middle of his blackened face was starting to run at the edges where he had already begun to sweat. Without a word he squatted beside Jac, tossed the robe back from his shoulders, and undid the dressing that covered the métis' wound. He then smeared the ugly, jagged gash with a piece of buckskin soaked in some greenish, evil-smelling salve carried in a hollow horn taken from the sack and bound it afresh with cured hide. The way he shoved his patient around as he treated him said little for his bedside manner, but then you don't expect a lot of courtesy from someone who was calling for your death a little over twenty-four hours ago. Finally he drew out a rattle with a bone handle and a head made from the painted skull of some small animal, possibly a prairie dog, tilted back his head so that the dead wolf's glass-bead eyes glittered in the light of the rising sun, shook the rattle perfunctorily three times in each of the four directions, chanted something in an emotionless drone, packed up, and left, dragging his half-developed leg behind him beneath the trailing robe. No pipe smoking, no ritual of purification, no change of song. Either he had disposed of all that the first time around or he didn't think his patient was worth the bother.

"Tender, is he not?" commented Jac.

"Wait till you get his bill," I told him. Then our guard jostled me from behind and we saddled up.

There are people who spend their lives studying the migrating habits of western nomadic tribes, for whom these next few pages might make fascinating reading, but I was too preoccupied to take notes even if I'd had the necessary material. Back-breaking hours in the saddle, sleeping on damp, hard ground with one eye open for rattlesnakes, wrists chafed bloody and hands swollen by rawhide thongs drawn too tightly during the hours of darkness when an escape attempt might be made, mosquitoes the size of horseflies that whined in our ears when we tried to sleep and drew blood, leaving crusts of it all around the hole, days so hot the sweat seemed to sizzle when it hit the air, nights so cold our perspiration soaked garments grew stiff and crackled when we moved, the salty leather taste of jerky morning and night, the ache in our jaws from trying to chew it, wading through fresh horse manure and old buffalo chips, horse froth drying white and stinking on our pants legs, warm water drunk from earthen jugs, blisters on our palms, boils on our backsides, dogs barking, babies crying, horses snorting, men sweating, dust, dust, dust. Dust in our eyes, noses and throats. Dust in our boots and pockets. Dust that rose and rose in great, strangling clouds that obscured the sun and stained sky and grass the color of old blood. Dust so fine we couldn't feel it between our fingers but which stirred and shifted in our lungs when we coughed, and we coughed often, hacking so hard it seemed our throats would turn inside out with the pain of it. Dust that never settled but continued to drift aimlessly hours after we had camped, etching swirling black shadows against the pale night sky. Dust so thick a finger drawn down a cheek left a furrow a blind man could feel. Each day was like the one before, only it was worse because we were older and less able to take it.

Meanwhile, to the east of us, a cloud only slightly smaller than the one we were trailing held parallel to our route along the horizon. When one of us finally made mention of it, Jac merely nodded and said, "He missed the train."

It was on the fifth night that Happy—thus we had

nicknamed the anonymous dour brave who looked after us—made his mistake. It wasn't that he was stupid or careless, nor that we were especially smart, but that circumstances made it impossible for any of us to be anything else. We were within listening distance of the Missouri River fifteen miles south of Fort Yates, camped in a grassy hollow just off the east bank, where patrols from the fort would have to cross over to engage us and the animals could graze without being outlined against the horizon and the sentries could lie concealed in the tall grass around the rim. Rounded stones, deposited when the prehistoric lake that had occupied the spot receded, studded the ground. Before this, Happy had always made sure that there were no such tools around before he settled his prisoners, but since there were too many of them here and most were anchored down more or less permanently, he compromised by choosing a spot where the stones were relatively smooth and devoid of those jagged edges that came in handy for sawing through bonds, flung away the undesirables, tethered us carefully and wrapped himself up in his buffalo robe to take up his nightly vigil. As usual, he was asleep within minutes.

I waited until I was sure he was under good and deep, then struggled into a sitting position and shifted around from rock to rock until I found one that felt like it might do. Hudspeth and Jac did the same. Mine was edgeless, but the surface was like sandpaper and might conceivably be expected to wear its way through the stiff, dry leather thong that bound my hands behind my back between now and sunup. I made myself as comfortable as possible and started rubbing.

The next couple of hours were the hardest. Every muscle in my body cried out for rest, and the tedious rhythm of my wrists scraping up and down the surface of the rock acted like the swinging motion of a baby's cradle, heaping a couple of hundred pounds onto my eyelids. I dozed off twice, the second time so deeply that when I jolted awake I had no idea how long I'd been out, and redoubled my efforts to make up for lost time. But by then the crisis had passed and staying alert was no longer a problem, because the pain made sleep impossible. It started as a dull ache between my shoulder blades and ended up a sharp, stinging sensation like something left by an angry hornet. Worse, I had begun sweating in spite of the cold, and salty rivulets came trickling down my wrists, burning against the raw flesh and drawing the thong even tighter. My hands grew slippery with blood from the chafing. With all this to occupy my mind I hardly noticed the numbness of my rump where I sat on the iron-hard ground.

I heard snoring and looked up to see that Hudspeth, seated a few yards away, had fallen asleep in the middle of his labors, his chin on his chest and the ends of his moustache fluttering as he inhaled and exhaled mightily through his big red nose. I whistled softly through my teeth at Jac, who was working away at a rock not far from the marshal, and inclined my head toward his dozing bulk. Jac nodded and kicked at the marshal's feet until he came awake with a start. He looked around in bewilderment for a moment, then caught on to where he was and what he was supposed to be doing and resumed scraping.

The damp chill of approaching dawn had seeped into my clothes when my thong came apart with a resounding pop. Pere Jac's parted at almost the same instant. We stared at each other for a second like a couple of kids who had risen ahead of the rest of the family on Christmas morning. Then we tore away the scraps and bent forward to undo the thongs on our feet. The marshal, who hated being last in anything, set his jaw and worked his hands until I could have sworn I saw smoke rising behind him.

I finished ahead of the métis and, once I had mastered the fine art of achieving one's balance after the circulation has been cut off for hours, crept over to see what I could do for Hudspeth. But he was less than two-thirds of the way through his bonds, so I left him there and went off in search of a knife.

The nearest one was on Happy's belt. Since he couldn't very well be expected to give it up without protest, I selected a likely looking rock from among the dozens imbedded in the ground around me and tested it for heft. Rocks are vastly underrated as weapons, as I'd learned at the receiving end last winter. Deciding that this one would suit my purposes, I pulled off my boots and tiptoed over to where the guard was lying enveloped in his hide cocoon.

Right away I regretted having named him Happy. You don't do that, any more than you make a pet of the hog you're planning to butcher for Easter dinner. It didn't matter to me how many white scalps he may have taken, nor how many half-grown girls he may have raped before slashing them open from belly to breast, nor if he preferred using both hands or just one when swinging a baby by its heels and dashing its brains out against a tree. Being shallow, I was concerned only with the fact that he had never done any of us any actual harm, other than causing us a little discomfort, and that only on orders from the top. It had me all torn up for maybe a second and a half. Then I brought the rock crashing down squarely onto his exposed right temple.

Even so, I was just in time, as at the last instant his eyes sprang open and he went for his knife. But there was no way he was going to fumble his way out of his covers before the rock struck. He arched his back, but by then it was just nerves because he was already dead.

I looked around quickly. The sounds I'd heard before were the same sounds I was hearing now, nothing missing, nothing new. Apparently the slight noises the Cheyenne had made in dying had not been enough to alert his confederates. I let out my breath, only then realizing that I'd been holding it all this time, and returned to my task. Freeing the knife took some prying, clenched as it was in his fist. At length, however, I had my hand around the smooth bone handle.

I felt a presence behind me and spun around, swinging the knife in a wide arc from left to right. Pere Jac leaped backward but not far enough to keep the flat of the blade from scraping the top of his breechclout.

"Sorry," I said, in the overwhelming silence that followed.

"My widow would have been gratified to hear that," he replied dryly. But the closeness of the call was discernible on his face.

"Next time maybe you'll remember to keep your distance."

"You will forgive me if in my prayers I request that there be no next time."

"There sure as hell won't be if you two don't quit jawing and cut me loose!" Hudspeth's whisper was as good as another man's shout.

I slashed both his trusses—hands and feet—and told him to stay put. Before he could protest I turned away and returned to the dead guard. Somehow I kept my jerky from coming back up long enough to roll the body clear of its wrap and silde the robe on over my shoulders. I considered discarding my hat, thought better of it when I remembered the merciless Dakota sun, and crumpled and jammed it into my belt instead. My chances of passing as an Indian were about as good as they were of surviving the next half hour, but it was all I had.

"Stay where you are!" I hissed at the marshal, who had been struggling to get up. "Maybe I don't look much like a Sioux or a Cheyenne, but I come a hell of a lot closer than you. Wait until I get you a weapon."

He didn't like it, but he was no fool. He kept his position.

I handed the knife to Pere Jac. "You they'll believe," I said. "Cut out three good horses from the relief string. Hit the sentry before he can cry out or we'll be skinned and dressed by sunup. I'll get us some firepower."

"With what? I have the knife."

"Weren't you watching the first time? When you get the horses, give us three owl hoots, then count to twenty. If we're not there by then, ride like hell."

He nodded and slid away into the shadows to the west, where the horses were hobbled.

It was pathetically easy. They say a leaf dropping will bring an Indian out of a sound sleep, but that doesn't hold true when the Indian is surrounded by hundreds of his own kind and he's played out from five days of hard riding. I thumped the first one just in front of the ear while he lay sprawled beneath on ornate blanket. It wasn't as thorough a job as with Happy. At the last moment he stirred in his sleep and I missed the vital spot, fracturing his skull but not killing him. That was all right, because I hadn't intended to do away with anyone in the first place. You just can't be as accurate with a hunk of stone as with a gun or a knife. In any case he was out of action, although still breathing. A search of his body yielded up another knife and a Spencer rifle tucked beneath the blanket. I checked the breech and had all I could do to keep from cursing at the top of my lungs. What had he planned to do if the cavalry attacked while he was armed with an unloaded piece?

I went over him again, more carefully this time, and

came up empty. I took a deep breath and let it out slowly, to think. Then I grinned and pulled open his buckskin shirt. There they were, seventeen .56-caliber cartridges, pierced through their lead noses and strung on a leather thong around his neck. I yanked it loose and loaded the rifle up tight, swinging the lever forward and back slowly and quietly to rack one into the chamber, then added another cartridge. I thrust the string containing the remaining ten in my pocket.

Having served its purpose, the rock was cast aside and the knife took its place. This one was store-bought, with a cowhide-wrapped haft and a blade of tempered steel, probably the former property of some long-dead soldier or scout. I laid the Spencer aside for the time being and, holding the knife underhanded, crept up to the next sleeping form.

I withdrew the blade and wiped it thoroughly on the dead brave's blanket. Then I began my search. This time I hit paydirt. Not only had he a fully loaded Spencer, but a revolver stuck in his belt as well. I looked at it in the light, and damned if it wasn't Hudspeth's Smith & Wesson. The odds against that happening weren't as great as you might think, since we were camped in the middle of the Cheyenne and they had been the ones who had captured Jac and the marshal. Twenty to one. No, make it eighteen, since I'd just disposed of two of his comrades. I'd have bet half a month's pay on odds like those. I thrust the revolver into my own belt, collected the rifle and the one I had taken from the other Indian, picked up that one's blanket, and gave everything but one rifle and the knife to Hudspeth. His bright little eyes lit up as he curled his hand around the Smith's heavy grip.

"Where in hell—"

I hissed. "Wrap that blanket around yourself and

keep your chin tucked in so the handlebar doesn't show. And ditch that hat."

Three owl hoots sounded faintly to the west. I put my boots on and helped him to his feet.

"Wait a minute!" He stood his ground. "What about Ghost Shirt?"

"For Christ's sake, shut up!" I would have throttled him if the circumstances were different and he weren't so big. We crept off.

Within a hundred yards of the horses I halted and threw out an arm to stop Hudspeth. Someone was speaking in harsh Cheyenne.

As my eyes grew accustomed to the shadows on this side of the hollow, I made out Pere Jac standing motionless among the horses' milling forms. At his feet, just as motionless, sprawled a figure which I took to be that of the Indian assigned to watch over the horses. Something about his position told me that his responsibility was ended. Jac was gazing up at the rim. I followed his line of sight and spotted an Indian sentry silhouetted against the lightening sky.

He must have risen from the grass when he heard noises. He had a rifle braced against his shoulder and was scanning the scene below in search of a target. He repeated his challenge.

I raised my own Spencer and drew a bead on his chest. I was set to fire when a shot rang out from an unexpected quarter. The sentry's rifle tumbled from his hands and he crumpled into the tall grass. Then a bugle sounded and the world fell apart in tiny, glittering pieces.

12 . . .

The first wave came thundering over the western rim spread out in charge formation, bugle wailing, Springfields popping, scattering the riderless horses left and right in spite of their hobbles. Officers' sabers flashed in the first pink rays of dawn. Sabers, by God. I gave Hudspeth a shove between the shoulder blades with the flat of my hand so that he lost his balance and pitched forward onto his face, and joined him an instant later. Hoofs shook the ground on either side of us. The wind of them bounding overhead stirred the hairs on the back of my neck. I heard the dust sifting down all around me, my senses were that acute. Not that it did me any good. It seemed we lay there for hours while rider after rider pounded past, although it couldn't have been more than a couple of minutes. Even so, at the rate they were traveling that added up to a hell of a lot of cavalry.

I waited until I was sure the last straggler had passed, then leaped to my feet, still clutching the Spencer. Hudspeth got up more slowly, but I could see he wasn't hurt, unless you count being mad as hell as a handicap. Pere Jac, who had himself flattened out when the sentry fell, was already up, clutching the mane of his own paint—dumb luck—and shouting something at me that I couldn't hear because hoofbeats were still echoing in my head. But I caught his drift and snatched at the mane of the horse nearest me, an excited army gray that was trying to gallop and gnaw at the thong that bound its forelegs at the same time. Hudspeth had the misfortune to grab onto a mustang that fit him about as well as a size 5 corset fit the Statue of Liberty, now arriving piecemeal from France. But we all had mounts and, as far as I could tell in the haze of settling dust, were still armed.

The Indians had been taken completely by surprise. They were running all over the place, whooping up their courage and firing their rifles at flitting shadows, grabbing for the manes and tails of panicky horses, while the soldiers rode through with their reins wrapped about their forearms and picked them off with rifles and side arms first from this side, then that. Gunsmoke glazed the battleground. Sabers slashed randomly at tipis and running figures. It was a killing frenzy. A brave armed only with a flint tomahawk leaped onto the back of a horse behind the soldier who was riding it, but before he could swing his weapon a bullet from a nearby Springfield splintered his head and he tumbled off. Another soldier leaned down from his saddle, revolver in one hand, and tore aside the flap of a squat tipi. The young squaw inside thrust the muzzle of a Spencer up his nose and pulled the trigger. His horse screamed and reared. He somersaulted backward over its rump and landed on his face, which didn't matter because he no longer had one. A fat squaw waddling as fast as she could go with a child in her arms ran straight into the downswing of a young lieutenant's saber. Her head came off slick as a kicked cabbage and her body ran for several more steps before it stumbled and fell, spilling the infant out onto the ground. A soldier's horse came clattering toward the yowling, naked baby where it lay sprawled in the grass. I turned my head away just as the first hoof struck.

Major Harms, or whoever was calling the shots if not him, was a student of General Nelson Miles. The second wave, which came in from the northeast, was backed up by squares of infantry, the kind of troops the armchair generals back in Washington City swore were hopelessly ineffective against Plains Indians, but which Miles had been using to great advantage since the beginning of the wars. By this time Sioux and Cheyenne snipers had taken up positions along the eastern rim, and as they took aim the horse soldiers hit them at breechclout level with their 45-70 single-shots. The cavalry just kept coming. I had no idea how many there were, but it was obvious that both Fort Lincoln and Fort Yates had been all but emptied out for reinforcements and that the Indians' superior weaponry wasn't worth a leaf in a torrent against numbers like these.

Now that the focus of battle had shifted to the other side of the hollow, a handful of troopers from the first attack took advantage of the lull in this quarter to grab a few scalps. I wasn't shocked. The first one taken was worth a bonus or a furlough depending upon who was in command, and anyway they weren't worth much to the corpses from which they were lifted. What bothered me was the officers back East who acquired the trophies without any risk except to their pocketbooks and either sold them at a profit or hung them in their parlors to add weight to their tales of personal prowess told to entice fashionable young ladies into bed. Barbarians come in all types and colors.

Jac and I cut away the hobbles on our captured mounts, including Hudspeth's, and were about to make a run for it when the marshal cried out and pointed behind me. I swung around, hugging the rifle to my hip.

Ghost Shirt, astride his roan, had broken through along with half a dozen warriors and was making for the high ground west of camp. At his side rode Lame Horse, minus paint. The soldiers who had been cutting dead hair fired in unison. Two Indians fell. Ghost Shirt clapped a hand to his head and reeled. His horse whinnied in terror, wheeled right, and blundered into the milling relief herd. The remaining braves, one of them the medicine man, returned fire. The troopers dived for cover as they galloped through, then sprang up and snapped shots at their backs. Another Indian tumbled from his horse, I couldn't tell which.

While the soldiers' backs were turned, the chief, his mount trapped among its fellows, lost his grip on the mane and slid like a rag doll to the ground.

"Get him!" I snapped at Jac, who was closest to the herd. "Before he's trampled."

He left his paint, calmer now that it had recognized its master, and sidled his way in between the horses. Hudspeth held my gray while I went in to help.

Ghost Shirt was lying on his face next to the roan. Together we turned him over. He had a crease on the left side of his head where a bullet had grazed it—I couldn't tell how badly, there was too much blood—but he was still breathing. So much for the god theory. Being the only one of us with a shirt, I tore a long strip from the tail of mine, used it to clean away what blood I could, and bound it tightly around his head. My Winchester was slung over his shoulder by a makeshift strap, a welcome sight but hardly a surprise. It was too good a weapon to leave in the hands of a subordinate. I transferred it to my person, unbuckled the gun belt containing my Deane-Adams, and strapped it on around my waist. That made me feel fifty per cent human again. I inspected both guns to see if they were loaded and found that they were, which completed the cure.

Then Jac and I heaved the unconscious Cheyenne up and over the back of his horse. The métis held the animal while I braided two more strips into an approximation of a rope and tied Ghost Shirt's hands and feet together beneath its belly. If he survived that, I decided, I might reconsider my opinion of his so-called immortality.

I picked up the confiscated Spencer from the ground where I'd left it, and then I said something that wasn't clever. I said, "Happy birthday," and handed it to Pere Jac. To show how much strain we were under, we both laughed like idiots.

Hudspeth had our saddles, bags, and blankets laid out on the ground when we emerged, leading the roan by its army bridle, and was cinching his rig onto the mustang's back. He could move fast when he had to. We'd left them where I'd killed the guard because it's hard to look like an Indian when you're carrying fifty pounds of leather over your shoulder, and Hudspeth had run there, loaded them up, and gotten back before his mount could stray out of reach, with bullets flying all over hell. He flicked his eyes over our burden and yanked tight the cinch.

"You got him," he grunted. "Good."

I could have clubbed him with the butt of the Winchester. Jac had his eight cases of whiskey and I still had my job whether we brought back the Indian or not. We had risked our hides to help him keep his badge, and all the thanks we got was something my father said when his hunting dog fetched its first duck. Even the dog got a pat on the head. But I supposed that was as high as he gushed, so I let it slide.

"Why don't you give me the mustang and take the gray?" I asked him. "You'll scuff your fancy boots dragging them on the ground."

"I grabbed it, I'll keep it. You'll find fresh jerky in

your saddle bags, both of you, and them buckskin bags hanging on your horns is half full of water. I got 'em from a bottomed-up tipi."

"That's not all you got," I said, one hand in my saddle bag. I drew out a box of Deane-Adams cartridges.

"I found that on the ground. The injun must of dropped it when he got shot."

I dropped it back into the bag. "Where's that Spencer I gave you?" I had just noticed he was no longer carrying it.

He snorted. "It wasn't worth the extra weight. The action was jammed full of powder. I wouldn't trust no gun of mine with no redskin if it meant my life. I heard once—"

A bullet nicked the top of his saddle. He ducked behind the horse, drawing his revolver. Jac and I shouldered our rifles.

"Come out of there, you onion-skinned sons of bitches!" A master sergeant's voice if I ever heard one, Ohio twang roughened by weather and grit and years of bawling orders at green recruits.

The herd had begun crowding around us, blocking our view of the cavalry stragglers. Now, gray light perforated the shadows and the horses shied away before the harsh bellow, and in the clearing beyond stood a heavy-chested trooper in a dusty uniform with a knife in one hand and an Army Colt in the other. There were others with him armed similarly, but he was the one who had shouted. A .45-caliber bullet had pierced the right cheek of the Sioux lying at his feet and carried away the left half of his skull on its way out. I had to admit that the trooper was dedicated. He had given up the chance at a furlough—or a bonus—in order to take a few prisoners.

I said, calmly as possible, "You need spectacles."

This being friendly country, more or less, we had doffed our disguises and put on our hats, not counting Jac, who wore none. The sergeant (his stripes were visible now) had expected Indians, and at worst he might have been prepared for other soldiers, but two white civilians and an elderly half-breed were too much for him to sort out at one time. But they're conditioned to hold onto their guns when in doubt, and this one held true to his training.

"Just who the hell are you, and what you doing with that there dead injun?" His features were Scandinavian, deeply tanned and dusted across chin and cheeks with blond stubble. He had pale blue eyes, which contrasted vividly with the burnished copper of his complexion, and yellow side-whiskers that came to the corners of a jaw so square a carpenter could have used it for a miter. The hand holding the gun had an equally square black thumbnail and knuckles banded with white scar tissue. He had burst them on his share of out-thrust chins.

"In the first place," I said, "he's not dead. As for the rest, we're civilian peace officers on special assignment with Major Quincy Harms and this is our prisoner." That was a gamble. If the sergeant and his companions were from Fort Ransom we were sunk.

He scraped his chin with the back of the hand holding the knife, ostensibly on the theory that it helped him think. Still he didn't lower the revolver.

"I don't know. You got a badge?"

That request was beginning to wear thin on me. I was standing behind the gray; resting the carbine across its rump, I fished out the star with my left hand and held it up. There's no doubt that pinning it to your shirt simplifies things, but anywhere you wear it, it's too close to your heart. Hudspeth pulled open his coat to show his. The sergeant squinted from one to the other in thoughtful silence.

"All right, so you got tin. That comes cheap. Anything else?"

"For Christ's sake, can't you see we're white?" One of these days, I thought, the marshal's nose was going to explode in a big red cloud.

The sergeant glared at him. He was going to say, "Shut up, fat boy," or something as inflammatory. It was on his lips. When he did, Hudspeth was going to throw lead and we would all die right there, smack in the middle of the earth's left armpit. I wondered how St. Peter would take it when he asked me what I was doing at the gates so early and I told him I had acted in defense of my partner's waistline, and the marshal was standing behind me in line broad as a chuck wagon across the beam. My grip tightened on the Winchester.

But I was disappointed, although I doubt that's the proper word for what I felt. Instead of saying it, the sergeant nodded curtly, as if he had just come to the decision that we were, indeed, white. He wasn't finished yet, however.

"What about Grandpa?" he challenged, jerking his chin toward Jac. "Don't tell me R. B. Hayes is deputizing half-breeds now."

I explained who he was and what he was doing there. The sergeant's eyes left me and took in our gear lying on the ground a couple of yards away. I answered his next question before he could ask it.

"Our horses were shot out from under us. Pere Jac, there, took a lance in his shoulder as he went down. We're in the midst of changing mounts."

I must have been pretty convincing, because the top kick glanced down impatiently at the Sioux he'd been preparing to scalp. He was losing interest. But for duty's sake he got in one more lick, a good one.

"What's so all-fired important about that particular injun?" he demanded. "There'll be hundreds to choose from in a few minutes."

"This ain't no ordinary—" Hudspeth began. But before he could finish he had something else to occupy him, namely the pain in his ankle where I had struck it with the side of my boot.

"It's one of Ghost Shirt's inner circle," I broke in quickly, to draw attention from Hudspeth's cry. "Tall Dog, a Cheyenne warrior. He may be able to shed some light on his boss's plans."

The sergeant snorted. "Hell, that's no secret. He was on his way to link up with Spotted Cat and his Arapahoes down south. What he didn't know was they surrendered to General Crook last week."

"Surrendered?" It flew out. Right after it did I knew it was a mistake.

He nodded. It hadn't dawned on him yet. "Every last one of 'em, right outside Deadwood. Not a shot fired. Christ, everyone's talking—" He broke off. Realization flushed over his face. He'd been about to holster his weapon, but now he raised it again. "Say, where you been? If you was with Major Harms all this time like you say, you would of knowed all about the surrender. It's all over the army. Speak up!"

I could have given myself a swift kick. Not because I had opened my trap without thinking, which was reason enough, but because of what happened next and what it meant. If I hadn't been all aglow inside over how glib I was and how I was going to talk us out of this, I might have seen it coming, as Jac had, and taken steps to counteract it—as Jac had. All the time the sergeant was questioning me, the métis had taken advantage of the fact that all eyes were on me and had sidled around the horses until he was standing within lunging distance of a quaking trooper who looked too young for the uniform he was wearing and who was having trouble holding onto his revolver with both hands. When the sergeant raised his Colt again, Jac dropped his Spencer noiselessly in the grass, curled one of his trunklike arms around the trooper's windpipe, pinioned one of his ankles in the crook of a knee so that he was balanced precariously on one leg, and thrust the point of his knife against the tender flesh beneath the young man's chin. At the same time, the half-breed bumped him from behind with his pelvis and the revolver sprang from his hands like a slippery frog. All without a sound, until the trooper went and spoiled it by crying out.

I was sure the sergeant was an old-line campaigner who knew better than to let his attention be distracted from his primary objective no matter what. I still think that, even though he did what he did. A man on the shady side of forty doesn't give up the reactions of a lifetime just because a little brown book tells him they're no good. He turned his head just far enough to see what the noise was about, realized his mistake, and turned back, but by then it was too late. The muzzle of my Winchester came swinging around, cracked against the back of the hand holding the Colt, and was staring at the third button down from the collar of his tunic by the time the revolver hit the ground. My nerves were strung so tight I nearly blew him into the next world when he doubled over, hugging his shattered hand between his knees.

"This carbine fires a forty-four caliber round," I told him, "and so does the revolver the marshal has trained on the man behind you. One of them is enough to make a corpse your loved ones won't want to kiss before they lower it into the ground, but they don't kill any deader than the knife Pere Jac is holding at Tom Sawyer's throat there. That leaves two soldiers uncovered. Are you a gambling man, Sergeant?"

He took enough time to swallow twice, but I can't say if he used it for that purpose. I was looking at his eyes. I saw in them that although he was still doubled over, the pain in his hand was no longer a priority. He was figuring the odds. So he was a gambling man. A smart one too, if what I read there next was on target.

It was. "Drop your guns," he told his men. When there was no response he repeated it, bellowing this time. Two Colts and a Springfield thumped the grassy ground.

"The belt gun too," I said to the man who had discarded the rifle. He hesitated, then unbuckled the belt one-handed and let it fall. Hudspeth stared at it.

"Hey," he said. "Is that a Smith American?" The trooper said it was. "I'll be damned!" He stepped forward, hugging his own Smith against his rib cage, and picked up the belt, which was loaded with cartridges.

"Get all of them while you're at it," I told him.

"You won't make a mile." The drillmaster's bawl had shrunk to a croak. Now that the decision had been made, the throbbing in the sergeant's hand must have been terrific. I risked a downward glance and felt a twinge of remorse. I hadn't meant to finish his army career. As far as a lifer like this was concerned, I supposed, I might just as well have killed him. I decided to let him have the last word. I was out of smart answers anyway.

The marshal came back carrying the discarded iron. I told him to unload the pieces and leave them there in a pile. We were carrying too much weight as it was, and I didn't want to leave the troopers unarmed in the middle of a fight. We were still on the same side, no matter how it looked. Hudspeth obeyed but retained the belt full of .44's.

I kept them covered while he and Jac, who had released the callow soldier, saddled up and stepped into leather. Behind us, the whooping and shooting continued, farther away now as the Indians were bottled up against the high southern rim of the lake bed. Bright yellow flames blossomed in scattered places as the tipis were set afire. Another ten or fifteen minutes and it would all be over for everyone but the buzzards. I leathered the five-shot, mounted, and together we broke into gallop and topped the western rise in the direction of the Missouri River. The troopers dived for their weapons, but by the time they had them loaded we were well out of range. Their popping was drowned out by the drumming of our mounts' hoofs.

We stopped at the river to water the horses and fill the buckskin bags Hudspeth had liberated from camp, then wheeled right and headed north. Ghost Shirt was still alive, no thanks to us. I had bunched my bedroll under his chin to keep his head up; the gash above his ear was bleeding again, but slower now. He was still out. I wondered if he would ever come to, and if he didn't, if Flood would still insist upon hanging him. I decided that he would. In the judge's case, the quality of mercy was strained through a sheet.

After a couple of hours of hard riding—tempered, of course, by the condition of our prisoner—we got off and led the horses to give them a rest. No one had spoken since leaving camp.

"Where to now?" asked the marshal. He seemed more out of sorts than usual, which was understandable after several miles on the back of a horse three sizes too small.

"The scenic route," I replied. "In another few miles we'll swing east for three days or so and then north again. We can't take the chance of being spotted by whatever troopers might be left in Fort Yates, and if

Dakota's like anywhere else there's too much civilization strung out along the river. It'll take us a hundred miles out of our way, but with any luck we'll be able to catch the train to Bismarck and be there by the end of next week. Whenever that is."

"That's one hell of a long ways to travel with a red-hot injun, even if he does live. Some of them Cheyenne got through back there, you know. And don't forget the army."

"The Cheyenne will be too busy licking their wounds for some time, and the army's got its hands full. Worry about them later."

"I got as much confidence in that as I do in Jac. He's the one said they wouldn't attack unless we was moving."

Jac shrugged, both shoulders this time. His wound was coming along. "I did not expect infantry support."

"Stop grousing," I said. "You didn't think we'd capture Ghost Shirt in the first place."

"Now the hard part begins." Pere Jac's face was wooden.

13 . . .

The first words Ghost Shirt uttered upon coming to were English, and they weren't very nice.

We had set up camp in the shadow of the buttes along the edge of the plateau twenty-five miles northeast of the hollow where the battle had taken place. Jac and Hudspeth were breaking out the jerky and I had a hand under the Indian's head and a buckskin bag full of water in the other when his eyes opened without any fluttering and he spoke the words, which needn't be quoted here. I clucked my tongue.

"Shame on you. Is that any way to talk to someone who helped save your life?"

He said something else just as colorful. Apparently he had picked up quite a few of our quainter expressions during the time he had spent among us in his youth. But he didn't resist when I forced the neck of the the water bag between his lips. He drank greedily. Then he closed his eyes again. I lowered his head gently onto the extra horse blanket I had folded beneath it. The even rise and fall of his chest told me he was asleep, or doing a good imitation of it.

"He ought to eat," grumbled the marshal. His jaw worked as he ground away at a piece of jerked meat. I shook my head.

"He needs rest more. When he's ready to eat, he'll eat. Besides, with his head in the condition it's in, he'd be lucky if he didn't break open the wound just chewing on this saddle leather." I produced my own strip, looked at it, sighed, took a bite, sighed again, and put it away. I was hungry, but my teeth were still sore from the last meal. "I hate Dakota," I said.

Pere Jac had finished his meal and was loking over his pony, grazing with the others at the end of their tethers on the other side of camp. He muttered an oath, the first I had ever heard from his lips.

"What's wrong?" I asked.

"Split hoof." He was inspecting the pony's right front. "He has not yet begun to limp, but he will. If I get another day's ride out of him it will be a holy miracle."

"That's what you get for not shoeing him," said Hudspeth.

"Are there any settlements nearby?" I asked Jac.

He released the hoof and straightened. "A ranch, three miles the other side of the buttes. It belongs to an old Scot named Tyrone, or it did. It has been many years since I saw him. Perhaps he is dead."

"Any horses?"

"He raises them, or used to. But he will charge an arm and a leg."

"So long as he don't charge money," put in the marshal. "We ain't got none of that to spare."

"Get it up, both of you." I got out my wallet and spread the bills on the ground. "Thirty-three dollars. See if you can sweeten it."

Hudspeth carried a dilapidated billfold with a picture of Lola Montez on the back of an advertisement for chewing tobacco. Reluctantly he drew out a pair of ten-spots and six ones and placed them next to mine. Neither of us was carrying pocket change because you don't go Indian-hunting with anything on you that jingles. I looked up at Pere Jac.

"No bills," he said. "How about this?" He reached into the leather poke he carried and handed me a lump of yellow something the size of a tooth, which was exactly what it was. I recognized it as the loosened gold molar he had extracted from his mouth the night we had met in the métis camp. I hefted it in the palm of my hand.

"Quarter of an ounce, maybe a little more," I judged. "Let's say nine dollars."

"It cost me twelve."

"Someone saw you coming. All right, that gives us sixty-eight dollars, enough to buy two good horses in Helena."

"It won't buy us one from Tyrone." He drew up the poke and returned it to his saddle bag.

"We'll worry about that tomorrow."

Tomorrow was bleeding into the purple overhead like cheap red dye when I awoke to find Jac standing over me, moccasined feet spread apart and the muzzle of his Spencer dangling in front of my face. I thought, *You can't trust anyone,* pushed it away before it could blow off one of my best features, and drew the Deane-Adams, pointing it at his groin.

The movement startled him. He stepped back quickly and glanced down at me as if he'd forgotten I was there. He hadn't been watching me at all, but something far beyond me. The muzzle of the five-shot brought him back in a hurry. Without a word he raised his arm and pointed in the direction he'd been looking. That trick being as old as the rock that had been digging into the small of my back all night long, I didn't look right away but climbed out of my bedroll and took two steps backward, keeping him covered. Then I looked.

My first thought when I saw the curl of black smoke

drifting up against the distant haze was that I had made a horse's ass of myself again. Then the significance of it hit me and that didn't seem so important any more. A spot of bright yellow flickered at the base of the curl. The group of dark lumps clustered around it might have been rocks, but they weren't.

"How long?"

"I cannot say. I noticed it at first light."

"Get Hudspeth up."

"Too late. I'm up."

I turned to my left. The marshal was standing next to his bedroll facing west, where the campfire was. No doubt about it, I'd been living too soft of late, sleeping too soundly. It didn't comfort me that I'd come off watch only three hours before. "Got your glass?"

He thrust it at me. "I reckon the injuns found the ammo in my saddle bags more interesting. But you won't see anything."

"My eyes are ten years younger than yours." I pointed the glass in the direction of the fire and twisted it. Behind me the sun had begun to top the buttes, casting their shadows just short of the other camp. When I had the flames in good and clear I shifted a little to the right. As I did so, one of the lumps stirred, cast something into the fire, and stood up. It was dressed in black. No, blue. It turned to look up at the buttes and sunlight glittered off the tiny, polished surface of what had to be a glass eye. I lowered the telescope.

"Shades of the U. S. Army," I said.

"Harms?" suggested Hudspeth.

"Worse, if what Jed Hoxie told us is worth anything. Sergeant Burdett."

"How many with him?" He took back the glass and trained it in that direction, as if the fresh knowledge might improve his vision.

"Eight or ten. Either they don't know we've got

Ghost Shirt or Burdett talked the major out of loading him down with more men that he needed. I'm betting on the second."

"How good you figure this guy is?"

"If he's good enough to have followed us this far, he's good enough for us not to worry about trying to cover up our tracks from here on in. We'd just be wasting our time. He wants us to know he's there, or he wouldn't have lit that fire. He hopes we'll panic and make mistakes."

While we had been talking, Pere Jac had begun to saddle the horses. "Speaking of wasting time," he said pointedly. We took the hint and turned to break camp.

I walked over to where Ghost Shirt was lying with a blanket drawn up to his chin and watched his face for a second or two. His eyes were closed and his breathing was even. "Get up,"-I said. "I know you're with us." I nudged him gently in the ribs with the toe of my boot.

Something the size of a newborn calf came roaring up from beneath the blankets and struck me full in the chest, knocking me down hard on my back. I found myself looking up into a savage face with hatred in its eyes and a double row of sharp, curving teeth in a gaping mouth. The jaws closed on my right arm when I went for my gun. I tried to extract it and felt the flesh tearing away from the bone. Hot breath seared my face. My ears rang with the thing's frenzied snarling, which grew shriller as I fought to keep it from my throat. It shook my wrist like a dead snake. I had about given up the battle when something blurred across my vision, there was a loud thump followed by an ear-splitting yelp of rage and pain, a name was called sharply, and suddenly the weight was gone from my chest.

"Are you all right, Page?" Pere Jac was standing over me, gripping his Spencer by the barrel like a club— which was an appropriate comparison, since that's what he had just used it for. Behind him, Hudspeth had his Smith & Wesson out to cover Ghost Shirt, who was on his feet now, and Custer, the yellow mongrel I'd seen him with back at the mission, who was at the Indian's side. The dog was scrubbing its head against the grass to clean the blood from the cut Jac had opened over its right eye. It was still snarling.

I got up, holding my torn wrist together with the other hand. Almost reluctantly, I peeled back the ragged sleeve to inspect the damage. It wasn't as bad as I'd feared, although it was bad enough. A good deal of meat had been exposed and rearranged, but as far as I could tell the muscle was intact. I tore a fresh strip from what was left of my shirttail and began to bind it up. Jac finished the job.

"All right," I said, once the blood was out of sight. "Where'd the animal come from and how'd he get into camp? It wasn't during my watch."

"Nor mine," said Jac. "I never left this spot."

We looked at Hudspeth. He fidgeted.

"It must of been after I stepped into them bushes." He jerked his head toward a prairie rose bramble fifty yards away. There was no apology in his tone. "It was only a couple of minutes. Hell, a man's got to—"

"Damn smart dog, picking just that moment to sneak into camp."

"He is smart."

It was Ghost Shirt who had spoken. He was down on one knee beside the dog with his hand on its bleeding head. Not stroking it or patting it, just holding it there, the way he might handle anything else that belonged to him.

"He is trained to follow me at a distance and to join me at night in silence." The commanding strain had not left his speech in spite of his captive state. Although he spoke without accent, the fact that he gave each syllable its proper value made it clear that for him English was a foreign tongue. "I did not train him to attack in my defense. That he does naturally."

He sneezed, winced at the shock to his own injured head, and climbed unsteadily to his feet. I was surprised. It was the first time we had stood face to face, and even then we weren't, not exactly. I knew that most Indians only ran to about five and a half feet, but from his reputation I had expected this one to top off a lot taller. The crown of his head came to my nose. It didn't make me feel superior, though. Some of the hardest fights I've had have been with runts.

He was a fine specimen, at that. The shirt he wore sashed about his waist, once red, now faded to a desert tan, barely contained his chest and shoulders, and his solid, heavy-muscled thighs strained the seams of his buckskin leggings. From there they swelled into powerful calves, then tapered to trim ankles and a pair of feet small and delicate-looking enough in their fringeless moccasins to arouse the envy of a beautiful woman. His reddish brown breechclout nearly swept the earth.

"Why'd you call him off?" I asked.

I got the hypnotic stare. "For his own safety. One more blow like the first would have killed him."

"Is he going to behave himself now?"

"He always has. I said that he is trained."

"Let me put it another way. Are you going to behave yourself?"

He smiled then, which took me aback. I hadn't seen him do that before. It didn't suit him. "I have not been unconscious all the time," he said. "I have overheard your conversation. With what will you threaten me? I am worth nothing to you dead."

Daring me. Just like a twenty-two-year-old boy. Aloud I said, "We'd rather keep you alive, sure, but we'd heaps rather stay alive ourselves. If you're the genius they say you are you'll try to fix it so we won't have to choose. Besides, there's a group of men in blue coats back there who don't care whether they bring you back sitting a saddle or draped over it. If you decide to pitch pennies you'd better be sure where they'll land."

I'd expected that last statement to go over his head, but he understood. He hadn't spent all his time while out East inside the classroom. Anyway, the smile was gone.

Hudspeth mounted the mustang. In spite of the situation and the pain in my wrist I suppressed a grin. He looked like a fat padre on a scrawny burro. He scowled at the dog.

"If that mutt goes with us he eats grass," he said. "We ain't got enough jerky we can afford to waste it on no mangy cur."

"He is Cheyenne. He will hunt for his food," said Ghost Shirt.

We straddled our horses, Jac favoring his wounded shoulder, me my wrist, the Indian his head. Only Hudspeth remained unimpaired, unless you counted the fact that he was deprived of his whiskey and that he was riding a horse that didn't fit him. Followed by a dog with a burst scalp, we must have looked like a hospital train returning from a battlefield as we steered single file down the narrow trail that led to the flatlands. I turned in my saddle for one final glance at our pursuers before we passed below the ridge. There was now no sign of a fire.

The haze burned off around five o'clock, when the air turned hot and dry as the inside of a brick chimney. The grass had gone from green to brittle brown. The harsh smell of baked earth stung our nostrils. Suddenly I missed the sultriness of the past several days. The back of my neck grew skillet-hot and water splashed into my mouth from the buckskin bag I carried seemed to evaporate before it reached my tongue. The landscape swam behind shimmering waves of heat.

Tyrone, it turned out, owned several sections on the western edge of the Drift Prairie, smack in the middle of which stood a tiny sod hut with a privy behind it and a corral roughly the size of Montana. Here and there horses grazed in groups or galloped off alone to kick up their heels in the open acreage. A windmill towered over the hut, its blades stock still. It was either tied down or the air was just as stagnant up there as it was at ground level.

To the northwest, beyond the fenced-in section, several hundred acres had been turned over quite recently. As a matter of fact, it was being turned as we approached it, by a pair of huge workhorses pulling a large plow with a scrawny old man at the handles. As he pushed, he kept up a steady rhythm of curses in a rich, bellowing cant that carried for miles. Since there was no one else around to receive them, it was evident that they were directed at the two grays straining at the traces. The horses didn't appear to be paying any attention to the abuses he was hurling at them as they worked. They were probably used to it by now and couldn't function without it.

We had reached the west end of the plowed field when the farmer rounded the opposite corner. Maybe I was getting old, but I was sure he hadn't noticed us yet. The bullet that struck the ground in front of my gray's hoofs and kicked dirt up over its fetlocks told me different.

14 . . .

"I spent too much time plowing these furrows to mess them up with a bunch of graves. But I'll make the sacrifice if I don't start hearing some names I trust damn soon."

However many years it had taken Tyrone to pick up the American way of speech west of the Mississippi, they hadn't been enough to eradicate his Scottish burr, which showed itself most prominently in the acrobatics his *r*'s went through before they left his tongue. His voice was deep and rich, the way it had been when he was cursing at the horses earlier. He was standing behind the giant grays holding a Remington rolling-block he had hooked from a special scabbard on the plow handle as he was coming around the end of his last furrow, so smoothly that I hadn't realized what he was doing until the shot rang out.

The breed spoke up. "Tyrone, do you not remember me?"

"Jacques!" It was strange hearing Jac called by his right name. I found myself resenting it without knowing why. For all his obvious delight, however, the Scot maintained his grip on the rifle. "Where have you been these twenty years? I thought you were dead."

Several items of gossip were exchanged, none of

which is crucial to this narrative. We did learn that the rancher was breaking ground for late oats after an argument with his feed supplier had resulted in their terminating their working agreement. Then Jac introduced us—all except Ghost Shirt, to whom he referred simply as our prisoner. Only then did Tyrone step out from behind the horses and approach us, still holding the rifle. His figure beneath the shapeless work clothes was small and wiry and he walked with a definite bounce. A worn tweed hat with a slouched, finger-marked brim was crushed on top of his head. The lower half of his face was completely hidden behind a reddish beard, streaked with white and cut square at the bottom. Over this swooped a moustache that must have dressed out at a pound and a half, the waxed ends of which dipped down to the corners of his jaw before jutting back up to tickle his ears. A pair of wire-rimmed spectacles glittered astride a bulb of flesh in the middle of his face. I placed his age at about sixty, but it could have fallen ten years either side of that. He got to within a few yards of us when he stopped short, his face reddened, and he raised the Remington to his stringy shoulder.

"Ghost Shirt!" He made it sound like one of the names he had been calling the horses. The dog, which had just caught up with us, hunkered down and growled threateningly at him through bared teeth.

"You know him?" I asked.

"I saw him in the stockade at Fort Ransom last March when I went there to raise hell about the Crows stealing my horses. What are you doing with him?"

"Judge Flood plans to decorate a pole with him in Bismarck if we can keep ahead of the army." I made a quick decision based on what Jac had told me of the Scot's character on the way there and gave him a run-down. He listened in silence.

"How far are they behind you?" he asked, when I had finished.

"Not more than a couple of hours."

"So why are you stopping?"

For an answer, Pere Jac stepped down and held up his pony's damaged hoof for him to see. Tyrone nodded.

"I can give you a good price on a three-year-old I broke last fall. What've you got to spend?"

"*You* broke him?" Hudspeth cut in. He had all the discretion of a heckler at a church service.

"Somebody had to." Tyrone glared up at him defiantly. "Every last hand I had lit out when Ghost Shirt broke jail. I was busting broncos before you were born."

"Did they have horses then?"

I decided to steer the conversation back onto the main track before bullets flew. "What can you give us for sixty-five dollars?"

The Scot discovered he had a mouthful of worms. There is no other way to describe that expression.

"You've guts, I'll give you that. Not that they'll do you any good now or in the long run. In your situation I could soak you a thousand dollars."

"Not when sixty-five is all we have." I sighed. All right, so maybe that was overdoing it a little. I was tired. "I guess you've got us figured out. I was saving some for emergencies. Sixty-eight dollars."

Worms again. "Get off my land."

"Seems to me it would be worth the difference to keep three of your fellow citizens from becoming criminals and robbing you." I didn't draw my gun. That would have been too obvious, and fatal under the circumstances. But I shifted my weight in the saddle to bring the butt of the Deane-Adams within easy reach.

"Is that how it is?"

"You certainly have a way with words," I said.

I'll give him credit for one thing: He didn't say, "You're sworn to uphold the law" or anything like that, although I could see that he was considering it. I had a whole speech made out for that one. But what he did say was just as predictable.

"This Remington is trained on your belly. Are you betting that your hand is quicker than my finger on this trigger?"

Another gambler. The West was full of them. I said nothing. There's a time to raise and a time to stand pat.

"Maybe you didn't hear his name before." Hudspeth was backing my play. "This here's Page Murdock. He's the one brought in that scalp hunter Bear Anderson last year in Montana, right under the noses of Chief Two Sisters and the *en*-tire Flathead nation."

I thought he was laying it on a little thick, but it appeared that Tyrone was not a man to be subtle with. His murky green eyes did things behind the spectacles. He was a strong man, and a brave one, but sustained tension is a hard thing for anyone to take. I knew, because I was on the other end of the same taut string. Five or six seconds shuffled by. My shoulder began to ache from holding my arm in the same position. I supposed the rifle was growing heavy in the old Scot's hands, although you wouldn't have guessed it by the way he held it. Finally he lowered the piece about the width of a butterfly's eyelash.

"You throwing in the pinto?"

Jac said he was.

"You're getting a good pony damned cheap."

I had handed the treasury over to Pere Jac on the trail. He reached into his poke, withdrew the crumpled bills and the gold tooth, and turned them over to Tyrone, who took them in one hand while he balanced the Remington in the other. I could have taken him then had I wanted to, but there was no longer any reason and anyway I liked him. Maybe I was looking at myself in thirty years.

He held up the tooth. "What's this?"

"What's it look like?"

"How do I know it's real?"

"Bite it."

"I'm not going to bite anything that was in somebody else's mouth."

"Then you'll have to trust us. Where's the animal?"

"In the corral next to the house." He pointed. "That's it, the piebald grazing at the fence. Watch him. He's spirited."

Jac mounted and said, "We will leave the paint as agreed. That and sixty-eight dollars should buy us the best horse in the West."

"That's the only kind I raise."

"Burdett and his men will be around before noon," I told the Scot. "When they come—"

"I know. Tell them you went the other way."

I shook my head. "They know better. Tell them the truth, but lie first. They won't expect you to level with them the first time around. Wait until they press you, then give it to them straight. It will save you a lot of pain. Real pain. These aren't your run-of-the-mill horse soldiers. They play for keeps."

"Who doesn't, out here?"

The piebald was a good pony, broke to saddle but not in spirit, as Pere Jac discovered when he went to mount after cinching up, and found himself swinging a leg over empty air. The pony was on the other side of the corral, tossing its triangular head and champing at the bit, by the time its would-be rider hit the ground amid a swirl of yellow dust.

"Maybe he doesn't like Indians," I suggested, helping

the métis to his feet. "Next time try mounting from the left."

Getting near it was a problem this time, but at length Jac got a foot planted in the left stirrup and his hindquarters in the saddle. His unfamiliar weight threw the animal into a panic, but after a couple of wild gallops around the coral the two were inseparable. The old man may have been half and half, but when it came to riding he was all Indian. I could tell he was satisfied, because when it came time to leave he ignored the gate standing open and bounded over the fence. It was a four-railer, and the stallion cleared it with room to spare.

By noon we had come upon the trail the war party had left coming out. Small wonder the army had found no difficulty in locating us. A grass fire left a harder path to follow. All those hoofs and moccasins and travois had churned the grass into a band of red dust a quarter-mile wide and eight inches deep, meandering drunkenly to the horizon. At that point we veered straight north. None of us felt any need to eat more earth, and there was no sense in making things easy for Sergeant Burdett.

A wind had come up from the northeast. It rippled across the tall grass so that the writhing blades resembled not so much the waves of the ocean (a favorite comparison among visiting Easterners) as the bristling hackles of a great angry beast. The first gust came out of nowhere as we topped a rise, lifting my hat from my sweat-greased brow with a sucking sound that reminded me uncomfortably of the noise made when a scalp is pulled away from the skull. I caught it just in time—the hat, not my scalp—and jammed it down to my ears. The air hitting my face was hot and stale, like an expelled breath. Then it died, but before the ground swell retreated over the last hill in the southwest it came up again, and from then on the intervals between gusts grew shorter and shorter until we were bucking a constant gale.

A jackrabbit exploded out from beneath the gray's hoof as we were cantering down one of the hillocks and thumped through the grass toward a burrow some twenty yards away. Ghost Shirt's dog was after it an instant later. There aren't many dogs that can catch a jack on the run, but Custer was no ordinary mongrel. A rabbit has only one trick, when you come down to it, and that's that it can stop and turn on a dime. Nine times out of ten nothing else is needed. It'll run so far, then halt suddenly. Almost invariably its pursuer, unable to duplicate the feat, will run right past, and before it can turn the rabbit has already reversed directions and gotten a head start that nothing short of a horse at full gallop can touch. Fifteen feet short of the hole this jack chose to rely on the odds and stopped abruptly. In the next instant Custer was upon it. There was a savage snarl, a squeal of pain and terror, and then the dog tore away its throat and settled down to devour the warm flesh. It was all over in less than a second.

"He won't eat grass today," I told Hudspeth. He made no answer. For another four or five miles, in fact, he said nothing. Then, as we were nearing the crest of yet another of the endless swells:

"We got company."

The marshal was riding at my left and a little to the rear. When I turned back to look at him he jerked his head backward. As he did the wind caught the brim of his hat and folded it back against the crown, Indian scout style. Weeks on the trail had beaten all the newness out of it. I looked beyond his shoulder.

He had sharp eyes, despite what I had said that morning when he was unable to spot the soldiers through the spyglass. Far to the southwest, a flying wedge made up of dark, irregular shapes had just come into view atop one of the undulating hills and was traveling with great speed down its face.

"Making up for lost time," I said. "The've gained an hour on us."

Jac said, "They cannot keep up that pace. Even so they will be upon us by nightfall. Something should be done."

"That's what I like, a man who makes decisions." That burning wind in my face had dried up my patience. It wasn't as bad as the "hot southerlies" that blew up from Mexico from time to time, baking the beds of rivers and turning grassland into desert, but it would do until one came along "How about making one that's worth something?"

Hudspeth reined in next to a burned-up wild rose bramble and leaped down from the saddle. My common sense was deadened by the heat. For a moment I thought he had decided to make a stand against eight or ten seasoned troopers and get it all over with, but when he stopped and twisted off the bramble at its stem I couldn't see how that fit and abandoned the theory. Sun and lack of rain had cooked its branches brittle and many of its tiny, shriveled leaves shook loose and rattled to the ground with a sound like shot falling through the trees as he worried it from its moorings. Then he straightened, holding the trophy as if it were a priceless artifact.

"Matches." He held out a hand to Pere Jac.

The métis caught on at the same time I did. After only a beat he reached into his belt and produced the square of oilcloth in which he kept his matches and tobacco. Hudspeth struck one on the heel of his boot and, shielding the flame from the wind with his body, touched off the bramble. The dry leaves caught like pitch and went up in a bright orange blaze. After returning the package to Jac, he mounted up, holding the makeshift torch at arm's length to avoid frightening the mustang, then leaned down from the saddle and set fire to the brown grass where he had been standing.

"Start riding," he shouted over the wind and the fierce crackling, controlling with his free hand the horse, which had begun dancing backward nervously from the spreading flames. "If this wind shifts we'll all be fried where we sit." He galloped west, touched off fires in two more places, then hurled the burning bush in the direction of the distant riders and wheeled to join us in our northern flight.

I heard a raucous noise just behind me and twisted in my saddle, drawing my gun. A yellow blur dashed past me. I realized then that it was Custer just catching up with us after finishing a fresh meal. The dog had darted straight through the flames without a qualm. It had its master's grit.

"Where did you get an idea like that?" I asked Hudspeth as he drew alongside me.

"From my parents, though they never knowed it." His face was flushed from the heat of the flames. "Once when I was ten years old I come home from school and found a smoking black hole where our cabin used to be. Land charred for a square mile. Turned out a spark from the ungreased hub of our neighbor's Red River cart sparked off a fire on our south forty. My ma and pa was inside eating when it hit the cabin. It come so fast there was nothing they could do. I buried what was left of them in one hole."

I never know what to say in a situation like that, so I kept my mouth shut. That's usually the best course anyway. Behind us, the grass went up like tinder as the high winds whipped the flames westward at unbelievable speed and sent a great cloak of black smoke spreading over the prairie. Over my shoulder I caught a glimpse of the dark-clad riders as they reined in a mile or so shy of the blaze, but then the smoke from three separate sources came together and blotted them out.

"And there came out a fire from the Lord, and consumed them," said Pere Jac, but he was speaking so low that I doubt anyone heard him but myself and his God.

15 . . .

Nothing breeds co-operation like a common enemy. Once the threat of Sergeant Burdett and his pack of two-legged hounds was ended, however, it came time to think about restraining Ghost Shirt. For this purpose I produced from my saddle bags the special pair of handcuffs a blacksmith had struck to my order in Montana some years back and used them to secure his hands behind him as we were preparing to bed down. I hadn't brought them out before because they were shiny and sent out a flash in the bright sunlight that a half-blind drummer couldn't miss, but with the hostiles, red and white, out of the running for at least the present it seemed safe to put them to work now. That the Indians had left them in the bag said something about the way things had changed over the past couple of decades. When the wagon trains began rolling west they would have sold their souls for such an attractive bauble, but now they shoved it aside in their search for ammunition. If they'd known what use I'd be putting it to the story would have been different.

A tiny spring inside the mechanism—an addition of my own—locked them automatically with a metallic snick when I closed the manacles about his wiry wrists. Since Indians are as dangerous with their feet as with their hands I used a length of rawhide left over from our captivity to bind his ankles where he lay on his blanket. He made no protest, but then I hadn't expected him to. His kind didn't do much talking when not among its own, and never when words were useless. The dog slunk toward him as I was tucking him in, but he snapped something at it in Cheyenne and it returned to its place beside the fire. That was wise. He knew that it wouldn't be able to resist attacking me next morning when I came near its master, and had no wish to spend the rest of a brief life in those irons. Hudspeth, Jac, and I took turns standing watch as always.

The procedure was repeated the next night. Mornings I released him from the cuffs to eat and undid the thong around his ankles, then after breakfast manacled him again, this time with his hands in front so he could ride, and kept him ahead of us on the trail to remove temptation. It was late in the morning of the second day since the fire that we came upon the rails of the Northern Pacific some five or six miles west of the James. We crossed them and set up camp just out of sight but not out of earshot of the next train.

Nearby was an ancient buffalo wallow, low on water but high on wallow, with a stand of half a dozen spindly cottonwoods growing on its north shore. That was an unexpected stroke of luck. More than half certain that we wouldn't survive to see the railroad, I hadn't given much thought to how we were going to stop the train once we got there. You don't just stand in the middle of the tracks and wave one down in the midst of hostile

Indian territory, not and expect to spend the rest of eternity as anything but a grease slick along the cinder bed. The sight of those trees in the middle of a barren land was enough to make me a believer in manna from heaven if I hadn't known that a water-loving cottonwood sprang up wherever a man spat. Fortunately, Hudspeth had seized a hatchet along with the other provisions he took from the Indian camp, and by the time I had Ghost Shirt trussed up to make sure he behaved, the marshal was three quarters of the way through the first trunk. When that was on the ground I spelled him on the hatchet while he and Jac lugged the tree down to the rails. When they were all lying beside the tracks we went to work cutting them into six-foot lengths. Within a couple of hours of our arrival we had a respectable pile stacked four feet high across the irons.

I was depositing the last spindly chunks atop the heap when something buzzed past my right ear and struck the end of one of the logs, splintering the bark. Then I heard the shot. I tossed away my burden and dived behind the woodpile as more firearms opened up from the same general direction, their bullets pelting the ground and spanging off the rails. One of them struck the heel of my left boot while I was in flight. I came down hard on the ties, rolled, and ended up in a crouch next to Hudspeth, who had been standing behind the pile when the commotion began and now was down on one knee in the same spot, his Smith & Wesson in hand. His moustache was bristling. A lot of things annoyed him, but none so much as being shot at. I drew my Deane-Adams.

Jac, who had been on his way back from checking on our prisoner, charging his pipe as he went, lay motionless on his stomach in the tall grass twenty feet away. At first I thought he'd been hit, but then I saw his ear twitch and I realized he was just lying low. His Spencer was leaning against the woodpile on the other side where he'd left it, the end of its barrel taunting me over the top of the barrier. My Winchester was still in its scabbard with the horses in camp. Two bad mistakes when you come to think of it, the métis going unarmed to inspect a dangerous captive and me leaving a firearm near that same captive, who was trussed up but still had a brain. Worse, we both knew better. Reaching the railroad against all those odds had made us all cockier than we had any right to be under the circumstances.

Beyond the stack of wood, where the shots had originated, yawned open prairie, unbroken except for an occasional brown bush, too low and spindly to conceal a man, let alone several. For several there were, unless that was a Gatling gun out there, which still meant more than one because you don't exactly carry that kind of firepower on the back of a horse. To look out there, though, you would have sworn we were all alone. Which meant only one thing.

"Burdett?" whispered Hudspeth at that point, as if he'd been reading my mind. I shook my head.

"Indians. Only they can hide like that in the middle of open grassland. And only they can use up that much ammunition without hitting anything worthwhile."

"You mean Lame Horse?"

"Who else? He probably saw us leave camp with Ghost Shirt at the Missouri and guessed where we were heading. He's been paralleling the tracks ever since or he would have been caught in the same fire that pushed back Burdett. How much lead have you got on you?"

"Just what's in my gun. The belt's back in my saddle bags. How about you?"

"Five in the cylinder and another ten in my belt. The rest is in my bags. If you carried a forty-five Peacemaker like almost everyone else I might risk giving you some. At least it wouldn't blow up in your face."

"Look who's talking, you and that little toy you pack."

I stoked up my courage and raised myself just enough to snatch hold of the barrel of Jac's rifle and hook it back over the woodpile. Three guns opened up as I did so. One bullet actually struck the wood four feet to the left of my exposed hand, their marksmanship had improved that much. A log thicker than most was dislodged from the top and landed with a crash across the rails. That let daylight in. I removed my hat to reduce the target and crawled on my knees to the end of the stack to take aim at a likely-looking movement in the grass thirty yards south of the tracks and squeezed off a shot. A jackrabbit barreled out heading east.

Hudspeth had better luck. Crouched peering through a chink where the uneven surfaces of two logs failed to meet, he spotted the white plume of a single eagle feather protruding above a patch of brush too far away for a revolver to reach with any accuracy at the same time I did, aimed high, and sent a lean, black-painted brave reeling over backward with a scarlet smear where his collarbone met his throat. That's why I said luck. It had to have been an incredibly bad shot to hit anything at that distance.

That lessened the odds somewhat, although I couldn't say by how much since there was no way of knowing how many Indians had slipped past the army besides those few we had seen with Lame Horse back on the plateau. But I was heartened by the evidence that the enemy was flesh and blood after all. No sooner had this one hit the ground than a comrade lost his head and snapped off a shot that whizzed two yards over Hudspeth's hat. I fired at the puff of gunsmoke. Nothing spectacular happened as a result, but there was no answering shot from that quarter, which may have meant something or nothing.

For a long spell nothing happened, unless you count being eaten alive by mosquitoes as the afternoon wore on and we were enveloped in shadow. Drought killed off everything but them, which figured. Nevertheless we were better off than Jac, who was forced to lie out there baking in the sun with the shade of the woodpile only a scamper away. The temptation must have been staggering. There wasn't enough Indian in him to keep his naked back from turning as red as Hudspeth's nose, but he was old-man stubborn enough not to move a hair. As for the full-bloods, they burned too, but more slowly, and since they were used to such hardship we couldn't claim much advantage.

The apparent impasse did prove one thing. If Lame Horse was in charge as I suspected, he came nowhere near Ghost Shirt as a strategist. He had pinned everything on wiping us out in the first volley, and when that failed he was at a loss over what to do next. Whether or not it had yet become evident to him, though, his course now was obvious. I said as much to the marshal.

"Wait for nightfall?" He repeated, in his stage whisper. "I thought injuns never attacked at night."

"That's true of some, but only because they believe that if they're killed their souls won't be able to find their way to the Happy Hunting Ground in the dark. Lame Horse is pretty sure of himself, and if he loses a brave or two it doesn't concern him as long as he isn't one of them. He isn't a company man like most of the others in his tribe. His performance back at the mission convinced me of that. And if he's as powerful a medicine man as I think he is the others'll do as he says because they're afraid of him. Which leaves us with a choice."

"What's that?"

"We can either die fighting or turn Ghost Shirt over to them. He's what they're after anyway."

"Think they'll let us go if we do?"

"I doubt it. That crippled bastard's wanted our scalps ever since that first night."

"So why did you even bring it up?"

"It was bound to come up sooner or later. Just thought I'd get it out of the way."

"Well, you know what my answer it."

There being hours to go before sundown, we settled in for a long wait. As I crouched there, taking an occasional potshot at nothing in particular to let them know we were still in the running but mostly just crouching, I realized what it was about Indian fighting I didn't like. It wasn't the danger. That was something I'd accepted the day Judge Blackthorne swore me in and I'd never questioned it. Rather, it was the waiting, the long periods of inactivity while something was brewing beyond my control. I'm not talking about tension, although there was plenty of that as vague movements here and there in the grass told me Lame Horse's braves were deploying themselves for the coming attack. What it was was boring as hell. A man can starve for weeks and still have enough fight left in him to give you a run for your money. By the same token, you can deprive him of water until you're sure he's long since dried up and blown away and yet have him slash your throat from ear to ear when you show up to view the remains. Bore him long enough, however, and his reflexes will slow and his brain begin to rot away. I'd felt this same way during the war when I was laid up in the army hospital, following the progress of the fighting in bits and pieces from the newspapers and, when I wanted accuracy, stories told by incoming wounded from Atlanta, Gettysburg and finally Appomattox. Even now, as much in the thick of things as back then I was out of it, I felt the same sense of stagnation and uselessness, as if I were missing something important.

The hell of it was that I wasn't. Unlike the Montana high country, where night falls with the unexpected abruptness of a guillotine blade, dusk seeped in over the prairie interminably through the pores in the vermillion and blue-black streaks that were smeared across the western sky on the heels of the departing sun, casting layer upon layer of gray wash over the landscape until the features bled together, and that's when the scenery we had been watching for hours began to move. They rose from the grass like shadows up a wall when the lamp is turned up, indistinct gray shapes scarcely darker than the charcoal sky that stretched behind them. The wind had died, but that didn't matter because they moved noiselessly, high-stepping deer fashion through the grass without so much as a rustle. It was eerie, unreal. I was almost afraid to shoot for fear that the dream would then become a reality. I shrugged it off— literally, for something cold had begun to inch its way up my spine—drew a bead on the shape nearest me with the Spencer, and fired. It advanced without faltering. The only explanation I could come up with for that was that they looked bigger than they were and I had missed. It was like fighting ghosts.

I was getting set to fire again when there was a move-ment to my right, Jac was on his feet, starlight glittered on something metallic in his right hand, he made a lung-ing motion, there was a solid sound like an axe biting into wood, and the shape I had been about to shoot at staggered backward three steps, doubled over, and sank almost gracefully into the grass. At that moment another shape that had been walking behind the first wheeled and swung the silhouette of something long and deadly in the métis' direction. Before it could squeeze the trigger I snapped off a shot, aiming low this time. The figure spun halfway around, dropped its rifle, and fell.

Having shot his wad when he threw the knife, Jac now was unarmed. I tossed him the Spencer and he caught it just in time to thrust the muzzle into the belly of a brave who had abandoned stealth to charge him with tomahawk raised, and blew him inside out.

That turned it from a ghost watch into a good old-fashioned Indian fight. They were charging on foot along a front twenty yards wide, those who had guns popping away at targets they couldn't see any better than we could ours, those who hadn't swinging tomahawks and clubs and trade axes and bows and lances and singing the war songs their grandfathers had sung when they went to fight the Pawnee and Crow. Hudspeth snapped off two shots in rapid succession, dropped one warrior and wounded another so that he released his lance and had to get down on all fours to grope for it in the tall grass, then swung left and splintered the bow of a third just as he was drawing back to let fly with an arrow.

"Cut out that goddamned circus shooting!" I shouted, for the gunshots were deafening.

"What circus shooting?" he demanded. "I was aiming for his head!" Then a bullet splattered the top of the log over which he was peering. He cried out and rocked back on his heels, rubbing his sleeve across his eyes.

"Hit?" I had to blurt it out the side of my mouth as I fired the Deane-Adams into the bulk of a shape coming up on me hard. It ran a few more steps and collapsed at the foot of the woodpile. I angled the revolver downward and put a second bullet in it for good measure. Playing 'possum is as old a trick as Indians have.

"Bark in my eyes." He rubbed them with the heels of his hands, the Smith & Wesson dangling by its butt from his right.

An Indian armed with an eight-foot lance stopped running, struck an athletic pose with his legs spread apart, and took aim with the steel-pointed weapon at the helpless marshal. I sighted in on him carefully and squeezed. The hammer snapped hollowly against an empty shell. I squeezed twice more. Same story. The brave's throwing arm was in motion when Jac caught him with a bullet from the Spencer. The lance left his hand before he sank, whistled through the air, stuck point-first in the top log just below the marshal's face, drooped, and fell. By this time Hudspeth had the bark cleared from his eyes and fired at a brave who had gotten down on one knee to draw a bead with his rifle. He missed, but the redskin flattened out in self-defense.

I punched my last cartridge into the chamber of my revolver. We were all scraping bottom now. There were more Indians out there than I'd expected after they had been playing it so cautious. If we all got lucky and claimed one for each round, that left a good half dozen to battle with our bare hands. I fancied my thoughts were much the same as those that had gone through Custer's head during his last moments. It was strange how often he had been on my mind of late. Or maybe it wasn't so strange.

My first shot after reloading spoiled my figuring when it sailed clear over the head of a befeathered brave near the center of the advancing line. As I picked him off with the second I was wondering if it might be possible to line a pair of them up and make one bullet do the work of two so I could get back on track. You might say I was a little off my feed by this time.

Then I heard something that made me regret all those church services I'd missed since I was five years old.

It was a godawful noise, shrill and deep at the same time, raucous and distinctly unpleasant, a wail of agony and yet a roar of triumph, like all the damned souls of Hell letting go at once. It had no comparison. Once you heard it you never forgot it, and when you heard it again, no matter where or under what circumstances, you didn't have to stop and think to identify it. You just knew it was a steam whistle.

It climbed to a scream, paused, and climbed again, finishing the second time on a growl. It might have been miles away and it might have been right on top of us. Owing to the nature of the sound and the warping quality of the dry night air, there was no way of telling just how close it was. For an instant while it was blasting I thought I spotted an orange flash on the distant horizon that might have been flames spouting from the stack of the engine, but it could just as well have been sheet lightning or my imagination. In any case, the effect of the noise upon the Indians was immediate and devastating.

In earlier days, before the Union and the Western Pacific had bisected the great buffalo herds and the iron horse was a thing unknown on the prairie, its cry might merely have made the braves curious, much as the rattle of pots and pans on a frontier where man had never before set foot might attract inquisitive deer. But just as a deer once shot at while investigating such a noise will react in the opposite fashion when he hears it again, so the Indians who had learned the hard way that the great flame-snorting beasts brought only death and misfortune to their tribes. For all they knew, this train might be carrying more troops from the seemingly inexhaustible store of fighting men that the Great White Father struck out like arrowheads in his eastern lodge to send against the nations. They stopped fighting suddenly and melted away before the harsh noise like tallow before a hearth. One minute we were going at it fang and claw, and the next we were alone in the midst of a silent prairie. After a few moments we heard the drumming sound of retreating hoofs, then silence again. Where the braves had picketed their ponies so that we hadn't seen them remains a mystery to this day.

As if to taunt them, at that moment the whistle blew again. This time for sure I saw flames on the horizon.

"Now, what made 'em break it off so quick?" Hudspeth wanted to know. We were standing now. Faintly I could feel the buzzing vibration of the distant train's wheels through the soles of my boots. "It's still a good five miles off. They had enough time to settle our hash and take a few souvenirs besides."

"Indians have no concept of time. Have you got anything in that gun besides air?"

He was still holding the S & W. Suddenly reminded of it, he glanced down, then returned it sheepishly to the pocket inside his vest. "No. But they didn't know that."

"Still breathing?" I called to the métis, who was standing with his captured Spencer in both hands. He assured me that he was.

The whistle sounded again, perceptibly closer this time. I handed my gun to the marshal. He stared at it, then at me.

"What's this for?"

"Protection in case they come back. Get this wood burning while Jac and I fetch the Indian. Jac, give him your matches. I hope you've got more in that rifle than Hudspeth left himself."

"One round," he said.

"Good enough." We left Hudspeth gathering dry grass for tinder and headed on up the slight rise that led to camp.

"That was fair shooting for a man who believes in turning the other cheek," I told the breed, who was walking behind me.

"A little religion is a good thing," he said. "In its place." I could tell by the way he said it that he was smiling, although it was too dark to see. "I have said that I will fight for what is mine."

The wallow looked naked now that the trees were gone. A spatter of starlight reflected off the surface of the puddles in its muddy bottom. I was wondering if it might be a good idea to water the horses now so that they wouldn't try to drink on their own after we turned them loose and get themselves mired down, when a flash of red and yellow flame splintered the darkness, a shot crashed, and something tugged at the left flap of my jacket, which was swinging free of my rib cage. Later I found a hole in it where the bullet had passed within an inch of my hide.

Pere Jac wasn't so lucky. He gave a little sigh, sank to the ground, and never got up this side of Purgatory.

16 . . .

It's surprising how much your eyes can see in an infinitesimal amount of time, even though it takes your brain five times as long to comprehend it. In the instant the shot was fired, I saw in the brief illumination of the explosion our prisoner swaying at the top of the grassy knoll, his feet still bound together, my Winchester braced horizontally across his back in his manacled hands, the muzzle pointed in our direction. The fight at the railroad had given him time enough to struggle upright and make his way over to the horses in order to get his hands on the carbine in my saddle scabbard. Likely he had fallen a few times and dropped the weapon more than once while freeing it from its holder and getting it into position, but those were minor setbacks for the Scourge of the Northwest.

I said that the brain is a lot slower than the eyes. Even so, I had all this put together between the time the bullet pierced my jacket and Jac hit the ground. By that time reflex had taken over and I was already moving. Meanwhile Ghost Shirt was struggling frantically to manipulate the Winchester's lever behind his back and rack in another shell, muttering curses beneath his breath in English, there being no equivalents in the

Cheyenne tongue. He was succeeding when I launched myself at him in a tremendous leap—I paced it off absent-mindedly on my way back later, it was twenty feet, not bad for a middle-aged peace officer—and piled into him, locking my arms about his waist. But before we connected time seemed to freeze, and I felt as if I were suspended while the carbine's lever clicked home and the young chief's finger closed on the trigger. In the instant of collision there was a roar so deafening it seemed to be inside my skull and the left side of my face caught fire.

We came together then, with an impact that tore the Indian off his feet and sent the Winchester flying from his hands. The horses, although picketed, had been milling around nervously as far as their tethers permitted ever since the first shot, and now were between us and the wallow. We landed right under the feet of my gray. It whinnied and did a quick dance to avoid us. One of its hoofs stamped dust out of the ground a couple of inches shy of my right ear.

The jar had knocked the wind out of the Indian momentarily, but before I could press my advantage he squirmed out of my grip. Bound though he was, he fought like a sack full of badgers. Every time I tried to straddle him and pin him down he kicked at me with his lashed-together legs or arched his back and rolled out of my reach. I was just grateful that his dog was still off somewhere hunting and unable to join in. The second time he got away I reached for my gun and grabbed a handful of prairie air. I'd forgotten giving it to the marshal. Angry at myself, I flung an arm out longer than it was designed to go and snatched hold of something that tore when I pulled at it. Ghost Shirt's collar.

He tried to squirm away again, but I had a piece of his throat as well and held on. His windpipe throbbed in my hand, struggling for air. I pulled myself closer and got a leg over him before he could put a knee where women and savages instinctively aim. Even then he pinned one of my ankles beneath his body and threw himself over on one hip, and I would have gone over had I not thrown out a hand to brace myself. My injured wrist all but buckled beneath the shock. By then, though, I'd felt something that sent new strength coursing through my strained muscles. I'd reached for the ground, but my fingers closed over something hard, cold and familiar. The Winchester. Holding him down between contracted thighs, I swung the carbine over my head by its barrel and braced myself for the downswing. He wouldn't live to see the train, let alone the scaffold in Bismarck.

I nearly wrenched my shoulder out of its socket when I swung and the carbine didn't move. Someone had clamped a hand around the stock. I blinked and looked back over my shoulder at Hudspeth's bulk standing over me.

His feet were planted apart the length of an axe handle, which made him about as flexible as an adobe wall. To hedge his bet, he had drawn my Deane-Adams and clamped it to my right temple when I turned my head. The barrel was still warm from firing. It struck me then that of late this particular firearm had not done me a whole lot of good.

"He's whipped, Page." His voice was tired and hollow, the full note of a gong muffled in rags.

"Jac," I said.

"Jac's dead."

I released my grip on the Winchester slowly. Beneath me Ghost Shirt's eyes gleamed dully in the starlight. I got up.

At the base of the hill, the woodpile blazed brightly, exposing a twenty-foot section of track. Here and there the upturned face of a dead Indian reflected the reddish glow. Closer now, the approaching locomotive's whistle took on added depth against a background of chuffs and clangs and humming rails. I went over to where the métis lay stretched out with the Spencer across his stomach.

"Match," I said, holding out a hand toward Hudspeth.

He hesitated. "There ain't but three left. We might—"

"Match!" I barked it this time. He handed one over without another word. I struck it on the seat of my pants, bent, and held it over the still figure's face, cupping my other hand around the flame to shield it from the wind. In its glow I saw that Jac had retained his perennial half-smile even in death. His eyes glittered between half-open lids. The seams in his face looked deeper than ever now that there was nothing to distract my attention from them. I suddenly realized that he was a good five to ten years older than my extreme earlier estimate. On the edge of the illumination a neat round hole four inches down from his collarbone showed how lucky the Indian's shot had been. A couple of inches this way or that and in six months it would have been just another scar.

The flame was burning my fingers. I shook it out and dropped the charred remnant into the pocket of my jacket. Force of habit. Fires were as hazardous in my native Montana with all its forests as in the grassy plains of Dakota.

The engine was only a mile off now. In two minutes it would be on top of us.

The same thoughts must have been going through the marshal's head, because he said, "No time to bury him." I ignored him and strode past him to the horses.

I had my cinch undone when he realized what I was up to and stepped in to give me a hand. In a few seconds we had all four of them unrigged. As they wandered off to graze we gathered up our saddles and bridles, leaving behind Jac's McClellan, and started back down. I took the time to spread the métis' saddle blanket over his corpse, not that it would afford any protection against the coyotes and magpies once they scented fresh meat. I then took charge of Hudspeth's gear while he loosened the cord that bound Ghost Shirt's ankles, heaved him to his feet, and pushed him stumbling ahead of him down the slope. At the bottom the marshal gave him a brutal shove that sent him pitching headlong into the grass. Then his ankles were drawn together once again.

By now the engineer had spotted the flames, slowed down, and was hanging on the whistle as if he thought the escaping steam might blow the obstruction off the tracks. I saw him in the glow of the flames belching out of the broad black stack, a smear of crimson face beneath a tall hat made of striped pillow ticking leaning out the window of the cab over an arm crooked at the elbow, sparks from the stack swirling about him like fireflies on their way to the cinder bed. Below him the steel driving arm flashed as it cranked at the wheels, at times seeming to come within two or three inches of his sleeve at the top of its cycle. Behind the engine, oily black in the darkness, rumbled the wood car, baggage carrier, and two passenger coaches followed by the caboose, the windows of all three illumined in yellow. The smoke pouring from the stack was a gray streamer trailing a mile behind the red lantern that swung from the railing of the caboose.

At any time that speeding behemoth could have rammed our flimsy barricade and sent it flying in blazing fragments all over the prairie, but the engineer didn't know that. When it became apparent that the offending substance would not go away, he hauled on the brakes. A jet of white steam erupted from beneath the boiler. Sparks sprayed from the shrieking wheels. Wood groaned, steel screamed against steel in a grotesque parody of human anguish. The driving arm reversed itself without pausing and the entire mass of metal ground to a shuddering halt three feet short of the pile of burning logs.

While all this was going on I had left our gear with Hudspeth and crossed over to stroll among the bodies scattered south of the tracks. I had my revolver, which the marshal had returned to me, fully loaded now from the cartridges in my saddle bags, in my hand in case any of the corpses should still be breathing. But none of them was, nor was any of them Lame Horse, which was what I had come to determine. All were Cheyenne. I left them and approached the engine, which was snorting and blowing like a stallion impatient to be on its way.

"Mister, you better start explaining." The engineer's demand was delivered over the breech of a pre-Civil War Walker Colt, for God's sake, a cap-and-ball six-shooter as long as a man's arm from elbow to fingertips. I smiled respectfully.

"You wouldn't want to use that," I assured him. "I'm law."

He thought that over. He was a wasted strip of leather with a wind-burned face cracked at the corners of his eyes and mouth and a perpetual squint. His side-whiskers were gray tipped with white and the hairs were long enough to curl in upon themselves. A smudge of soot stained his moist right cheek. He was sweating, but not from the tension of the moment. The heat inside the cab from the open firebox was withering. I kept my eyes on him and on the fireman standing behind his shoulder, a big man whose short-cropped black hair reminded me of greasy wool. At first I'd thought his face was blackened from his exertions before the flames, but now I realized he was a Negro. He was naked to the waist, and his slabbed chest glistened like new iron beneath a sheen of sweat and a sparse covering of coiled hair that ran in a thin line down his stomach into the damp waistband of his pinstriped pants. At the moment he was trying without success to get the engineer's attention by tugging at his sleeve and calling him "Boss" in a voice as deep and clear as the echo from the bottom of a barrel.

"So you're law." It wasn't the most clever thing the engineer could have said, especially after he'd had all that time to think up a good retort. But a friend of mine was dead and I was in no mood to render him senseless with my wit, so I let him go on to the obvious. "Let's see some proof."

"This proof enough?"

Hudspeth's growl, coming from the other side of the cab, took all the sand out of the man with the Walker. He didn't even bother to turn around and confirm the fact that the marshal was standing on the step plate with his freshly loaded Smith & Wesson pointed at his back. He just sighed and laid the relic in the palm of my free hand, the one that wasn't holding the five-shot.

"That's what I was atryin' to tell you before," the Negro informed him.

They were convinced, of course, that they were being held up. I couldn't blame them. I hadn't seen a mirror for some time, but looking at Hudspeth—dirty, unshaven, his clothes wrinkled and torn—I got a fair idea about how much I looked like a lawman after all this time on the trail. I don't suppose I smelled like one either, but whether that made any difference amid

the occupational scents of wood smoke and oiled steel
and their own perspiration was open to debate. Whatever the case, I was climbing aboard to display the
badge and lay their fears to rest when the fireman
released the brake.

The locomotive jolted forward, throwing me off balance and wrenching the handrail on the other side out
of Hudspeth's grasp. His gun went off into the ceiling
and he dropped out of sight. As I threw my arm out to
catch myself, the Deane-Adams struck the wall of the
cab, jarred loose from my grip, and clattered to the
steel floor. I fell four feet and landed on my back on
the ground, the Walker bouncing from my left hand
as if propelled by a spring. When my wind returned I
found myself staring down, or rather up, the bore of
my own weapon in the black man's hand. I spent more
time on the wrong end of that piece. There was no
doubt about what he had in mind. The cylinder was
already turning when I clawed my badge out of my
pocket and thrust it at him.

For an agonizing moment I wondered if it would
mean anything to him at all. Everything depended upon
how he had been treated by lawmen in the past. Then
the cylinder rolled back to its original position and he
backed off without lowering the gun.

"What's going on, Gus? Why aren't we moving?"

The newcomer had appeared from the darkness at
the rear of the train. Round and cherubic, he carried
a lantern and wore a baggy blue uniform with brass
buttons and a black-visored cap set square on his
shaggy head. With him was a taller man whose erect
carriage and squared shoulders made me think he was
more accustomed to a uniform than the well-tailored
suit and vest he was wearing, but a uniform far different from his companion's. His reddish hair was graying
at the temples and had a windblown look. Like myself

when in civilization, he was clean-shaven, a rare enough thing in that bewhiskered era, his spare cheeks and firm jaw shadowed in blue where the razor had scraped them without missing a stubble. While the conductor appeared to have eyes only for the railroad personnel present, the tall man took everything in with cool eyes under brows so pale they were visible only because of their contrast to his deep tan, which had only recently begun to fade. I figured him for cavalry.

Gus, it seemed, was the engineer. He had alighted from the cab to reclaim his ancient revolver. When it was safely in his belt he rattled off his version of the events, gesticulating at the flaming woodpile, now past its peak and burning spottily where the logs were not already charred, at the marshal, who had recovered himself and was standing on the top step of the cab, his gun trained on the Negro's back and his badge gleaming ostentatiously on his lapel, and finally at me where I sat on the ground eyeing the muzzle of the Deane-Adams in the fireman's hand.

"Well, what more proof do you want?" This from the tall man, addressing my guard. He had a raspy voice—roughened, I supposed, from years of barking orders under fire—but with an undercurrent of smoothness that suggested breeding beyond that offered by the manual of protocol.

Still the Negro hesitated. A glance passed from the tall man to the conductor, from the conductor to the engineer, and finally from him to the fireman, whereupon the last sighed and returned the gun to me. I holstered it and got to my feet with a helping hand from the tall man. A ridge of calluses ran across his palm and between his thumb and forefinger where the reins are held.

"Cavalry?" I asked, just to confirm what I already knew.

He laughed, white teeth gleaming against his burned skin. "Lord, no! Horses are for racing and drawing buggies. Lieutenant Colonel Andrew Locke, 16th Engineers, retired."

I grinned in spite of myself. "You're the first ex-military man I've met since the war who didn't claim to be a full colonel."

"There aren't many of us left. I wish you'd introduce yourself. Old soldiers are always being pumped for colorful stories, and I'll need a name to go with this one." He indicated the bodies of the slain Indians, almost invisible now that the fire was dying. He seemed to be the first to notice them, judging by the way the others suddenly forgot all about us and stared at the carnage. At first glance the corpses did look like discarded railroad ties scattered over the right-of-way.

I gave him our names and told him that we had fought the Indians over a prisoner trussed up on the other side of the tracks. "We're commandeering this train to take him to Bismarck," I finished.

The engineer and conductor raised their voices in protest. The colonel, however, merely rubbed his chin thoughtfully.

"I don't think I can let you do that," he said finally.

"You don't have any choice." I turned to the engineer. "Get up steam."

"You don't understand." Locke remained calm. "This is a private express."

"Yours?"

He shook his head, then looked thoughtful again. "Perhaps I can work it out. Will you come with me?"

"Where and why?"

"The last car. A few minutes now might save you an hour."

He sounded sincere, which added to my distrust. But

time was running short. At any minute Lame Horse and his Cheyenne might overcome their fear of trains, and I had no illusions about the ability of six men to stand them off with only (so far as I knew) four guns and a museum piece among them. Ignoring Gus's protests, I yanked the Walker from his belt and handed it up to Hudspeth. "See that the fireman stokes the box, and put Gus to work clearing the tracks. I'll be back in five minutes."

"Someone's got to watch the pressure gauge," the engineer snarled.

"The conductor's not doing anything."

Colonel Locke and I mounted the steps to the platform of the second coach, where we stopped before the door that led inside. He turned to me and his voice dropped below a murmur.

"I have to whisper," he said. "The old man has ears like a cat. Just keep quiet and agree with everything that's said."

Before I could question him he rapped softly on the door. Immediately a voice that had to belong to either an orator or a wounded moose boomed an invitation from within. We entered.

It was just as well that my companion had advised me to keep silent, because I was struck dumb by my first glimpse of the coach's interior. I had expected an ordinary day carrier, narrow and cramped with a double row of hard seats facing each other in pairs on either side of a bare aisle. I wasn't prepared for a palace.

The dominant color was wine red. It covered the two easy chairs in plush velvet, tickled my ankles where I stood on the carpet, threw off a sheen from the curtains on the windows and from the drapes that concealed all but the brass lion's paws that were the feet of a huge four-poster bed in the far corner from view.

A chandelier the size of a bull buffalo's head dangled from the paneled vault of the ceiling, its crystal pendants sparkling in the light of two globe lamps, one of which stood on the bar—a bar, by God, of polished oak with a decanter of what looked like burgundy and two long-stemmed glasses atop it—the other on a reading table beside the larger chair, overstuffed with a winged back and arms of curved walnut. The man at the bar pouring amber liquid from a second decanter into a glass was also overstuffed, but unlike Judge Flood, whose excess tonnage hung out everywhere, this one's was all up front in a solid, rounded globe of belly that started at his collar and swelled out so far that I doubted he could clasp his hands over it without straining his arms, then swept back to balance between his normal-size thighs like a hot-air balloon supported upon a pair of uprights. He was in shirtsleeves and vest, the obligatory gold watch chain describing a grand arc across the biggest part of the bulge. Upon it were strung ornaments representing various guilds and lodges the way an Indian might display scalps on a thong.

"A brandy man, I'll wager," he announced over his precise operation with the decanter and glass. His voice was not a bellow like Flood's, nor a rumbling bass like that of the black fireman, but its resonance carried the best qualities of both. It was a voice trained to ring in the rafters of a great marble hall. He spoke as if he'd been expecting me and as if we'd already been introduced. "I trust this cognac will cut the dust to your satisfaction. It's not Napoleon, but with the country just emerging from a depression it's inadvisable to flaunt one's affluence. That is the phrase you Westerners use, is it not? 'Cut the dust?' Or perhaps I should say *we* Westerners, since I am to be one henceforth."

"I'm partial to rotgut," I said, but accepted the proffered glass from a strong, stout hand with a thick gold band around the wedding finger.

His eyes twinkled at what I suppose he considered a prime example of frontier wit. They were the kind of eyes that twinkled easily or flared hot with anger or grew soft and gentle, all at a moment's notice and upon command. Like those of Major Harms they were brown, but with a dash of yellow, like the cognac. His face was round but not bloated, the dewlaps folded neatly on either side of a fleshless beak and darting immediately into the cover of his whiskers, which, beginning at the tops of his cheekbones, grew into a magnificent noose-shaped mass that concealed his vest as far as the second button. He had started growing them before I was born. They were a shade darker than the iron gray of his hair, thinning now but in the best way, retreating in twin horns of pinkish scalp to the left and right of a healthy widow's peak that topped the bulge of his forehead in the style of a Crow pompadour. He would never be as bald as Judge Flood. I looked to the colonel for an introduction.

He, too, had been been extended a glass of cognac. He sipped at it, then touched his lips with the corner of a silk handkerchief and returned the latter to his breast pocket.

"Sir," he said, addressing the host, "this is Page Murdock, deputy marshal for the federal court of Judge Harlan Blackthorne at Helena, Montana Territory. Deputy Murdock, allow me to present Senator Harold Firestone, late of the United States Congress and former Governor of the State of Illinois." He paused, then added, for the other's benefit, "Deputy Murdock is sympathetic."

17 . . .

I sipped at the cognac while my host studied me with new interest. I could tell it was good liquor because it didn't have much taste. The ideal spirit, I imagine, has no flavor at all. But that wasn't what concerned me at the moment. I was wondering what a politician was doing away out here in the middle of nowhere and just what it was that I was supposed to be sympathetic with. Out of the corner of my eye I caught a subtle signal from Colonel Locke reminding me of his earlier admonition. I decided to trust him for the time being and kept my mouth shut.

"Tell me, Mr. Murdock," said the senator. "What is it about this country that you despise? The greed for territorial expansion or the corruption in lofty government circles? Or is it something else? Something personal, perhaps? I am curious to know."

I was glad I wasn't supposed to say anything. I stood there like a plaster Cupid while he waited for an answer. He was a couple of inches shorter than I and had to cock his bearded chin upward to engage my gaze. There was a hard glint in his eyes now, one of suspicion. Or maybe I was reading something into them that wasn't there. The silence was growing threadbare when Locke plunged in.

"Deputy Murdock is a frontiersman, Senator. He feels that civilization is encroaching upon his world and blames Washington City for its systematic destruction."

Firestone kept looking at me. "And how did you learn of our mission? It is supposed to be a secret." This time I caught a genuine trace of distrust in his tone. The colonel had his work cut out for him.

"Deputy Murdock is a friend of a friend," he said cryptically.

To my surprise that bit of nonsense seemed to satisfy the senator. I got the impression that he was eager to place his trust in me and was prepared to meet me more than halfway. "Very well," he said. "I caution you to remain silent.. As far as anyone else is concerned, I have retired from politics and am on my way to assume the supervision of my cattle herd in Montana." Then he softened again, visibly, and smiled, crinkling the skin around his eyes. "I knew that you were in sympathy when I looked out the window and saw you boarding this coach. I said to myself, 'Here is a man who will not accept abuse lying down.' I assure you that you are not alone, and that when we reach our destination you will find many others who feel as you do."

"He has a partner," Locke put in. "A marshal named Hudspeth."

He seemed unruffled. "He, too, is sympathetic?"

"He's my partner," I said. Now I was doing it. Five more minutes with these two and I'd be speaking in riddles for the rest of my life.

"Then he is welcome also." He turned to Locke. "Place their belongings in the baggage car and see that they are made comfortable in the other coach." Back to me. "We will talk more later, after we have both rested.

Travel exhausts me. I am afraid that I am no longer the campaigner I was in my youth." His eyes clouded over and I could see that he really was played out, as much as a man can get in this life. His complexion was sallow and the whites of his eyes were turning an unhealthy ivory around the edges. If he wasn't dying I had never seen it before.

Locke kept silent until we were back outside and beyond earshot of the rolling palace. Then he produced a metal flask from an inside breast pocket and tipped it up, letting the contents gurgle twice before he lowered it and replaced the cork. He looked as if he needed it, so I didn't blame him for not offering me a swig. He and Hudspeth would get along.

"When did he snap?" I asked then.

"A year and a half ago, when he lost his bid for a third term in the Senate." He returned the flask to his pocket. I noticed a similar bulge on the other side of his coat, but not from another flask. I wondered if this was some new style I hadn't heard about, or if it was just that a man whose drinking habits required a portable supply found it necessary to carry a hideout gun as well. "He was planning to go for President in eighteen eighty, and had his eye on that election. When a thirty-two-year-old war veteran knocked him out of the seat he'd held for twelve years it was too much for him. Ostensibly, he's on his way to take over the ranch he owns south of Medicine Hat. He thinks he's going there to meet up with his private army and prepare to cleave off Idaho, Washington, and Oregon and start his own country."

He paused to let that sink in. It didn't take as long as he expected. I said, "When a politician loses his grip he doesn't fool around, does he?"

"It's really not so farfetched when you think about

it. Every politician harbors a secret desire to be king of something."

"I wouldn't know. I stopped voting after the last election."

He smiled without mirth. "The Hayes steal. That little stunt did more to undermine popular confidence in the democratic system than four years of civil war."

"Is there an army?"

"Forty men in army surplus, armed with war-issue Springfields. No ammunition. He'll finish out his life in that lonely spot, drilling his tin soldiers and strutting around like a Mexican general in the uniform he designed for himself. He'll be out of the way and harmless."

"Who's paying the soldiers?"

"He is. You don't spend half your life in public office in this country without becoming a millionaire. The bank draft he's carrying in his vest pocket would feed a family of ten for thirty years."

"Is that why you're armed?" He started. I smiled. "Next time you have a suit made, tell your tailor to leave more room around the left shoulder. What is it, a shoulder rig or a pocket like Hudspeth's?"

He swung open the left side of his coat to reveal a glossy leather holster beneath his armpit, tilted forward to bring the ivory-handled butt of a small Remington within easy reach. The rigging was concealed beneath his vest.

"What are you, his bodyguard?"

He shrugged. "Bodyguard, adviser, companion—"

"And keeper?"

That didn't bother him. Not much did, I guessed. "It pays well."

"Better than the army? Why'd you leave?"

"You can only go so far in the service, unless you've

distinguished yourself in battle, in which case the White House is the logical next step. I don't like politics. Besides, men who erect privies for generals' wives don't get their names on the front pages of newspapers."

I didn't ask him why he felt riding herd on a madman had any more future than service in the 16th Engineers. At best it would just make him angry, and I didn't know how much reserve he had or how good he was at getting that Remington out of its nook, and didn't care to find out at this point. That was one thing about life in the West. With everyone packing a weapon you had to be careful what you said or did. I reversed directions.

"What's a friend of a friend?"

His face cleared at the question. He was glad of the change. "Conspirators in high places," he explained. "Firestone is convinced that the country is rife with them west of the Mississippi. Not that it isn't, and on the other side as well, but not the kind he thinks. He hopes to strike the first blow for revolution."

"Oh, Christ, not another one."

He laughed, a trifle too heartily. "There's small danger of that happening outside the twisted confines of the senator's skull. Let's go see if we're ready to push on." He almost threw an arm around my shoulders as we struck out toward the other end of the train, there was that much politician—and liquor—in him. But there was enough soldier in him to refrain, and to change the sweeping gesture at the last moment into a tug on the back of his collar as if it had become twisted.

"How do you plan to explain the Indian?" I asked.

"Don't worry about that. The old man never leaves his car. Just to be safe, though, you might consider locking your prisoner in with the baggage."

"No good. I'm keeping him in sight to end of track."

"Then lock yourself in with him."

"Not without windows." We had reached the engine, where the fireman was busy chucking wood into the box while the engineer, having cleared the debris off the tracks, leaned against the wall of the cab with an eye on the pressure gauge. The conductor stood about studying his watch and looking impatient. Hudspeth glared at them from the ground. Jac's Spencer was in his hands, my own Winchester lying at his feet with our gear, which he had carted from the other side of the tracks. Ghost Shirt, who had accompanied it, lay propped up on one elbow nearby, in as comfortable a position as he could manage considering his trusses. The steady throb of the boiler drowned out whatever conversation there might have been.

"You're entitled to the truth," I told Locke in a voice too low to carry past him. "The Indian is Ghost Shirt, chief of the northern Cheyenne. His medicine man is the leader of the braves who are out to bust him loose. I don't know how many he's got with him, but it can't be a lot or they would have rushed us in a body hours ago. That doesn't count for much, though, because they're used to being outnumbered. In any case I doubt that we've got any such edge. I thought you should know what you're letting yourself in for before we set out."

He turned that over for a while, inspecting it from every angle. He didn't look alarmed, but then it was hard to say how he looked when he was. For him, the deadpan he showed me may have been the way he expressed fear.

"Tell me," he said at length, "would it make any difference if I said no?"

"At most it might cost Hudspeth and me some ammunition. One way or another we're taking the train."

"That's what I thought. So why tell me at all?"

"Maybe I was touched by that little speech you made about the democratic system."

I don't know if he heard the answer. He was busy studying Ghost Shirt, who was busy studying him back, although not quite as clinically. It looked as if the Cheyenne was eyeing Locke's throat where the blood bubbled close to the surface. The links joining the manacles jingled ominously behind his back.

"Let's not tell the others," the colonel advised. "Gus is too contrary and Ephraim, the black, is too smart. They're better off not knowing."

"You're the colonel."

"Go to hell."

At last the locomotive was ready to go, snorting power and straining at its leash. Hudspeth stood guard over our prisoner while Locke and I loaded the saddles and paraphernalia into the baggage car (minus the rifles, which Hudspeth and I retained), then, after I had cut loose the bonds on the Indian's ankles and hoisted him to his feet, mounted the cab to keep temptation from Ephraim and Gus during the long journey west. That must have taken some heavy soul-searching on his part, considering how much he hated train travel. The conductor, for whom the colonel vouched, was allowed to return to his caboose with a strongly worded admonition—mine—not to speak to Firestone about the Indian. Madmen make me nervous, because you never know how they're going to react. To preserve his ignorance we elected to escort Ghost Shirt to the empty coach through the baggage car. We were entering the latter, Locke in front, me in the rear, the Indian sandwiched between us, when the car rocked beneath a sudden weight and something the color of tobacco spit swept past us into the interior, whirled about, and stood in the middle of the darkened aisle, legs spread and showing its teeth in a grin of warning. A growl rippled from deep in its throat. The colonel slid a hand onto the butt of the gun beneath his arm. I reached past our prisoner and placed a hand on his shoulder, stopping him.

"Don't risk the shot. He belongs to the Indian. As long as you don't threaten his master he's sweet as a drugged rattlesnake."

"You'd better be right." He advanced a cautious step. The dog went for his leg with a bellowing snarl. He leaped back, tearing his pants leg on a fang.

"Good advice, Murdock," he said acidly, drawing the Remington. The mongrel hunkered down growling, its hackles bristling.

"Call him off!" I rasped in Ghost Shirt's ear.

He shrugged. "I am not sure that I can. He hates soldiers."

"How can he tell?" demanded Locke. "For that matter, how can you? I'm not wearing a uniform."

"A snake is a snake, with or without his skin."

"Call him off or you'll lose him," I snapped.

The Indian spoke to the dog in soothing Cheyenne. The animal appeared to be listening. After a moment its hackles flattened and it lowered itself the rest of the way to the floor. Only the warning growl remained.

"Walk," said Ghost Shirt.

Locke grunted and stepped forward reluctantly, gun in hand. The growling increased in pitch as he circled around the animal, but it kept its position, one eye peeling back, until Ghost Shirt and I had passed, when it got up and fell into step behind us. At the last moment I ducked through the connecting door on the Indian's heels and pushed it shut on the dog's snout. It yammered savagely, I caught a glimpse of bared yellow fangs in the space between the door and the jamb, and then, with a double thump, the dog was separated from us by a barrier an inch and a half thick. It whooped and the door bounced when the weight of its forepaws slammed against it, but held. Claws scraped frantically at the wood. I hoped for the colonel's sake that there were enough walls between his employer and the animal to muffle its angry yelps.

While the bodyguard went on to resume his duties in the private car, I pushed Ghost Shirt into a seat of the more conventional first coach with his back to the rear of the train so that I could sit opposite him and watch the connecting door, committed the Winchester to the overhead rack, and unlocked one of the cuffs. Then I brought the wrist that was still manacled around in front of him and secured the empty iron to the wooden arm of the seat. He bore it all without complaint. From the way he placed his free hand to his bandaged head I figured it had begun to ache again, but that could just have been a ploy to throw me off guard. With a prisoner as crafty as he was, having to watch him every minute was enough to give a man a headache of his own.

With the thought, I suddenly realized how desperately tired I was and dropped into the seat facing him as if my knees were operated by hydraulic pressure and all the water had suddenly drained out. I was getting old. I had lost count of the days I'd spent on the trail, but I knew I'd been out longer than this in the past, gone through at least as much, and still had enough sand left to rack up points in Purgatory by visiting certain establishments on Helena's east side. Now I didn't think I could stand the walk. The West had sucked out my youth and left me a brittle shell. For the first time I understood how Hudspeth felt, and it scared me. Mine was no profession to age in.

The train started forward, taking up the slack between the cars with a lurch that rocked us in our seats. I sneaked a look at the Indian to see how he reacted, but from his stoic expression I gathered that a train ride was nothing new to him. I kept forgetting his eastern sabbatical. The scenery outside began to roll past, slowly at first, then picking up speed until my own reflection was all I could make out against the night-backed glass. But before it did, I saw the corpses of the slain Indians scattered beside the cinder bed, dim but unmistakable in the light of the smoldering fragments of wood the engineer had tossed off the track. I wondered how Locke was going to explain them away to the senator, or if he had contrived some way to keep him from the windows until the danger was past. Given his special talents, either was possible.

At twenty-five miles per hour the whistle sounded hoarsely, sending vibrations tingling through my boot soles. It was a hoot of derision for the pioneers whose wagons and oxen had crawled over the same ground at the rate of five miles per day only a few years back. In four hours we would cover more territory than Hudspeth, Jac and I had covered in as many days. Every minute we kept rolling was another half mile between us and the surviving Cheyenne. Still, I felt no relief. One of our number was dead, and one hundred miles separated the rest of us from absolute safety. I didn't think Lame Horse's medicine could resist odds like those.

18 . . .

I hadn't been sitting there ten minutes when the train's motion and my own exhaustion combined with the delayed effects of the senator's cognac and I fell asleep. How long I slept I couldn't begin to guess, but when I awoke with my forehead clammy against the window I had a stiff neck and the inside of my mouth tasted like the water in a buffalo wallow. It couldn't have been too long, because the first thing I saw when my eyes opened was my prisoner watching me with a predatory alertness. When I stirred, his eyes darted to the dusty floor and the stoic expression returned like a trained hawk recalled to its master's arm. I determined not to fall asleep again, but just to curb his ambition I slid over, trapping the gun in my holster between my hip and the wall, removed the key to the manacles from my left hip pocket, and transferred it out of his reach to my right. The Indian observed all this, but you wouldn't have known it from the bored look on his face. I watched him in silence for some time.

"Is there any special reason you hate the whites so much, or is it just the usual?" I asked finally. A little salty conversation seemed like just the thing to clear away the fog.

There was another long silence during which I gathered that he wasn't in the mood to answer. That came as no surprise. He hadn't said ten words to me in English or any other language since we'd met. I had given up on him and was trying to make some tune out of the noise the wheels made as they chuckled over the rails when he spoke. The sound of his voice made me jump.

"How does one describe a snake to a man who has never seen one?" He spoke low for an Indian, eschewing the high-pitched oratory by which his people set such store. "If you say that he slithers, that he speaks with a sibilant, and that he spits venom, do you convey his worst qualities adequately? Or is it better that you show the wounds where his fangs have struck?"

On "struck," he tore open his faded shirt with his free hand and yanked it down over his shoulders, twisting as he did so to show me his back. I winced. In the coal-oil light the scars stood out like long white worms against his burnished skin. One of them curled up over his left shoulder to the base of his neck. I could picture the man who wielded the whip letting the tasseled end slide of its own weight down across the torn flesh after the blow had landed.

"Who did that?" I fought to keep the grimace from my tone.

"My white schoolmaster in Iowa." He sat back, shrugging the shirt back over his shoulders. The muscles in his chest rippled with the movement. "I made the mistake of letting him see me talking to a white girl before class. He was a big man, and I was not yet grown. He lashed me to a tree in front of the school with his belt and horse-whipped me in front of my classmates. All the time he was beating me he quoted passages from an article he'd read that compared the American Indian to the Negro and said that each was incapable of learning anything but the most rudimentary rules of survival. A month later his house burned down."

"What took you so long?"

"He had a strong arm. It was three weeks before I stopped passing blood."

"What happened after the fire?"

"Nothing. I stole a horse and left that night to return to my people."

"And you base your hatred for an entire race on that one incident?"

He shook his head. He had the bearing of a proud animal, despite the irons. "That was only the climax. You are not Cheyenne. How can you know what it is like to be told all of your life that your people are the finest that has ever lived, and then find yourself surrounded by strangers to whom you are lower than a maggot in a buffalo chip? Strangers who lack the courage to tell you so to your face but whisper among themselves when they think you cannot hear? Among the People, if one brave is angered by another he does not gossip like a squaw behind the other's back, but calls him out to settle the matter by contest of arms. I have more respect for the man who whipped me than for these others, for he at least was man enough to make his feelings known. You can fight an insult, strike back after a blow, but what can you do against a thought? An Indian is nothing if not direct."

"Is that how you felt when you sneaked back and fired his house?"

That one caught him off guard. For all his reputation, he was still a spoiled boy, unaccustomed to having his word questioned. I pressed on before he could reply.

"Everywhere I go I keep hearing about the Noble Red Man who neither lies nor cheats," I said. "I haven't caught up with him yet, but when I do I'm going to tell him he's spreading a false impression. The greatest liar I ever knew is summering in the Bitterroot Mountains right now, along with five or six hundred of his Flathead followers. He'll pass you the pipe with one hand and lift your scalp with the other. Yet not a drop of white blood flows in his veins. Explain that."

"If he shows two faces it is the white man who taught him how."

"Then he learned his lesson well. Don't put me down as an Indian hater. I think you have a legitimate beef. But why can't you face the fact that you're no better than anyone else? That you're just different?"

"Does it not shame you to think that you are stealing our land?"

"I never stole an acre."

"But you did not try to stop those who did?"

"For the simple reason that it was none of my business. I believe in letting a man fight his own battles. Who spoke for the Comanche when your own people drove them out of the Black Hills into the desert? Or for the peaceful tribes they forced out generations earlier? Or for the Cheyenne when the Sioux pushed their way in from Canada? You're not complaining because we're not as good as you are but because we're not better. You're a hard man to please."

"You use words like a weapon, white skin."

I sighed. "I didn't expect to win you over. After twenty-two years, though, I thought it was time you heard the other side." I paused. "You know that Lame Horse is after your job."

If I'd expected that to surprise him, I was disappointed. He went on studying the floor between his feet as if his future could be read in the patterns his moccasins had made in the dust. "Some of my warriors have told me this. They are wrong. He knows his place."

"The problem is you don't agree on where it is. I

saw that argument you had with him back at the mission. I didn't have to understand Cheyenne to know he's got ambitions."

He met my gaze then. A faint smile played over his lips. "At last you have become tangled in your own net of words. Have you not already said that it is Lame Horse who tried to free me tonight?"

"Naturally. There's no guarantee that you'll hang soon even if we get you to Bismarck. With all the publicity you've been getting it's a real possibility that the sob sisters back East will pressure the President into commuting your sentence to life in the penitentiary. As long as you live you pose a threat to your successor. Dead, you're a martyr and powerful medicine, nothing more. The best thing that can happen to Lame Horse is that you get killed in the confusion while he's trying to break you loose."

"Only a white would think such thoughts."

There we were, back at the beginning. Nothing brings out the stubbornness in an Indian like cold logic. I changed the subject.

"Where'd you get the dog?" I nodded in the direction of the baggage car, where the mongrel could be heard whimpering frustratedly and digging splinters out of the door. Like its master, it never gave up.

"Why do white men place so much value in owning things? He is my companion, not my property. I got him nowhere."

"Meet him, then."

He ran the fingers of his free hand over his plaits—searching, most likely, for lice. He found none. He was cleaner than most Indians, a condition ingrained in him during his stay with the whites, whether he liked it or not. "We met in the Black Hills, in your year eighteen seventy-two. We have been together ever since."

"Who bobbed his tail?"

"The white trader who claimed to own him. I cut off one of his ears to show him how it felt."

He watched me out of the corner of his eye for some reaction. It was his turn to be disappointed. I have a high threshold of shock. "Why did you name him Custer?"

"Their hair is the same color." He toed the dust. "Was the same color."

I stared at him, but he didn't add anything. "It really goes deep, doesn't it?" I asked him. "The hate."

"Before I was born," he said, eyes still on the floor, "when still in my mother's womb, I saw the plight of my people as clearly as others see it now. The spirits sent me this vision so that I would be prepared to take up the reins and lead the People to their rightful destiny. I knew before I took my first breath that the way would be hard and my enemies many. Still I did not turn away. I have seen our braves slain and our women and children defiled. Always I held to my course. While a single Cheyenne breathes I will not lay down my arms in defeat, not if it means the death of my people and the end of our way of life for a thousand generations."

It was a sad speech. Sad not because of the certain doom it carried, but because he didn't believe it, not one word of it, any more than I did. His exposure to our culture had ruined him for his own beliefs. I might have felt sorry for him if the memory of Pere Jac's death weren't so fresh.

I was about to pursue a different line when Colonel Locke came in bearing two glasses filled nearly to the brim with cognac. I sat back as if caught whispering in class.

"I thought you might be getting thirsty back here." He held out one of the glasses.

I didn't take it. "There's one missing."

He stared at me for a moment, uncomprehending.

Then his eyes slid toward the Indian and understanding clouded his features.

"Keep your liquor," snapped Ghost Shirt, before the colonel could say anything. "It is one of the main reasons for our troubles. The Comanche do not touch it and they are still a great people."

"Next time offer him one." I accepted the glass.

Locke made a nonchalant gesture of concession with his free hand and lowered himself onto the edge of the seat across the aisle. He did all this on board a moving train without spilling a drop from a full glass. I wondered how much it would take to get him drunk enough to lose his natural poise. He took a sip and frowned at the glass as if its contents weren't strong enough.

" 'It's not Napoleon,' " he said, swallowing his voice in imitation of the senator's stentorian tones, " 'but with the country just emerging from a depression it's inadvisable to flaunt one's affluence.' "

Pleased with his impersonation, he smiled and crossed his legs, holding the long-stemmed vessel delicately between thumb and forefinger. I noticed that his socks were handwoven and bore a tiny gold monogram. So his job did pay better than the army. I didn't look close enough to see if the initials were his or if he wore Firestone's brand.

"Is it worth it?" I asked.

He looked at me, still smiling, and raised his brows. Tiny threads of blood gave the whites of his eyes a pinkish cast.

"The money," I said.

He glanced down at his glass and saw in it what I was talking about. Then he sipped again. "Is it any of your business?"

"It is if trouble comes and you're too soaked to remember one end of that shoulder gun from the other."

"In my valise are three sharpshooter medals I won

during my last hitch. I was so blind drunk when I took two of them they tell me I couldn't see my group when it was shown to me."

"What about the third?"

"I couldn't locate a bottle in time. Worst score I ever made. But I won just the same."

"You're having fun with me, aren't you?"

"My valise is in the baggage car. Shall I fetch it?"

I didn't bother to answer, which for him was answer enough. Relieved, he started to sit back, then remembered that the way he was perched left nothing behind him for support, and straightened again. "Good. I didn't want to have to shoot that damn dog."

"How's the senator?"

"Sleeping, thank God. I gave him enough laudanum to keep a horse happy for a week. Diluted, of course. Like his reason."

Again I said nothing. If he insisted on acting like a supercilious ass it was no business of mine. He was good at it, though. I almost believed him.

At length I had to give in and say something. If I hadn't, the monotonous sway and rumble of the coach would have taken me under for sure. "I was just asking Ghost Shirt why he named his dog Custer."

"No surprise. I met the man in Washington when he was testifying against Secretary Belknap. A mutual friend introduced us in a restaurant. I was with a young lady at the time. The way the Boy General preened himself in her presence you would have thought he was a pup in its first heat. I don't think he even knew I was there after we shook hands. And him with that vision of a wife of his sitting right across from him. I proposed a toast to him in Chicago when the news came in about the Little Big Horn. They were still talking about it when I left."

"The Little Big Horn?"

"No, the toast."

I said Locke was poised. I'll add that he was charmed to boot. How else explain his timing in having just drained the last drop from his glass when Gus hit the brake?

As if shoved violently from behind, Ghost Shirt pitched out of his seat so hard he sprained his wrist when the manacles binding him drew taut and the seat's wooden arm split down the middle with a sharp report. Later I found that even the steel links between the cuffs had been stretched out of shape. Colonel Locke slammed shoulder-first into the back of his own seat, but caught hold of it before the backlash could throw him into the one opposite. Seated as I was facing the rear, I was spared the first trauma as my seat back absorbed most of the concussion, so that I did no more than spill what was left of my drink over my shirt and lap, but when the coach bounced back I duplicated the Cheyenne's headlong dive. There was no chain to stop me, and only a last-minute twist to the right saved me from a broken neck when I came into contact with the seat opposite. A sound like walnuts being crushed in another room filled my ears as my shoulder struck the wooden framework. I hoped it was the polished hickory giving away and not my shoulder, but I doubted it because an instant later the pain came and my brain cells began to blink out in clusters. All around me oaken pegs groaned beneath the pressure of a well-built coach tearing itself apart, and a screech like half a dozen eagles being castrated all at once burned a red-hot hole through my eardrums.

Then it was all over and the car had settled and my brain cells opened up one by one, allowing me a rare view of a cobweb sagging hammock-like an inch from my eyes in the corner I had somehow managed to jam myself into. It wasn't what you expected to see first thing upon coming back from the dead. Even so I could have kissed it. My left shoulder, numb now, gave up on me when I tried to push myself up off the floor where I was kneeling, but with the help of my right hand on the window sill I was able to hoist myself back into my own seat. My knees tingled sharply. I looked down and saw that they were bleeding through my trousers. Six months later the last sliver from my shattered glass would work its way out of my flesh.

I was sitting at an angle, or rather the coach was, the curtains on the windows dangling at a forty-five-degree tilt from the rods. Across from me, Ghost Shirt had slid back into a sitting position and was busy testing his fettered wrist between thumb and forefinger for breaks. It wasn't broken, but it was beginning to darken and swell. Locke, across the aisle, picked his glass up from the floor, still intact, and set it on the seat facing him. Of the three of us, he alone had emerged unscathed from the upheaval. Fools and drunkards.

The silence parted when a window at the other end of the coach, jarred loose from its frame, fell forward, executed a complete flip, and crashed to the floor. Then the quiet closed back over it, swallowing the last tinkle so effectively that after a moment it seemed as if there had been no such disturbance. We stared at each other like mourners on all-night watch over a corpse. At length:

"This is getting to be a habit," said Locke.

That did it as far as the tension was concerned. I got up, swaying to catch my balance on the tilted floor. Pain blazed through my left shoulder when I grabbed at the back of the seat for support. I stifled a curse.

"I'm going up front," I told Locke before he could ask questions. "You'd better see to the senator." I pulled my carbine down from the rack and headed toward the door without waiting for an answer.

The locomotive was perched at a crazy angle, its stack heeled away over to the left and pouring smoke out of it at a tilt that suggested a strong wind, although there was none. Steam rolled out through the spaces between the wheels and swirled in the yellow beam of the lantern mounted over the boiler. In it I saw the twisted ends of the rails pointing heavenward at an even sharper angle only a few yards ahead. Someone or something had torn them up and given them enough English to derail a train whose engineer had not been as alert as Gus. That individual was climbing down from the cab as I approached. He spotted me and, out of instinct, snatched for the Walker Colt that was no longer in his belt. I held up my hands, palms forward, to show that I was friendly.

"How come you were able to stop in time?" I asked him.

"Two-mile grade up ahead." His southwestern twang held a sharper note than usual. "I was slowing down some to take it when I seen the ends of them rails glint in the lantern beam. I didn't have to see no more. Hold-up men done the same thing down in Colorado when I was with the U.P. in seventy-one. We keeled over then, and I lost one of the best firemen I ever had. Not this time, though. This time I got her stopped quick enough. Quicker'n I expected, truth to tell." He hooked a finger inside his mouth. He was bareheaded, and in the reflection of the light coming off the bent irons I saw a thin trickle of blood leaking out of a split lip and down his chin. It mixed with the smudge on his cheek when he rubbed it, so that I couldn't tell what was blood and what was soot. Like the rest of us, he had kept moving when the train stopped.

"Are you all right?"

"I've lost teeth before. Forget it. Worry about getting them rails fixed before any holdup men come around.

That's what I thought you was when you come up on me so sudden."

"I wish that's all it was," I muttered.

"What's that?"

"Can't you put her in reverse and take her back to Fargo?"

"Not enough wood."

"We've got three cars and a caboose. If you've got a fire axe we're in business."

"Nothing doing. I got retirement coming up and I ain't about to tell James J. Hill that I burned up four of his cars, one of 'em a private Pullman. No, sir."

"Would you rather face whoever tore up the rails?"

"Same difference."

"What if I told you it was Indians did it?"

He squinted at me through the gloom. Suspicion glittered in the slits of his eyes. "You know something you ain't telling?"

"It would take too much explaining. What about it? Hill or the Cheyenne?"

He turned that over, frowning. Then he shook his head curtly. "No, by God! Hill's got nothing to do with it. I ain't never run from no fight before and I ain't about to start now. We're staying and fixing the rails."

I was in no position to fight reasoning like that, especially since I had made much the same speech to Hudspeth on the east bank of the James River when I was younger and more foolish. I sighed. "All right, I guess I can't make you. You're the only one who can run the train. Have you got the tools?"

"A crowbar and a pair of sledges in the cab. No spikes, but we can use the ones what's there if they ain't been busted or throwed away. Might be we can get it done before morning, if the irons ain't too bad twisted and we don't get jumped first."

"That's a hell of a lot of ifs."

He shrugged.

"How are the others?"

"Ep's burned some, not bad. You better see to your friend, though. His head damn near busted the throttle when we stopped." He went ahead to inspect the damage to the rails while I mounted the cab.

I announced myself first and was glad I had. Ephraim, the fireman, was waiting for me at the top with the aforementioned crowbar raised over his woolly head. The light of the flames crackling in the open box turned his skin from iron to bronze and made the burned flesh on his right breast and cheek look worse than it was. His hair was singed where it met his forehead. He must have stuck his head right into the box when the wheels stopped rolling. His eyes had a hunted animal look. When I got close enough for him to see me clearly he relaxed and dropped the bar clanging to the floor.

"How bad?" I asked, indicating his burns.

"I done had worse, I 'spect." His dungeon-depth voice was soothing. There was a church choir in Helena that would have given anything to have that bass in its ranks, if he weren't black. "I'd sho' feel better, though, if'n you'd ask your friend there please don't open no holes in this child's hide with them there cannons he's aholdin'."

I looked in the direction he had nodded, where Hudspeth was sitting on the floor with his back propped up against the opposite wall of the cab, his Smith & Wesson in one hand, the obsolete Colt in the other. He had the Spencer pinned beneath his not inconsiderable bulk. His forehead was smeared dark with blood, but I could tell by his heavy breathing that he was conscious.

"It's me," I told him. "Murdock."

"I knew that." He spoke laboriously. "It's the nigger

I was watching. He tried to take the Walker a minute ago."

"To pertect us," flared the fireman. "I heerd footsteps acomin' and thought it was them holdups come to shoot us. He was gonna put one in this child's belly when I backed off," he added.

"Give him the Colt," I told Hudspeth.

He stared at me, his barrel torso heaving. His breath was coming regularly now. I decided he wasn't hurt badly. "You must of thunked your head harder than me," he said at last.

"I don't know how you feel about it, but I prefer to fight one enemy at a time. You and I aren't going to stand off the Cheyenne all alone. Give him the Colt."

"Injuns, sho' 'nuff?" Ephraim rolled his eyes at me, the whites showing in the light of the fire. He sounded more eager than frightened. Black or white, they were all the same, these Easterners, coming out here thinking the West was something put on for their own entertainment. I ignored him. Hudspeth took nine, then handed over the Walker as I'd known he would all along. We had gotten to know each other pretty well during the time we'd spent together.

"I hope you know what you're doing," he growled.

"So do I." I gave the revolver to the fireman. He accepted it enthusiastically, checked the cap beneath the hammer, thrust it into his belt.

"Lame Horse isn't as impulsive as I thought," I said. "The way I figure it, he put his braves to work tearing up the track with their lances and trade axes on their way to where they met us, just in case we made it on board. We've got till dawn before he catches up to us, maybe less. If we don't get those rails fixed by then we'll have to fort up and hope for the best. Does it hurt?"

Hudspeth rubbed the bloody spot above his eye with

the heel of a hand. It was congealing now over a jagged gash an inch and a half long. "Not so much that a belt of good whiskey couldn't cure it," he said.

I grinned. "We'll see about that after I check up on our prisoner."

Custer was whooping it up fit to be tied as I mounted the platform between the baggage car and the coach, whining piteously and doing his best to turn the door into kindling. He reminded me of an old hound I'd once had who would set all the other dogs to howling for miles around every time I stepped outside without him.

It struck me then. Drawing my belt gun, I propped the Winchester against the wall, kicked open the door of the coach, and threw myself into the first seat on my left, landing hard on my hurt shoulder.

That was a mistake. Somewhere someone crushed a fresh batch of walnuts and sparks of white-hot pain swirled before my eyes. For an instant I was blinded. Through sheer act of will I forced myself to see through the swimming red haze. Gun in hand, I scrambled over to the opposite seat and peered cautiously over the back.

I hadn't missed much. Ghost Shirt was gone, along with my handcuffs and six inches off the arm of the seat he had occupied.

19 . . .

The door opened at the other end of the coach as I was getting up from between the seats. I raised my revolver to the level of the handle and thumbed back the hammer. My injured shoulder throbbed a half-beat off from the rapid banging of my heart. Colonel Locke came in and closed the door gently behind him.

"Sleeping like a baby," he said, turning. "I must have given him a stronger dose than I thought. Did you—" He stopped when he saw the gun.

"Ghost Shirt," I barked. "Did you see him?"

"Why, no, I—" He realized the implication of my words and glanced at the seat in which he had last seen the Indian.

While it was still dawning on his sodden consciousness I retrieved my carbine and pushed past him roughly, heading for the door through which he had just passed. Outside I leaped to the ground and looked up and down the length of the train as if expecting the fugitive to be standing there waiting for me. He wasn't. I did find the piece of wood he had taken with him when he finished the job the sudden halt had started, lying on the ground south of the tracks, but that was no clue at all, as he might have flung it there to throw me off while he lit a shuck north.

The first thing Locke and I did was search the train from top to bottom. I had learned my lesson the time a defendant on trial for murder in Judge Blackthorne's court made a run for it while court was in session and officers scoured Helena for two hours without result, only to have the janitor stumble upon him crouched in the rear of a cloakroom down the hall from the judge's chambers. We divided the train down the middle—or nearly so, Locke wanting nothing to do with the baggage car and its fanged occupant—me taking the front as far back as the coach, the colonel seeing to the caboose and the senator's car just in case our quarry had slipped inside after his own exit. We checked under the carriage and up on the roofs. I even risked my skin looking through baggage, where I knew he couldn't be from the way the dog was acting. The third time it went for my leg I should have shot it, but I didn't. I'm like that sometimes. I considered letting it out to see if it would lead us to its master, but gave that up because there was no way of telling whom it might attack when it did. Besides, the dog was Cheyenne. Silly as that sounds, I've seen horses brought up on Indian tradition throw their new riders when tracking down members of the same tribe for unfriendly purposes, and it was just possible that this mongrel would lead us into God knows what rather than betray the whereabouts of the man who took care of it. We didn't have time to find out. So when I left the car I made sure Custer was still inside.

I met Locke outside the coach. He was carrying the lantern I had seen the conductor with earlier.

"Anything?" I demanded.

"Just the conductor."

"What did he see?"

"I didn't ask. He's dead."

"Ghost Shirt?" I snatched his sleeve.

He shook his head. "Not unless he rammed the poor man's skull into the steel railing on the back of the caboose. That stop splattered his brains all over the platform. I dragged his body inside."

"Well, that's that." I put away the Deane-Adams. "He's either taken off on his own or gone to meet Lame Horse. I hope he decided to go it alone."

"Why?"

"Lame Horse doesn't know our firepower since we came on board. He may hold off attacking until dawn just to play it safe. If Ghost Shirt gets to him with what he knows, they'll hit us right away. What are we, twenty miles from where you picked us up?"

He calculated. "More like fifteen."

"Two hours, then." I had him hold up his lantern and looked at my watch in the yellow light. "Seven if they wait till morning. With luck we'll have the repairs done by then. How much have you got in that flask?"

He had produced the item in question and helped himself to a swig. He touched his lips with the back of his hand, held up the vessel, shook it and listened to the contents sloshing around inside, frowned.

"Two swallows."

"Not enough." I held out my hand. When he gave it to me I tipped it up and finished what was left in one long draught. As the warmth of it spread through my system: "Mind if I borrow this?"

"Be my guest."

I climbed to the platform of Firestone's car. Since Locke was his bodyguard I paused outside the door and shot him a questioning glance. Although perplexed, he nodded his permission. I entered the sanctum.

The lamp on the bar was still burning. Fortunately it was bolted down or the entire structure would have gone up in flames after that last stop. Even the chandelier, its chain clamped securely to the ceiling, was still intact. In the corner, the curtains on the great four-poster had been left open just enough for me to see Senator Firestone's mountainous belly quivering beneath the counterpane as he slept in the grip of his opium-induced dreams.

Someone, probably the colonel, had had the foresight to place both decanters in the cabinet beneath the bar after his last visit, and neither was damaged. I uncorked the flask and poured into it what was left of the cognac. Locke had been hitting it hard, but there was more than enough to fill the pint container. The colonel was standing in the doorway as I turned to leave.

"This must be a first," he observed. "A reverse conversion."

"It's not for me."

"I've heard that before."

"Nobody likes a drunk with a sense of humor." I put the flask in my hip pocket and accompanied him outside. "I don't suppose you've any firepower aside from that Remington," I said when we were back on the platform.

He shook his head. If I hadn't known how much he'd consumed already that night I might have sworn he was dead sober. He changed roles as often as a repertory company.

"How about ammunition?"

"Under the bar. Two boxes."

"Get them." I stepped down and struck out toward the engine.

Hudspeth, on his feet beside the locomotive as I approached, wasn't surprised to learn that our prisoner had escaped. "Figured as much, the way you two was scrambling all over the train a while ago." He patted his forehead from time to time with a bloodstained handkerchief. "Course you know if he gets to Lame Horse we're dead as rocks."

"Maybe not. Maybe they'll leave us alone once they have him."

"You said yourself they won't."

"It doesn't cost us anything to hope."

The engineer appeared from the front of the train. As he crossed the beam of the powerful mounted lantern I saw that his lower lip, although no longer bleeding, had swollen to nearly twice its normal size.

"Give Gus the Spencer," I directed the marshal. "We need as many hands as we can get. You can't fire two guns at once, and you've got enough ammunition to stop a war with just that Smith." I indicated the cartridge belt he had liberated from one of the troopers at the Missouri, strapped around his waist.

"Got me a gun." Gus patted the butt of the Walker Colt sticking up above the waistband of his pants.

"I give it to him," announced Ephraim, descending from the cab. "It's his'n anyways."

"From now on you're a rifleman." I took the Spencer from Hudspeth and gave it to the fireman.

"She's loaded up tight," said the former, as Ephraim inspected the breech. "Used all the shells there was left. What was that you said before about bringing whiskey?" His eyes shone eagerly as he looked at me.

"Sorry. All out."

His shoulders sank.

"Will brandy do?" I held out the flask.

He seized it with a noise a hungry St. Bernard might make accepting a raw steak. Suddenly his jaw tightened. He lowered the flask and rammed the cork back in with the heel of his hand.

"Reckon not." He thrust it back at me.

We stared at each other for some time in silence. Then I felt a slow grin spread over my face. I was a father watching his son take his first step unaided. "Keep it," I said. "For later."

Ephraim cleared his throat loudly enough to drown out the ticking of the boiler as it cooled. We all looked at him. "Seems a shame to just put it away like that," he ventured.

It might have been that my eyes played tricks on me in that poor light, but just then it looked as if the ends of Hudspeth's handlebar moustache twisted upward in the first smile I had seen on his face since we met. He turned the flask over to the fireman, who held it out in front of him for a moment, admiring it. Then he yanked the stopper and did for a quarter of the vessel's contents in one healthy pull. Drawing the back of his hand across his mouth, he returned the flask with a grateful nod to the marshal, who offered it to Gus.

The engineer shook his head. "I'm a man of temperance," he explained. "When I ain't, I don't do a lick of work for days, and from the looks of them tracks that's one thing we can't afford."

"Can they be fixed?"

"Won't know that till we try." He walked around Colonel Locke, who had just joined us bearing the two boxes of cartridges for his shoulder gun, and came back from the cab a minute later carrying a heavy sledge in each hand. "Who's first?" He held out one of them.

I stepped forward without thinking and took the hammer in my left hand, the right still holding the Winchester. The weight of the instrument when he let go sent a bolt of lightning straight up my arm to the shoulder. I dropped it and was following it to the ground when Hudspeth caught me in both arms.

"Let's have a look at that there arm," he said, lowering me to the prairie. I lay on my stomach while his powerful fingers poked and probed my shoulder in the light of Colonel Locke's lantern. The little shocks I felt as he did so were bearable after the big one I'd just experienced. His whistle of surprise was long and low and faintly reminiscent of the train's throaty blast.

"Iron-butt Murdock," he snarled finally. "Waltzing around with a dislocated shoulder like it's a stubbed toe. Here." He thrust something in front of my face. After a beat I recognized it as the knife I had given Pere Jac after capturing it from the Cheyenne back at the Big Muddy.

"What am I supposed to do with that?"

"You'll figure it out. Open up."

I did as directed. He jammed the hidebound handle into my mouth. I bit down on it. It tasted of leather and old sweat. He took my left hand in his own left, got himself set amid a general rustle of clothing, and then I felt the weight of his boot against the lump of displaced bone behind my shoulder. Realization came to me in a rush of panic. I tried to get up, but the pain and his boot held me down. I was wobbling the knife handle around in my mouth to find voice enough to protest when he pulled the arm tight and threw all his weight forward onto his foot.

Multicolored lights danced and exploded behind my eyelids. My blood sang in my ears. I bit down hard. My teeth ground through the rock-hard leather and into the wood beneath, dislodging splinters into the pocket beneath my tongue. Hudspeth's grip tightened crushingly on my hand and he heaved every ounce of his two hundred-plus pounds against the stubborn knob. It fell into place with an audible pop.

He was still panting from the effort a moment later as I pushed myself to my knees with my good arm and then got up, swaying on willowy legs. It took me a while to spit out the last of the splinters. "You bastard!"

He snorted. "That's the thanks I get. Back in Bismarck you'd pay a doc two dollars to do the same thing and be grateful to him afterwards."

"Where'd you learn to do that?"

"I didn't. Just thought I'd give it a whirl. It worked, didn't it?" he added, reading the expression on my face.

"Maybe I can do the same for you someday."

"No thanks. You done enough to me this trip." He accepted one of the sledges from Gus. "You won't be swinging no hammers for a spell. Which works out, us needing someone to look after the long guns just in case that injun's still around."

The engineer set the other hammer down on its head and turned toward the cab. "Come on, Ep, let's fire her up and back her down onto the level."

"No," said Hudspeth.

Gus stopped, turned back. "You want her to flop over whilst we're working?"

"We'll need all the weight we can get on them rails to hold 'em down. Think you can take her forward all the way to the end?"

"The end is right! Hell, all she needs right now is a stiff breeze to turn her into scrap. I ain't about to go back and tell James J. Hill—"

At this point the marshal interrupted with a suggestion as to what he could tell James J. Hill that I won't repeat. What he said next was more significant. "All right, if you won't do it I'll get someone who will. What about it, Ep?"

The engineer made a nasty sound in his nose. "He don't know the first thing about it! He's just a—"

"Sho' can, Marshal," the fireman broke in. "Can and will. Mr. Gus, he been trainin' me to be an engineer."

"You won't never make it now, boy!" He spat the words. "I'll sure as hell see to that!"

"Shut up."

Hudspeth was mostly bluster, but when he said that, people generally obliged him. His gaze lashed from the engineer back to the fireman. "Get up steam and take her as far up on them bent irons as she'll go."

Ephraim double-timed it back to the cab.

"Just don't forget that I didn't have nothing to do with it," Gus insisted.

Hudspeth beat me to it. "Who the hell cares?" He hoisted his sledge over his shoulder—making the engineer duck—and strode off in the direction of the damaged rails.

Locke, hefting the other hammer, smiled at his retreating back. "Not bad for a man who doesn't drink."

I kept my mouth shut.

At length Gus unbent enough to go back and release the private car and caboose from the rest of the train so that if it did go over it wouldn't take one of our more distinguished citizens with it. Meanwhile, Hudspeth and the colonel put the sledges and crowbar to work straightening out the worst kinks in the irons as Ep performed double duty as engineer and fireman, going back and forth between the box, the wood supply, and the throttle, all the time maintaining a vigil on the gauge to keep the boiler from doing the Indian's job for them. All this time I stood over the rifles watching everything and feeling useless. My shoulder felt worse than it had before the marshal had put it right, but at least it was in a position where I could depend upon it in a pinch. When at last the engine was ready, Ep gave two blasts on the whistle to clear everyone out of the way, released the brake with a sigh of escaping steam, and gave the throttle a nudge that started the engine rolling forward.

The rails, or perhaps it was the train itself, groaned ominously as the incline was scaled. The wheels found traction only every third revolution, spinning in between with an unearthly squeal, and the twisted steel rails bent downward beneath the creeping weight. Not enough, however, to keep the top-heavy engine from swaying like an Indian medicine man in a deep trance. I wiped that image out of my thoughts the instant it occurred. Indians and medicine men were on my mind too much of late.

A yard short of the irons' uprooted ends, the cab began to tip. I cringed in anticipation of the inevitable.

"Back up!" Hudspeth bellowed, drowning out the engine's snuffling wheeze.

The driving arm stopped, then began cranking backward even as the wheels on the far side were leaving the track. They fell back with a bang as the train lurched into reverse. As soon as the danger zone was past the marshal signaled stop by waving the lantern. The boiler exhaled its pent-up breath.

Ephraim alighted carefully, negotiating the extra couple of inches between the damaged rail and the ground in a smooth striding motion. He whooped his relief.

"You folks nearly had crushed nigger for dinner, and that's a fact," he said.

Gus, more active now that his own moral crisis was over, used the crowbar as a lever to take the twist out of each rail, holding it taut while Locke and Hudspeth secured it by pounding home the spikes first in one, then the other. The engineer then resumed his place at the throttle and backed up the locomotive a step at a time to make room for the repairs as they progressed. Ep spelled Locke to free him for crowbar duty, his great black muscles writhing with each swing of the sledge. The noise of steel on steel rang out over the prairie for the first time in five years.

· It was back-breaking work, as the corkscrewed track had to be held straight while each spike was being driven, and the vibration of all that pounding made the hands holding the bar tingle until they grew numb and slipped off, and the end of the bar bounced up like a snake striking for the arm or skull that was not pulled out of the way fast enough. The second time that happened it caught Locke high on the right temple with a solid thump, stunning him. Hudspeth handed his sledge to Gus and took the colonel's place until he had recovered himself enough to resume his task. In this manner the labor went on into the early morning hours.

Standing out of the way watching them, shifting my weight from one foot to the other, I had grown so drowsy by about three o'clock that the first owl hoot didn't register. I perked up at the second one. Hollow and echoless, it sounded very far away. A pause, then a third. It would have been soothing but for my knowledge that it wasn't far away, and wasn't made by anything that remotely resembled an owl.

20 . . .

Nor did it stop at the owl. A moment later there was an answering hoot from another quarter, and then, farther off, the complicated scan of a mockingbird. Closer —too close—a mourning dove's sad refrain tooted like air passing through a pipe. We might have been in an aviary.

They weren't fooling anyone, not out there in the middle of a lonely prairie with no place for a bird to roost, and they knew it. They were just reporting their positions to each other in the only way they knew how, a highly efficient form of field communication that went back some two thousand years. More important, they were trying to scare us. Fright is the strongest medicine there is, and no one ever used it to greater advantage than the war-loving Cheyenne.

At the first calls Hudspeth and the others had stopped working and gone for their arms.

"Go on working." I spoke loudly enough to be heard over the engine without shouting. "If they don't know how many men we have, acting scared is the quickest way of telling them."

"And if they knows?" said Ephraim.

"Then we'll die no matter what we do."

"I'd heaps rather die fighting." This from the marshal.

"Either way you end up a handful of bloody hair. Go back to work."

There was a pause while they bounced glances around among themselves. Slowly they returned their guns to their proper places and took up their tools. Steel clanged.

Time crawled after that. I figured that if Lame Horse knew our strength he'd attack within half an hour of his arrival. I spent every minute tight as a coiled rattler. As the half hour drew to a close and minute piled laboriously upon minute without a bullet in my back, I began to relax by degrees. If they were planning to hit us before dawn we'd be five minutes dead.

A metallic glimmering over the eastern horizon foretold that event some three hours later. "Break it off," I snapped, surprised at the sound of my own voice after all those hours of silence.

The others looked up from their labors. Aside from that nobody moved.

"Ain't finished yet," Gus protested. "Next train comes down this track, without no warning—"

"That's their lookout. If you're really worried about it you can leave behind that red lantern on the caboose as a signal. Don't forget to couple those last two cars. Locke, Hudspeth, put the tools away and join me in the coach. No hurrying. We don't want them to know we're leaving just yet. Start stoking, Ep."

"Just who made you ramrod of this here outfit?" demanded the marshal.

"A sore shoulder. Get moving." I picked up the Winchester and threw the Spencer to the fireman, who caught it in one hand. The first bullet found him in that position. He spun and fell, spread-eagled with the rifle flung out to the side. Another one clanged against the boiler, then another and another, whistling off the base of the stack. More kicked up dirt all around us. At that moment, a line of shadowy riders spilled up out of a cleft between the rolling swells to the south like ants from a kicked hill. They were snapping off wild shots and yammering at the top of their lungs.

"Get on board!" I shouted, backing up and firing the Winchester from my hip as I went. I nearly tripped over Ep, who was still kicking with a hole the size of a man's fist over his left breast. Tossing the carbine to Hudspeth, I called for him to cover me as I gathered up the Spencer and a handful of the fireman's belt and dragged him to the coach. My shoulder was forgotten.

"I need a fireman!" Gus shouted from the cab. "Locke!"

The colonel waved his understanding and ran a zigzag pattern between flying bullets toward the engine. His Remington bucked twice in his hand, its muzzle flashing. An Indian who had been galloping up on him shrieked and back-flipped over his horse's rump. Whinnying, the animal lost its momentum, executed a wide, clawing turn to the right, and took off bucking for the open prairie, narrowly missing Hudspeth as it brushed between us.

A Cheyenne slug splattered the corner of the coach an inch above my hat as I hoisted Ep's limp, heavy body onto the platform and bounded up behind him. Either their marksmanship was improving or God was on their side. Hudspeth, hammering away with the Winchester at every target that presented itself, swung aboard directly behind me.

Indians were clattering all over the place now. Crouched on the platform, I fired the Deane-Adams at an occasional flash of horse and rider in the light of the lamps still burning inside, without visible result. I heard the snapping of a light gun in the direction of the engine, and once the deeper roar of the Walker, and hoped Gus wouldn't forget to pick us up. Ghost Shirt's dog was going wild in the baggage car, which was no longer connected to ours.

The grayness to the east had given way to dirty pink. I had enough light to shoot by, but if there had been a friend among the riders harassing the train I wouldn't have known him from the others. I figured there was little chance of that and kept popping away at the fleeting forms.

Over everything, the panting of the engine grew loud and rapid. I was relieved to see for the first time that the rear of the baggage car was looming near, and threw out a hand to brace myself against the railing just as we made contact with a smashing jolt that threw me sideways into the marshal, pinning him between my shoulder and the wall. The couplings caught and held. We began rolling forward at a painfully slow pace, but picking up speed as we went.

I placed a hand over the gaping mass of gore that was the fireman's breast to see if his heart was still beating.

Warm blood squirted between my fingers. At that moment his great chest swelled with air and expelled it in a long, drawn-out sigh. I waited, but it didn't fill again and no more blood came. Gus was right. He would never be an engineer.

Hudspeth had ducked inside the coach to see to the other side of the tracks. After a space I felt the platform rock beneath me and figured it was him returning. At the same time, a solitary rider sitting a black and white pony drew abreast of the coach and swung the muzzle of a Spencer in my direction. It was Lame Horse.

Hudspeth had extinguished the lights inside the car, but there was enough natural illumination now for me to recognize the shiny, ebony-painted face with the jagged streak of yellow lightning slashing from his right temple to the left corner of his jaw. The necklace of shrunken human fingers bounced on his breast as he galloped to keep up with the accelerating train, slapping his reins one-handed back and forth across the animal's withers. You had to hand it to him for spunk. Hitting a moving target from the back of a horse in full gallop is next door to impossible, yet here he was fixing to do just that. He set a lot of store by the medicine in that necklace. Using it as a guide, I was steadying the foresight of my revolver on the top of the vulnerable arch below his breastbone when something burst behind my eyes and the lights went out.

The blackout lasted less than a second, but by the time my senses came swimming back I found myself sprawled on the platform, my head humming and my right leg swinging over the edge where the wind of our passage set my pants cuff to flapping. The Deane-Adams was nowhere to be seen. My first thought was that Lame Horse got lucky, but then I realized that the blow had come from behind. I looked up to see a familiar figure crouching over me.

My handcuffs dangled glittering from the swollen wrist of the hand holding the engineer's Colt by its long barrel like a club. That meant that he had been inside the cab, which in turn meant that he had been hiding in the one place I had given only a cursory search, the wood car. He had sprung from beneath a layer of camouflage, dispatched Gus and likely Colonel Locke, and scrambled over the roof of the baggage car to do for me. All this came to me in the instant of awakening. The moment he saw me lying helpless at his feet, Ghost Shirt let out a whoop and, swinging the revolver over his head as if it were a tomahawk, leaped up to hail Lame Horse.

The medicine man was ready for him. Within arm's length of the platform now, he thrust the bore of his rifle into his chief's midsection and blew him into history.

The force of the bullet slammed him against the door of the adjacent car, where he sank down with surprise on his face and both hands buried in what remained of his stomach, his feet still on the platform of the coach so that he formed a human coupling between the cars. Behind the baggage door an animal throat let go with a howl that made my scalp crawl.

Lame Horse was losing ground now to the train, which although it had begun to lose momentum with no hand at the throttle was still traveling too fast for a horse to keep up, but he had time enough to turn the heavy rifle on me. Before he could pull the trigger I snatched up the Spencer that was lying beside Ep's corpse and slammed an ounce of lead into the middle of his war paint. The yellow slash dissolved behind a cloud of red. He clutched at his face with one hand, but it was just his nerves reacting. I didn't see him topple. By then both horse and rider had slid out of sight behind the corner of the coach.

The train was moving perceptibly slower now. Hudspeth emerged from the coach carrying my Winchester in one hand and his own Smith & Wesson in the other. He helped me to my feet.

"What the hell happened?" he wanted to know. "I leave you alone for one minute—"

I ignored him. Ghost Shirt was still breathing. I stepped across to the other platform, where he lay with his mouth working soundlessly. Planting a finger in one ear to close out the noise of the train, I bent over him and placed the other ear so close to his lips that they almost touched. For a moment I froze in that position, straddling two cars and leaning against the door of baggage to maintain my balance. Then the Indian's neck muscles let go and his head rolled of its own weight to one side. The hypnotic light drained slowly from his half-open eyes. I straightened.

"What did he say?" The marshal's voice was so hushed I may only have guessed at his words.

"Something about Lame Horse," I said. "It wasn't, 'Forgive them, for they know not what they do.'"

When the train had rolled almost to a stop we sprang down and made our way to the locomotive. There were no Indians in sight. In the cab we found the engineer slumped over the throttle, the back of his head a pulpy mass covered with matted hair. Locke was leaning against the wood supply busily tying his handkerchief around his right wrist. A dark stain was spreading over the fine silk.

"He hit Gus with a chunk of wood the size of a man's thigh," he explained as we mounted the cab. "The damn fool was too busy replacing the one bullet he'd fired from that cap-and-ball to notice him. I had just put away my gun. Ghost Shirt searched me, but I guess he didn't know about shoulder holsters. I went for it while he was picking up Gus's revolver. I wasn't fast enough.

The Remington went over the side and I played dead. Did you see which way he went?"

I nodded. "He isn't playing."

"This one's skull must be near as thick as yours, Murdock," said Hudspeth, examining the engineer. "He's still breathing."

"How bad is the wrist?" I asked Locke.

"Just a graze. I would've given anything for one like it when I was in the service. The wound pension would have served me in good stead."

"Trouble." The marshal hefted the Spencer, which I had exchanged for the return of my carbine. I turned in the direction of his gaze.

A dozen Indians were approaching slowly on horseback from the east. Some of them led other horses, across the backs of which were slung their dead. The brave mounted at the point, powerfully built like Ghost Shirt but several years his senior, wore his hair in a pair of plaits that hung almost to his belt, the ends tied with bright red ribbon, and had his face painted black on one side, red on the other, with a white line the width of a finger separating them down the middle. Across his chest he sported a breastplate made of bones fitted together by a squaw's patient hands. The Cheyenne at his left carried a rifle upright with its butt resting upon his thigh. A scrap of white cloth swung from its bore.

"It's a trick," said Hudspeth.

"If it is they're taking an awful chance. We'll let them come."

They stopped a few yards away. The silence that ensued was broken only by the occasional shuddering snort of an exhausted mount. Finally the man holding the flag of truce spoke. A young brave with a pouting expression beneath his dead black paint, he had the high, thin voice of a born Indian orator.

"This man is Broken Jaw, of the Cheyenne nation."
He indicated the breastplated warrior, whose hard eyes
remained fixed on a point somewhere above our heads.
"He wishes to say that the white men fought bravely
and well this day, and that he is not angry with them
because of this."

I said nothing. Indians take a long time to get to the
point.

"He wishes also to say that while there was one
among the Cheyenne who did not behave this day as a
Cheyenne should, and whose soul will wander forever
the Place of the Dead in disgrace because of this, the
black white man who died this day will take his place
beside Heammawihio, the Wise One Above."

I perked up at that. Broken Jaw had witnessed the
medicine man's treachery as well as Ephraim's death. In
that tribe, the worst thing you can say about a fellow
warrior is to accuse him of not behaving "as a Cheyenne should." I wanted to hurry the spokesman along,
to find out what he was getting at, but if I tried I'd
only be butting my head against twenty centuries of
tradition.

"But there was a great sadness this day as well. Tomorrow the heavens will weep and the sun will hide its
head."

At last we were making some progress.

"Broken Jaw has come to claim the pod in which
dwelled the soul of Ghost Shirt so that he may prepare
it for its final great journey in a manner befitting a great
warrior of the Cheyenne."

"Tell him his wish is granted," I said, after I had
translated that into plain English.

The spokesman told him nothing, but then he didn't
have to. It was obvious Broken Jaw understood most of
what had been said. I told Locke and Hudspeth to wait
there and turned my back on their protests as I led the

party back to the baggage car. There, the head warrior dismounted to gather up the body.

"One moment," I said. He watched in silence as I produced the key to Ghost Shirt's handcuffs and removed them from his lifeless wrist. "So his soul will not wander in chains."

There is no word for thanks in the Indian languages, because none is needed. I saw the gratitude in Broken Jaw's eyes as he nodded at me.

The renegades had come away from the fight at the Missouri with no lodge poles with which to construct a travois, and so the pod in which Ghost Shirt's soul had dwelled was committed to the indignity of being draped over the back of an empty horse. Then Broken Jaw and the Indians who had helped him mounted up and left without a word. They didn't break into their death chant until they were almost out of sight on the eastern horizon. By then it was hard to distinguish the toneless dirge from the morning breeze that had just begun to stir the grasses on the prairie. Sometimes, when I'm alone and the wind comes humming beneath the cornices outside the window in gusts that rise and fall with no recognizable pattern, I hear it still.

21 . . .

Gus sat on the floor of the cab with his turbaned head in his hands, his legs dangling over the side. When he spoke he lisped wetly through the space where his bottom two front teeth had been before the train's sudden stop had rammed a healthy share of the ironwork into his mouth. That stop seemed a week old now. It was midmorning. Taking turns with a shovel they had found in the cab, Locke and Hudspeth had just finished burying Ephraim and the conductor deep enough to keep the wolves and coyotes from scratching them up for a day or two.

"Can you run the train?" I slipped my arms into the sleeves of my jacket, which I had taken off to clean the wound, apply the bandage and a liberal dose of cognac from the community flask. The left one went on carefully. My shoulder was beginning to set up.

"I need me another fireman. Lately I been going through 'em like cigars."

"I can still stoke wood." Locke returned from the rear of the train, where he had gone to check on the senator. A fresh shine in his eyes told me he'd made a stop at the bar, where burgundy was still available. "I'm learning to enjoy physical labor all over again."

"We'll cure that soon enough," said Gus.

"How's His Lordship?" I asked the colonel.

"Happily ignorant. I gave him a drop more laudanum. He'll sleep the rest of the trip."

"Is that how you usually handle him?"

He shrugged. "It can't do him any harm. His doctors say he has a stomach cancer. He won't see winter."

"Does he know?"

"If he didn't, do you think he'd be in such a hurry to make a name for himself in history?"

"All right, then, get her up." I turned toward the passenger coach, where Hudspeth was waiting.

"What time is it?" the engineer demanded.

I hauled out my watch. "Quarter of nine."

He swore, scrambled to his feet, got dizzy, grabbed the side of the cab for support, swore again. "There's a freighter due in Bismarck at noon. If it's nine she's an hour late now. We got to get moving."

The rest of us had managed to keep up a head of steam without a crash course in locomotive operation. Gus released the brake and the train was churning at a stiff clip by the time I reached the coach. I grabbed hold of the platform railing with my good arm and swung aboard.

"Figure on keeping a pet?" Hudspeth was sitting in the first seat facing the door on the right, Locke's flask in hand. His nose was flushed and all was right with the world.

When I raised my eyebrows he gestured with the flask in the direction of the baggage car, where Custer was barking up a storm.

"Damn!" I plunked into the vacant space beside the marshal. "I got so used to his racket I forgot to turn him loose when the Indians left. Gus won't stop now, not with several hundred tons of freight breathing down his neck."

"Shoot him when we get to Bismarck."

"I suppose we'll have to." I sighed.

"What do you mean, we? I ain't no dog killer!"

We stared at each other. For no reason at all we burst out laughing. We hadn't forgotten Pere Jac or Ep the fireman or Ghost Shirt and all our wasted efforts. It was just that after everything that had happened to us since we'd made this trip in the other direction, we had either to laugh or shoot each other, and we'd both done enough shooting to last us for a while. We roared until our sides ached, and for the next four hours we didn't dare look at each other for fear of starting it all over again.

The usual curiosity seekers were gathered on the platform in Bismarck as we eased into the station. I felt a pang, not of remorse at the end of a mission that should never have been undertaken in the first place, but for the trouble ahead. Curiously, my chief concern was for my partner. I wondered what would happen to him when Judge Flood learned we had failed to deliver his stepping-stone to the Congress. I got up, took down my carbine, and handed him the Spencer—his by inheritance.

"We'll let the local law take charge of the mongrel," I told him. "Pick up our gear afterwards."

"Suits me." He heaved himself to his feet. He really was a big man, six foot one and solid as two hundred and fifty pounds of salt pork. I let him go ahead of me down the aisle.

I was behind him on the coach platform when something exploded and his chest was enveloped in smoke. I was forced to let go of the Winchester as he fell backward into my arms, losing his own rifle. Mine clattered on the railing and dropped through the slot between the cars before I could catch it.

"You son of a bitch, this is for the fire."

I scarcely recognized the voice rising above the hubbub of panic-stricken spectators, because I'd heard it only once before. Dry and whispery, like sand sifting through a screen, it went with the man it belonged to, whom I placed right away. Sergeant Burdett, his shiny rain cape thrown open to expose his gun belt, stood alone in what was now a cleared space on the station platform, a heavy Army Colt smoking in his gloved right hand, its muzzle pointing at me. His good eye was cocked in my direction, its dead mate and the powder-burned cheek in shadow beneath the shiny black visor of his Yankee cap. He gave everything time to sink in before his finger tensed on the trigger.

Senator Firestone chose that moment to come waddling along the station platform from the direction of his private car, leaning backward to balance the forward pull of his enormous belly. He'd just awakened. Pink scalp showed in patches where his hair stuck up in tousled spikes and his eyes were still puffed from sleep. He walked right up to Burdett as if he were approaching the Senate podium.

"What do you think you're doing, soldier?" he demanded in his trumpeting baritone. "You're upsetting everything! Early, much too—"

The Colt roared twice. I heard both slugs slap his great mound. He staggered backward, puffing and blowing through his whiskers, and sat down on a packing crate beside the station door. He died in that position, looking like a passenger who had fallen asleep waiting for the train. By that time Burdett had forgotten all about him, and swung the revolver back to me.

I reached over and tore open the door of the baggage car. Eighty pounds of crazed animal bounded out through the opening, hesitated on the car's platform for half a heartbeat, then leaped eight feet for the first uniform it saw. Surprise and fear kindled in the sergeant's eye. He fired, blowing a hole through the bellowing monster, but not in time to stop its spring. The bellow soared to a shriek and it piled into its killer, bearing him down to the platform. Burdett's own roar was nearly as bestial as he shoved the lifeless weight from his chest, but before he could raise his Colt, Hudspeth, propped up on his left elbow where he had fallen after the first shot, pumped six bullets from his Smith & Wesson into the sergeant's heart as fast as the cylinder would turn.

The sigh of steam exhaling from beneath the boiler was the loudest sound when the marshal reached inside his still-smoldering coat and drew out Colonel Locke's steel flask. A thumb-sized hole was punched in it near the base.

"Bastard," he grumbled as he shook the last drops out of the aperture. Burdett's bullet rattled inside. "Wish I could do it all over again."

Judge Blackthorne was in a foul mood when he came back from court. His false teeth were clamped so tight they creaked and his robes, cut for a man an inch taller, made an angry noise as the hem scuffed the floor. He didn't look at me seated in the chair before his desk as he undid the cord behind his neck and spiked the sober black garment on its peg.

"Rough session?" I asked.

"Damn Philadelphia lawyers." He shrugged into a shiny black coat with beaverskin facing on the lapels and sank heavily into the high-backed leather chair behind his desk, where he sat working his porcelains for some time in silence. Then he pounced.

"Why in the name of sweet Jesus did it have to be Harold Firestone? Have you any idea how many friends that man had in the Congress? Have you any idea how hot they've been making things for me since the news got out?"

"It wasn't my choice. And stop acting like I'm the one who pulled the trigger. You got my report." Written in our own special code, it had run to eleven pages and cost more to send out collect over the wire than I would have paid for two good horses, saddles included. His reply, not in code, had been much more brief and, I suspected, considerably toned down by cooler heads at Western Union. Now I went over it again, filling in the blank spots. The words came easily since I had repeated the story several times at the top of my lungs for Judge Flood's benefit. Refusing to speak until we saw him had cost Hudspeth and me two hours in the Bismarck jail. Local law and the marshal had not gotten along for years. Following our report—received in stony silence —Hudspeth had bought a ticket on the next train to Fargo, where he planned to rent a horse and pay a visit to the métis camp to inform Pere Jac's widow and family of their loss. Blackthorne listened with his short beard on his chest and his fingers laced across his spare middle. He was proud of that trim waistline, although he did nothing whatever to maintain it.

"It fits with what I was told by the commanding officer at Fort Ransom," he grunted, when I had finished. "The slant was different. That man doesn't like you much."

"I got that impression."

"You know, of course, that the papers are calling the incident at the station a planned assassination."

"The papers are always good for an afternoon's entertainment."

"In this case we're encouraging it. It's better for all concerned if the public thinks the killing of ex-Senator Firestone was carried out with malice aforethought by a demented army deserter. Which is technically correct. Sergeant Burdett had orders to return to camp if he was unable to prevent you from reaching the railroad. He went on alone after the others turned back."

"Except that it was Firestone who was demented, and that Burdett didn't know him from Adam when he put him under. He just got in the way. He took one look at that uniform and thought it was one of his own toy soldiers jumping the whistle on his grand revolution. Where does that leave Hudspeth and me?"

"Nowhere. Officially, you weren't there. As the senator's bodyguard, Andrew Locke was the one who shot the assassin. The earlier reports will be forgotten eventually for lack of substantiation." He tried out his diabolic smile, but it wasn't the same with his teeth in. "I'm sorry, Page, but there's no glory in it for you this time. In the long run, though, it can only help your reputation to leave the public ignorant of your part in the thing. It really was a wasted trip, with nothing to show for it."

Nothing but a pile of corpses, I thought. Aloud I said, "Sorry to disappoint you."

He shrugged. "Don't apologize to me. I'm ahead of the game. I had a debt to pay and now it's square. Now I don't owe Abel Flood a damned thing, the hypocritical bastard."

"I wish you'd told me he was a hypocritical bastard before I left," I snapped.

"I figured you'd find out soon enough. Have you put in a voucher yet for that lost gun?"

I patted the new Colt in my holster. "This will do until I find another Deane-Adams."

"Not much chance of that, here in Colt country. Where are you going?"

I had gotten up and put on my hat, a new one to go with my first bath and shave in many days. "To get as close to dead drunk as my credit at the Belmont will take me." I took a step toward the door.

"No need for that." He opened his bottom drawer and tossed me a full bottle of the expensive Bourbon he had shipped in quarterly by the case from Kentucky. I caught it in one hand.

"Don't turn cow eyes on me," he snarled. "It's coming out of your salary."

I said something a man doesn't usually say to his boss and expect to remain employed, and left.

Don't look for anything like an ending of this, because no such thing exists, not in real life. Too many details overlap, and offshoots of one incident go on to weave themselves into something else that sprang out of something else before that, just as the Civil War never ended but went on in Mexico with much of the original cast. For me the Dakota episode was over. I don't know about the others.

Colonel Andrew Locke dropped out of sight after we had parted in Bismarck and I never heard from him again. If he found the upward mobility he was looking for when he left the army, it wasn't in any profession that got headlines or I would have caught wind of it one way or another. I doubt that he stuck with what he'd been doing. There isn't a lot of call for bodyguards who let their charges get killed, no matter what the papers said about their quickness on the trigger after the fact. The best guards never get their names in print.

Speaking of names, Abel Flood's didn't appear on the ballot during the 1880 presidential election because he died on the bench late in '79. He succumbed quietly to a stroke while court was in session, and all the parties involved with the case under consideration went on screaming and yelling the way they always did so he could hear them until someone noticed that he hadn't moved or blinked for ten minutes. The next day the Bismarck *Tribune* devoted eight columns to his three decades of service and the territorial governor decreed that flags throughout Dakota be flown at half-mast for thirty days in his memory. A street was eventually named after him, then dropped in favor of another after local law enforcement reminded the mayor that every major cathouse in the city was located along the original.

I was told by a friend that Major Quincy Harms had issued an order to place me under arrest the next time I entered Dakota following the death of Sergeant Burdett, but I don't know that for certain because I never found reason to go back. In the winter of 1882 he and two of his officers were separated from the rest of the command by a sudden blizzard during a raid on a camp of renegade Sioux. His body and that of his adjutant were found in a cleft between two buttes after the spring thaw, but they never recovered the third, which led to some ugly rumors about the others that persist to this day.

Whether he retired, quit, or was sacked, A. C. Hudspeth left Bismarck within a year of our adventure and rode for a time with a Wild West show operating out of Chicago. I know that because I saw his name on a poster in Rock Springs, Wyoming, while escorting a prisoner back to Helena for trial. According to the date on it I had missed him by a day. After that I scanned the newspapers fairly regularly in the hopes the show might come to my neighborhood, but I never heard of it again and it's likely it folded along with the dozens of others that couldn't hope to compete against a name like Buffalo Bill. Sometime around '85, an old girlfriend who knew more about my past than I preferred wrote me from the home she was sharing with her new husband in St. Paul that a candidate named Hudspeth had just made a bid for public office there on a law and order ticket. That didn't sound much like the marshal, unless he had caught the bug from his employer, but then I suppose if it weren't contagious we wouldn't have politicians at all. Whatever the case, he lost by a landslide. That must have been particularly hard to take for a man who didn't like the taste of dregs.

Everyone knows what happened to the Indians. The railroads resumed building the following year, settlers poured westward, and no man, primitive or otherwise, stands in the way of progress for long. Many Ponies, the Miniconjou chief who was more interested in pleasing his new squaw than fighting the white man, died doing both at what the official military histories would one day christen the Battle of the Missouri, while sharing a buffalo robe with his eighteen-year-old bride in their tipi. His fellow tribesman Tall Dog was captured and taken under heavy guard to Fort Abraham Lincoln, where, according to the report, he hanged himself in the guardhouse with a lace from one of his moccasins. Broken Jaw buried his dead in state on the west bank of the James and was leading his decimated band back to the Mormon stronghold when the reinforcement troops General Sherman had promised Fort Ransom fell upon them and cut them to pieces. In so doing, they lost three troopers to every brave. If you flip through a recent book entitled *Conquest of the Frontier* you'll see a picture of Broken Jaw's bullet-riddled corpse propped up on a door alongside those of two of his warriors, taken by a New York photographer while on a visit to the fort.

And last month in Washington City, the Smithsonian Institution opened a new exhibit centered around a glass jar containing a gray something said to be a piece of Ghost Shirt's brain.

WESTERNS THAT NEVER DIE

They pack excitement that lasts a lifetime.
It's no wonder Zane Grey is the bestselling
Western writer of all time.
Get these Zane Grey Western adventures
from Pocket Books:

_____83102 BORDER LEGION $1.75

_____82896 BOULDER DAM $1.75

_____83422 RIDERS OF THE PURPLE SAGE $1.95

_____82692 DEER STALKER $1.75

_____82883 KNIGHTS OF THE RANGE $1.75

_____82878 ROBBERS ROOST $1.75

_____82076 TO THE LAST MAN $1.75

_____83534 UNDER THE TONTO RIM $1.95

_____82880 U.P. TRAIL $1.75

_____83022 ARIZONA CLAN $1.75

_____83105 BLACK MESA $1.75

_____83309 CALL OF THE CANYON $1.75

36